# BOSSY
## *Brothers*

# TONY

# *ja* HUSS

# BOSSY Brothers TONY

## JA HUSS

# ABOUT THE BOOK

*Belinda Baker and I were not made for each other.*

We are not soul mates, or lovers, or even frenemies.

She is the one who needed to get away.

What we had together wasn't blind love, it was sick rage.

We were a match made in hell, it was hate at first sight, and when she walked away from me and never looked back—it was a relief.

It was bliss.

So why did I travel two thousand miles so I could be near her?

Why can't I stop thinking about this girl I never want to see again?

Why. Am I. Here?

And what do I have to do to make her disappear for good?

*Bossy Brothers: Tony features two girls falling for the wrong men and two men falling for the right girls. A family of tatted up brothers and a town filled with secrets and danger. A story of earned chances and first dates. Of coming to terms with the past and finding a way into the future. It is book six in the Bossy Brothers series and should be read after book five, Bossy Brothers: Alonzo.*

## CHAPTER ONE

**TONY**

**_She cried after we had sex._**

Every single time.

It wasn't a sobbing cry. It was mostly silent tears, but they were tears all the same. They would well up in her eyes for a few moments, gathering there like perfect little pools of sadness, and then they would run down her cheeks. And if she was wearing make-up, there would be little black streaks after the tears settled.

God, that was hot.

And I remember thinking to myself... *Dude. There is something seriously wrong with you.*

Because I liked her tears.

No. That's not even close to accurate. I *loved* her tears.

I don't want her to be sad. That's not it. I don't want to hurt her, it's not about that. But both of those things needed to be there for those tears to... you know, get me *off*.

But here's the weird thing about her—she likes it rough. She has always liked it rough. So I would get rough with her. At first it was a little bit of pressure on her throat as I fucked her from behind, my fingers just barely pressing on that heartbeat throbbing on her

1

neck. And God, she would moan. That turned into slapping her ass. Grabbing her tits. Pinching her nipples. You know, normal rough shit.

But she didn't cry during any of that. She didn't look scared at all, to be honest. She liked it. And I'm not a scary fucker. Not really. So she wasn't afraid of me.

No. It was something else. Because she only cried after she came.

And it got to a point where that's all I wanted. Once I had figured out this little display of hers, I went after it. I would get her off as quick as I could. Do anything she wanted to make it happen.

And then I would wait for it. I would wait for those tears.

If she was face down, or I had her pressed against a wall or a door, I would spin her around and fuck her another way just so I could come as I watched the tears fall down her cheeks.

There really is something wrong with me.

I tried talking to my brother Alonzo about this once. But how does one even begin to explain this fucked-up darkness inside my head? I couldn't find the words, and he looked at me like I was a freak, and then I waved him off and said forget it.

That was a long while back. Rosalie Thompson was put into the witness protection program eight years ago. She saw something she shouldn't have seen and we had to get rid of her. She got a new name. Belinda Baker. She got a new job—tattoo apprentice, I guess? She got a new town. Fort Collins, Colorado.

God, that year was a mess.

But the point is—she was out of my life and that weird craving for sex tears went away.

No other woman I've been with has cried after sex. And I never had an urge to make them cry. That's... sick. And I didn't do any of that with anyone else.

So it's not me.

It's her.

In fact, it was so much her and not me that after she left town—well, after we had our FBI contact force her into the witness protection program—I kinda forgot all about my tear fetish. Literally have not thought about sex tears in eight years.

And then one day, just a couple months ago, she came back. Rosalinda—as I like to call her now because I can't deal with just giving up on her old name and accepting the new one the witness protection program gave her—appeared down in Key West, on my fucking street, with my brother's long-distance fling and some tattooed asshole called Vann and ruined everything for me.

One look at her. That's all it took. Just one fucking glimpse of that girl and all those freak thoughts about fucking her as she cried were back.

The only thing that saved me was the whole secret mission Alonzo and I were in the middle of. I didn't really have time to think about her. The days were flying by, and shit needed to get done, and people from the past were popping up all over the place.

So I didn't have time for a tear fuck.

And then our little secret mission was over and she was gone.

Just... gone. Doing her thing.

But I was OK with that. I was. Because I knew she'd come back. And then all the stress from the secret mission would be over, and we'd... I don't know. Meet each other's gaze from across a crowded room or something. And we'd both let that urge to be tear-fuck buddies take over again and… I'd get my fix.

It was a bad fantasy from the beginning because, as any addict would tell you, that fix is what fucks it all up.

Rosalinda is my drug.

I imagined we'd do that for a while. Maybe a long while. Until we got sick of each other and one of us tried to walk away. But then we'd be miserable, but unable to admit it. And spend, oh, three or four years being 'that couple'. The ones who hate each other but can't stop fucking.

And then…I don't know. We'd move on, I guess. Get the therapy we so obviously needed and pull our shit together. Find new partners who didn't come with tears, and fights, and hate sex.

Be happy for once.

But here's the ironic part about all this—she didn't come back.

She went home to Colorado. She went back to her new name, and her new job, and her new town, and didn't even send me a text to say goodbye.

So… I guess I have to face the facts.

It's not her, it's me.

Because I just came two thousand miles, under the pretense of 'family business,' to stalk her. I left my boat tour business in the hands of my ridiculous brother-in-law, Jesse Boston, to be here. And ever since I arrived I've been sneaking around, hiding in the shadows, watching her in secret.

I'm obsessed with Rosalinda.

She has crept back into my brain and turned me inside out since she showed back up in Key West.

I need to figure out how to get rid of her. At any cost.

Because if I don't, she is going to *ruin me*.

## CHAPTER TWO

**BELINDA**

*The bookstore girl has potential.* She's aloof, sketchy, suspicious, and never looks anyone in the eyes. I like all these things about her. I also like the plaid skirts and dark tights with the rips in the knees that she wore all winter. She dyes her hair blue, wears black eye makeup, and her name is Midnight. I was pretending to browse the used books when I heard a man call her that during a whisper fight. Her look is *Twilight* meets *Reality Bites*.

Midnight. The bookstore girl.

She is my last chance.

For a new best friend, that is.

My real best friend, Tara, moved down to Key West to be with her new soulmate. And now listen, I would not admit this to anyone and I will deny it to my dying breath if asked, but I was secretly hoping that whole soulmate thing with Alonzo Dumas wasn't going to work out. I was secretly praying that Tara would be back in Fort Collins working in the library like nothing happened after she realized that Alonzo wasn't her man.

But I've given up hope. Alonzo *is* her man. He is her soulmate and she's not coming back. So unless I move down there, I need a new BFF.

I'm not knocking Key West. It's a very nice place filled with very nice people, but it's also where my ex lives. And he… just… no. We're not doing that again. Ever. I am done with him. Because here's the thing—he's the reason I'm here in the first place. He was the one who got me mixed up in this stupid FBI witness protection program. That was eight years ago and let me tell you, running away from gangster-type people and leaving everything you knew behind—including your mother!—and then starting over in a strange place that is cold and snowy for half the year, that wasn't fun.

It was torture. I was lonely, and miserable, and the only reason I didn't fall into a serious depression was because I stumbled into the downtown tattoo shop called Sick Boyz Ink and met the men who run that place.

Actually, of the four brothers who work there, only one really mattered. Vann Vaughn. He's the youngest. His brothers are fine—the twins Vonn and Vinn and the oldest, Vic. But it was Vann who changed my life and got me a job there working the cash register and checking people in. I worked my way up to apprentice after a while and now that place is like my second home.

Literally. Because my first home is the little apartment above the Vaughn family garage just down the street.

The Vaughn brothers are my life. And I love them. I do. They're great. Especially Vann. He's always on my side.

But a girl needs a *real* best friend. Being sorta friendly with your co-workers doesn't count.

I've tried buddying up with the Vaughn sister, Veronica. But she's already got a crew of girls and they are tight. Plus, they're all in the motherhood stage of life. Settled with their men and houses. So they were a no go.

Then I tried to entice a few of the waitresses at the Fort Collins Theatre coffee shop into being friends, but they're all students at the university a couple blocks down the street. Too young, too giggly, and it only took one two-minute conversation with a couple of them to realize I wouldn't fit in. Most of the people in this part of Fort Collins are students. All they think about are tests, and Jell-O shots, and school spirit.

Then a new coffee shop opened up right next to Sick Boyz called the Great Cup. And the baristas in that place were all older. A few men in their early thirties, two women in their late twenties, and one… matron, I guess, maybe in her fifties. Vann and I went in there on their opening day—which was packed—and we each got a coffee and some free pastry they were giving away. But… wow. The coffee sucked so bad I decided right there and then I could not be friends with these people.

Vann still goes over there though. Maybe once a week for lunch. He's probably the only regular customer they have left after the word got around that the coffee sucked. But he doesn't get coffee, he gets one of those cheap pre-packaged sandwiches and a fruit smoothie. I don't know why, because that sandwich looks even worse than the coffee tastes and he usually throws it out anyway. But he says he's down with supporting all the local businesses in Old Town.

So whatever. His business.

My point is—my best friend options are severely limited because all the other regulars in the downtown neighborhood where I live and work are old. Middle-aged ladies running candle shops, consignment stores, or real estate offices.

The only other exception is the Anna Ameci's Italian Restaurant girl. Soshee. And she has declared herself my mortal enemy because she's in love with Vann Vaughn and she figures we have a little side action going.

Which we don't. Vann might have big dreams of getting in my pants, but it's not going to happen. I've known him for eight years and I've never even flirted with the idea of kissing him, let alone a full-on friends-with-benefits arrangement.

I tell him he's too young for me. There's a four-year age difference. And it did kinda start out that way because when we first met he was only seventeen and I was twenty-one. But that's not the real reason. I count on him for certain things. Things like the job and the apartment above his family garage. If things go south between us over some stupid casual sex, all the stability I've built over the past eight years will disappear.

And I can't do that again. I cannot lose everything and start over. It was hard enough the first time but a second time might kill me.

So… bookstore girl really is my last chance.

I've come in here to browse books every day for a week now. I'm just trying to get her used to me first. If I've pegged her correctly, she's one of those unfriendly people who trusts no one, hates the world, and has mastered the act of glaring at people while looking completely unaffected.

Like me.

I shake my head and chuckle into a stack of old smelly paperbacks as I think that. But it's true. We're just… unapproachable. And suspicious of new people. And never looking for something. We let things fall into place. We take it as it comes. We *deal*.

So I can't exactly waltz right up to her and say, *Hey, would you like to be my new BFF?* Because if I did that, she'd say, *Who the fuck are you?* and then snarl, *Get the fuck out of my store, you creepy stalker.*

So I stand there in the back of the bookstore, absently flipping through a tired old paperback with Fabio on the cover, trying to think up the perfect opening line.

"Hey," a cheery voice says behind me. "You're the tattoo girl, right?"

I turn and then back up and hit the stacks of books in surprise. Because this question came from Bookstore Midnight. "What?" I say, caught off guard and kinda confused by her upbeat tone.

"You work next door, right? With those hot tattoo brothers. I've been thinking about getting some ink. But I don't know. It's so permanent." She chuckles. "I'm more of a temporary tattoo kind of girl. I can't take the pain."

I squint my eyes at her. "Temporary tattoos?"

"I know. I'm a wimp. But I've noticed you in here a lot over the past week. Is there anything specific you're looking for? Something I can help you with?"

I look at the paperback in my hand, briefly consider playing it off and buying it, then set it back on the shelf. "No. I was just…" She's still smiling. And it's creeping me out. "Sorry. I'm… this… I gotta go."

I head for the door and don't look back. But I still hear her super-happy, "Bye! Come back soon!" before the door closes behind me.

I walk around the side of Sick Boyz and lean against the brick wall in the alley, frowning.

Wow. Did I ever peg her wrong.

'Can I help you?' 'Come back soon?' What the fuck is that? And temporary tattoos?

I shake my head and make a face. A blue-haired girl with the name Midnight doesn't say or do those things.

"Fuck," I mutter, turning around so I can kick the wall. "Fuck!"

Bookstore girl was my last chance. There's literally no one left in Old Town Fort Collins to be friends with.

Maybe I could try again? Make it work?

No. No, no. 'Tattoos are so permanent?' 'Can't take the pain?'

I shudder.

Nope. That girl is all kinds of wrong.

"Hey! There you are. What the hell are you doing, Belinda? We have people who need checking in."

I glance to my right and see Vann coming around the corner of the alley. It's nice out today. Nice enough for him to be wearing a t-shirt that shows off all the tats running down his arms. His long legs cross the distance between us in just a few strides and then he stops to peer down at me with a smile. "What's up?" Vann is perpetually good-natured.

"Have you ever talked to the bookstore girl?"

He makes a face. "The fake blue-haired one?"

"Yeah."

"No. She's dumb."

"How do you know?"

"Because she's…" He pauses for a moment. His smile falters, but he recovers before it can truly turn into a frown. "She's not real, Belinda. Stay away from her."

"Not real how? Not that I don't believe you. I do. You're right. There's something wrong with her. She was… *polite* just now when I was in there."

"Yeah." He laughs. "Girls who look like her aren't polite. It's a carefully cultivated look. Like yours."

"Wait. Am I fake?"

He smiles at me. I'm talking full-on beaming grins at me. "No, toots. You're not fake at all. You're the definition of real."

"Toots," I say, tsking my tongue. "You know I hate that name."

"But it's cute—"

"If you call me 'cute' one more time, I'll clock you, Vann."

He shakes his head and points at me. "See. Now that threat? That's all you, *toots*. Totally you."

I frown. And sigh. "I'm not really real, am I? I'm an invention of the FBI witness protection program."

"Just stop it."

"Hey, wait! Do you think she's one of us? That could explain the inconsistency between her cool dark look and her stupid helpful attitude."

Vann looks towards the street, kind of in the direction of the bookstore. "No." He shakes his head and that almost-frown is almost back. "No," he says, looking back at me. "She's definitely not one of us. But never mind her. Come on, we've got customers."

He takes my hand and starts to lead me back towards the front of the shop, but I immediately pull away and slip my fingers out of his grip.

"Jesus Christ, Belinda. I wasn't trying to hold your hand. It was a casual gesture."

"I know," I say. "But my hand is all sweaty and I didn't—"

"Whatever."

I know I frustrate him. I know he wants more. I know this because he's told me lots of times. He likes me. A whole bunch.

And I like him too. Just not in the same way.

Vann Vaughn is my rock. He is the most consistent, most true, most real thing about my life these days.

And I will not fuck that up by sending the wrong signals and getting his hopes up that we will turn into something more, because we won't. Ever.

Plus, even if he is mad at me for pulling my hand away, he'll get over it.

He always does.

Like I said—he's my rock.

## CHAPTER THREE

*When my older brother*, Alonzo, said one of us needed to come up here to Fort Collins and check out this rumor that the Northern Colorado witness protection program was being run by sketchy black ops FBI agents, I volunteered.

Here's why this is important. Alonzo and I, along with our father, run an illegal smuggling ring down in Key West. The only reason we're not in prison for this is because these same sketchy black ops FBI agents were covering for us.

I do admit that we should've been more suspicious of this little arrangement. But we're good people and we figured these sketchy black ops agents were too. That they weren't *really* sketchy, just sneaky. And they, like us, disagreed with the United States immigration policy and wanted to do the "right thing".

We now realize that we were naïve. These black ops partners are sketchy, have some as yet unknown ulterior motive for helping us, and they didn't save Rosalinda when they offered to send her up here to Fort Collins to start a new, safe life—they were most likely just keeping her out of the way until such time as she could be useful.

The problem is we can't prove this. It's all conjecture.

Enter me. That's my job. That's why I'm here. At least, the official reason.

I don't like Vann Vaughn. When he showed up in Key West with Belinda and her friend Tara—who is now Alonzo's full-time, real-life girlfriend—I hated him immediately. He's good-looking, he's charming, and he has inserted himself into Rosalinda's life in a way that kinda pisses me off, if I'm being honest.

But. He did mention that he had some inside information about the witness protection program as it pertains to his home town of Fort Collins, Colorado.

So I tolerated him and before we all went our separate ways, we got his theory. Which goes like this:

The FBI in this area are all corrupt. He offered up some evidence for this idea—all of it based off an encounter his brother-in-law, infamous custom motorcycle mogul Spencer Shrike, had with the FBI about a decade ago. He spilled some details about that involved crazy assassins, a secret shadow government called the Company, and, of course, a dirty FBI agent who was exposed and took the fall for a bunch of complicated illegal shit that his brother-in-law and friends were actually responsible for.

But he figured that wasn't the end of it—just a new beginning. And all the "witnesses" who have been sent up here ever since were a part of some bigger, darker scheme.

And since Alonzo and I had a part in the plan to send Rosalinda up here to start her new life, we're also—unwittingly—a part of this darker scheme too.

And that will not do. We do not risk our necks and our freedom twice a year to smuggle good people into the United States for a chance at a better life just to let our supposed partners take us down in the endgame.

So that's the official version of why I'm here. I need to talk to Vann, get more info, poke around town, find some other witnesses to corroborate his theory, and then take that back home to Alonzo and our team so we can stay a few steps ahead of the dirty FBI.

Because we have a sneaky feeling about all this cooperation they've been handing out over the years.

A sneaky feeling that we're the fall guys in some grand plan. That they've been setting us up and we're about to go down for all kinds of sins that have nothing to do with smuggling refugees.

Rosalinda works at Vann Vaughn's family tattoo shop called Sick Boyz Ink. I'm standing across the street from it right now. Hiding in the shadows of an alley next to a restaurant called Anna Ameci's.

It's one forty-five AM and Old Town Fort Collins is still pretty busy. There aren't a lot of bars on this part of College Avenue, but there are enough to keep the crowds steady. And the Fort Collins Theatre, which doubles as a restaurant and coffee shop, is running some kind of black-and-white movie fest so there's a ton of people over there milling about near the street.

My focus is on Sick Boyz, where there is also a crowd of people, all of them college students from the university just a few blocks south of here. A few ponytail girls, a few sporty guys, and the blue-haired girl who I know works at the bookstore next to the tattoo shop.

She's in the alley between the two establishments, leaning against the side-entrance door to the bookstore, talking to another girl who is holding the leash of a frantic, yippy white dog wearing a green and white CSU sweater.

Plus there's a ton of people just walking by. Not just students. Regular young couples and a few older ones too.

Rosalinda gets off work in fifteen minutes and then she either gets into Vann's truck for a ride home, or they walk the two blocks down Mountain Avenue to his family mansion. She lives in an apartment above the detached garage.

Mansion is probably a generous word for this house. It's big, I'm not saying it's not. Huge, actually. And Mountain Avenue is lined with similarly large houses on this particular block. Some blocks further down have smaller homes. Some much smaller. Almost cottages. But this block is where the rich people live.

Except the Sick Boyz people aren't rich and the house is mostly a falling-down mess. There's a few reno projects going at the moment. New roof in progress. New porch halfway finished. Someone started to paint it, but then maybe ran out of paint?

In fact, all the reno projects are in some halfway stage of completion. I'm sure the neighbors are thrilled.

Anyway, the point is—she leaves work at two AM and most nights she's with Vann Vaughn. Sick Boy number four. The youngest tattoo-artist brother working in the shop.

He has a thing for Rosalinda.

Lucky for him, she doesn't feel the same way back.

If she did feel the same way back, I'd have to step in and take control of that situation. Because she's still mine. She will always be mine until we kill each other, or get sick of the hate fucks, or get that therapy we desperately need.

Or something.

But she doesn't feel the same way about Vann, so I'm ignoring him and stalking her.

I've been stalking her for three days now. And tonight there is no Vann to get in my way. It's his night off. So tonight, when she comes out of the shop at two AM, she will be alone. And tonight, I will follow her in the shadows. And then I will take her by surprise. Scare her a little, probably. At first, anyway. She might hit me. No, she will definitely hit me. Probably grab my hair with both hands, knee me in the balls, and then punch me in the mouth.

Or at least she'll try.

But just before she does all those things, I'll spin her around, cover her mouth with my hand, and lean in to her ear and say something hot like… "I'm gonna fuck you now, Rosalinda."

And then she'll know it's me. And she'll be pissed. But not *that* pissed. And she'll let me drag her around the side of her garage-slash-apartment and fuck her up against the weathered old wood siding.

I really hope there's enough light to see her tears.

Maybe I should reconsider the fuck spot?

I'm thinking about this when she comes out of the shop. But… she's not alone.

She's not with Vann. She's with Sick Boyz number two and three. The twins. I'm not sure which is which, but it doesn't matter. They live at the Vaughn family mansion. They are walking her home.

Plans interrupted, but no big deal. I'm not one of those rigid dudes. I can bend. So maybe I have to put a little more effort into that final leg of this plot. Or maybe I have to actually sneak into her apartment after she goes inside. That could be fun. So I deal with the twins by keeping a safe distance as I stalk them, taking in small details about Rosalinda that I hadn't had time to notice before. I catch a glimpse of her pink ponytail under the streetlights. It appears and disappears as they walk down the block. Pink. Black. Pink. Black. A lot of hair has fallen out of the elastic holding the ponytail up. And I wonder if she wears it like that on purpose or if she's just had a long day. She wears skirts a lot. And cowboy boots. Sometimes she wears jeans, but they always have rips and tears in them. Rips and tears that look genuinely worn instead of artfully placed by some fashion designer.

That's her new Colorado look. Her new Belinda look. Her new *life* look.

I call it the long-rough-day look.

But every glimpse of her I've seen since arriving in town, she's been smiling.

*So which is it, Rosalinda? Are you weary? Or are you excited about this new life?*

This girl *is* Belinda. She is almost nothing like the Rosalie I once knew. I saw it immediately back in Key West and it kinda pissed me off. Not that she turned into someone new, but that her new look was as alluring to me as the old one.

I almost feel like she did that on purpose.

Like she's been planning this moment for eight years. Like everything she's done since she was brought to this town totally against her will and forced into taking a new name, and a new job, and a new look was done with the express purpose that when I came looking for her—and she knew I'd come eventually—I'd see it.

I'd see that she moved on, and forgot all about me, and embraced something new.

Does she cry after she fucks her new men?

I can't think about it. I'll just get irrationally jealous. And it is irrational. Because I do not want her. I don't. I might not understand why I'm here, or what I'm doing, or how I'll feel after I fuck her tonight—but I do know how it will end.

It will end with us going our separate ways.

That's the only way it can end.

I do not love her. She does not love me.

We are sickly twisted. Illogically entwined. Irrationally connected.

None of it makes sense and this connection needs to be severed for good. I'm counting on this ex-sex hate fuck—or possibly fucks in the plural—to break my obsession so I can figure out what's going on with the witnesses and then get my ass back home where I belong.

So I forget about the men she might or might not be fucking, and instead I concentrate on the twins because I know she's not fucking them. Not with their little brother, Vann, throwing himself at her every chance he gets.

Everyone in the little group in front of me is wearing boots. I recognize the dull thud of footsteps on the concrete sidewalk. Vaughn brothers number two and three are much taller than Belinda. They tower over her, glancing at each other frequently, only occasionally looking down at the small girl between them. But they laugh easily. Telling inside jokes, maybe, or recounting some customer experience they shared today.

All three of them wear black leather jackets Belinda painted. I noticed that the first day I saw her with the brothers. Her artistic style is easily recognizable. Maybe the only thing about her that hasn't changed in the past eight years. She has a color palette that she almost never deviates from. Muted grays and pinks. The occasional splash of sea blue and light violet.

It's very Key West.

And you'd think that grown men calling themselves Sick Boyz would go for a color scheme that's a little more... *masculine* with their leather-jacket paint jobs.

But the designs on the jackets aren't feminine at all. Even with the muted colors. Her designs are skulls and flowers. Birds and hearts. And if I were to just describe that to someone and tell them she was a tattoo artist, it would make sense.

But it doesn't make sense. At least not to me. Her designs aren't something you see in tattoo form. They are street art of the highest quality. That's what she used to do back in Florida. She would paint murals. It was graffiti at first, but she did one actual commission on the side of a building near her mother's motel before she left.

Things changed a lot over the years she's been gone. That building was sold, the mural painted over, and that was that. All evidence of her art was wiped away. I told her she should put her designs on canvases, but she didn't listen to me.

But I guess... she *did* listen to me, didn't she?

I understand the draw of painted leather jackets, but she's not fooling me with this tattoo artist dream. We had one last fight before she left Key West to go meet up with her new best friend, Tara. It was a brutal fight over her decision to leave Key West again and go *home*.

Like this place is her home.

It's not.

Our words came out like sharp daggers, meant to wound more than kill. But it wasn't her words that pissed me off when we had that fight. It was her tears.

I hated them. And I get it. It's not fair. How can I love the after-sex tears and despise the fight tears?

I can't explain it, but it makes perfect sense in my head.

She dug in her heels during that fight, insisting that this tattoo shop, these Sick Boyz, this town—all of it was her future.

Key West was over.

*We* were over.

I walked away first. I said something mean, turned away, and never looked back.

Because *of course* we were over.

That wasn't what I was trying to say. At all.

And yet here I am. Stalking her at two AM on a dark night. Two thousand miles away from where I should be.

I think I'm in the middle of a crisis. That has to be it. I mean, of course I'm in the middle of a crisis. My family runs a human smuggling ring in Florida propped up by some, most likely, sketchy FBI agents. And now those sketchy people propping us up aren't on our side anymore. They might even be angry enough with us to hurt us. Not just a get-you-busted kind of hurt either. They do carry guns, after all. People get killed when mutually beneficial deals with sketchy organizations suddenly become *un*-mutually beneficial.

So yeah. That's a fucking crisis.

But that's not what I'm talking about.

Like, I don't even have time for that actual, real-life crisis shit. Because Rosalinda. I don't know what it is, I just can't get her out of my mind.

So. The hate fuck. I've done some research and there is evidence that this is a cure for old wounds and past-the-expiration-date relationships.

That's how I'm rationalizing my odd behavior. I just really don't have any other explanation for it.

The three of them duck into a driveway and I walk a little faster now that there's no chance of them noticing me. But by the time I get to the mansion where they live, all three are inside.

The main house is mostly dark. But there's a glow leaking into the front rooms from the back of the house and I can see tall shadows crossing in and out of view as I invade their privacy with my unwanted voyeurism.

The garage apartment has no windows on this side, so I can't tell if Rosalinda went home to her place or is inside the main house.

I take a chance and slip around the side of the garage, heading for the back where there's a set of stairs leading to her deck.

When I round the corner to the back of the house I bump right into her.

"You asshole," she growls, taking a step back. There's a little bit of light from the porch above us, just enough to see her eyes blazing. "I knew that was you."

"Relax," I say, taking a step back as well.

"Relax? Why are you stalking me?"

"Stalking you?" I laugh. "I'm not stalking you."

She puts her hands on her hips and lifts her chin up. "Really? Then what the hell are you doing here, Tony? Not exactly your neighborhood."

I could make something up. Or just tell her the half-truth. That I'm here checking on the witnesses because there's something amiss and it might affect the secret missions I run down in Key West with my brother.

But I take too long to decide and she moves on. "We're over," she says.

"Yup," I agree. "We are."

"So leave."

"Fine."

But I don't move. And neither does she.

"Well?" she growls. "What are you waiting for?"

My eyes lock with hers. Could I walk away at this point? I'd like to think so. But then things would just get worse. I could become truly obsessed instead of marginally possessed. "Better to just get it over with."

"What?" she snaps.

My hand comes up almost of its own accord. I take two steps forward and it slides right up against her bare throat, my palm fitting there against the soft skin of her neck like that's where it belongs. I feel her swallow and take a breath.

But she doesn't move. She says nothing.

I lean in and kiss her.

She doesn't kiss me back. Not right away. But I don't give up easily. I nip her lip and press my palm against her throat a little harder. She gasps and her mouth opens. I slip my tongue in, expecting her to bite it. That's typically her next move.

But she doesn't do that either. Her lips go soft and then they press against mine, kissing me back.

And then I'm pushing her up against the side of the garage, my body angling in to trap her there, my knee between her legs. Her hands come up to my shoulders, gripping them tight enough for me to feel the dig of her nails through my hoodie.

And we kiss. And this kiss is pure lust. It's forceful, and heated, and filled with memories of all the times we've done this before.

I'm immediately hard. Ready to take this to the next step.

Not take her upstairs. Fuck that. I'm gonna do her right here. Outside. Her back pressed up against the splintering wood of this dilapidated garage.

But her fingertips grip my shoulders even tighter and then she pushes me back, dragging the back of her hand across her lips, glaring at me. "Fuck you, Tony."

"Let's do it." I go back in and kiss her again.

But this time, she does not kiss me back.

This time she whispers one word. Barely audible. "Stop."

I take a deep breath that sounds more like a growl than a sigh and step back. "You know you want it."

She sets her jaw and shakes her head. "Nope. I'm not getting involved with you again. I'm so over it. I'm so over you and this fucking act of yours."

"Act?" I laugh. "It's not an act. I need you, Rosalinda. I need you to *fuck me* so I can *forget you*."

She blinks at me, then huffs out a laugh. "I forgot about you so long ago, I barely remember what it was like back then, Tony. They say when you break up with someone you only remember the good parts. Well, that's not my problem." She places both hands on my chest and pushes me until I have to take two steps back. "My problem is that I only remember the bad."

She slips past me and climbs the steps up to her deck, disappearing from view. But a moment later I hear the jingle of keys. The creak of a door. And then the finality of this encounter as she slams it closed.

## CHAPTER FOUR

# BELINDA

*I lock the door* and lean against it, my heart hammering inside my chest. What the fuck just happened?

Tony Dumas is here. Outside my apartment. Right now.

I rush into my bedroom, head straight for the window, and push the curtains aside just in time to catch him flipping up the hood of his jacket as he rounds the corner to the front of the garage.

I step back, hit the bed, and take a seat.

Did that really just happen? Did my ex just travel more than two thousand miles to... what? Stalk me home from work and kiss me good night?

*Don't be an idiot, Belinda. He came here to fuck you and then forget you. He literally just said that! To your freaking face!*

And Rosalinda? What the actual hell? Like I'm some conjoined twin or my own split-personality version of Brangelina. Which so pisses me off.

But never mind that. He came here to get me out of his system because we have this... this... *sick thing* between us.

This sick thing where we get off on the hate and the venom. Where we crave the anger and rage. Where getting off isn't enough—we must be filled with wrath and fury when it happens.

I grab my hair and it takes every ounce of self-control I have not to scream in frustration.

But I hold it in, flopping back on the bed to stare up at the ceiling. Why? Why did he come here? Why did he start this again?

It took me months to stop thinking about him after we broke up the last time. Months of lying in my bed, straining to hear footsteps outside my mother's apartment connected to our Key West motel.

Footsteps I recognized.

That's how I knew he was behind us tonight. I heard him. I didn't say anything to Vinn and Vonn because that would turn into something... well, not good. Toxic masculinity at its finest, probably. A whole bunch of posturing and implied ownership.

It's been eight years. I was doing good. I've had a couple dozen nearly normal relationships. Well, encounters. More like booty calls. But still, they didn't involve hate-fucking.

I was in a good place before that last trip to Key West. And even then, I was very proud of myself for walking away. For not giving in to the urge to walk into his cottage—just across the fucking street from the one I was staying in—and start it all up again.

And just a few days ago I was thinking, *Yeah. I'm good. It's all good. I'm over it. I'm over him. Goodbye, Tony Dumas. So long, asshole. Hope I never see your face again.*

But now?

I reach for the pillow, place it over my face, and *scream* into it.

Then I do it again. And again.

Because I might not want to admit it, but… Oh, my God. I fucking wanted to give in. So bad.

I wanted to bite his lip, and claw his face, and make him… *make me*.

I reach for my phone in my jacket pocket and I'm just about to pull up Tara's contact when I remember she's back there. In Key West. With Tony's stupid brother. Two hours ahead, so it's four in the morning her time.

I throw the phone across the room. I regret it immediately. That regret is coursing through my veins before it even hits the wall. And then I'm down on my knees, scrambling on the floor trying to find it.

Great. I hold it up to the light filtering in from the window. The screen is cracked. I've only owned this phone for six months. The screen on my last phone was so messed up I couldn't even use it anymore. And I had to wait months for that fucking upgrade.

I hate Tony Dumas. I hate him with a passion.

Hate. That's the only emotion I've ever felt for him.

So why is he allowed to have this goddamned hold over me? I don't get it.

And why does my best friend have to live so far away two time zones over? She would get it. If we were together, she'd tell me something profound. Some reasonable explanation as to why I'm still dealing with these lingering feelings. And you know what? She'd probably be right. Because she'd probably share my problem with her boyfriend—Tony's freaking older brother—and he'd have some older-brother superpower insight, and then… bam. Everything would make sense. I'd fall out of hate-fuck lust with Tony, and I'd move on to someone else.

Someone who didn't think a good time was stalking a girl home in the middle of the night and hate-fucking her against the side of a garage.

Someone who didn't pull me into their dark side and make me like it afterwards.

God. That infuriates me.

Because I don't like it! I'm just… addicted to it!

Not it. That's not right.

I'm addicted to him. Just him.

I need someone who is not him. Pretty much anyone, actually. I'll take anyone.

Someone who is the total opposite of Tony.

Hmm. I pause to think about what the opposite of Tony might look like. Just so I can have a visual. Just in case said opposite of Tony appeared in my life. I should maybe be on the lookout for him.

Tony has naturally dark hair but he's been in the tropical sun for so much of his life, it's been bleached to a dark coppery bronze. His eyes almost perfectly match his hair, a magical kind of brown. A brown that reminds me of those polished tiger's eye stones you find living in large bins inside remote gas stations in random towns in Utah, or the perfect blend of tea I once found in the new-age shop that used to be next door to Sick Boyz, but is now a used bookstore. Delicious brown.

Which means the next guy needs light eyes and lighter hair.

Tony is well-muscled and he's got ink, but listen. I'm not letting him strike those two attributes off my checklist. Fuck that. I work in a tattoo shop. Knocking off all inked men means every male who comes through the door is off limits. And let's be honest here—I'm not exactly a social butterfly. I don't even have a best friend at the moment. So even though I don't want to find my next obsession at the tattoo shop, it might be my only option.

But definitely no sailors. Or fishermen. I'm done with men of the sea. Forever.

And there it is. That feeling in my gut. That sick, sick feeling of loss I get every time I even think the words 'sea' or 'ocean.' Or 'fishermen' and 'sailors.'

Loss. Like… a true kind of grief. The kind of grief I feel for my mother when I let thoughts of her creep in too.

I don't understand feelings. They're so stupid.

Not only does Tony not deserve me, missing him and what we had in the past should not be up there on the sadness scale with missing my mother. That's so wrong. *I'm* so wrong!

No. *He's* so wrong!

Tony is a freak who gets off on putting his hands on my throat. He loves fucking me like I'm his toy. His whole world revolves around control, and darkness, and rage.

So why do I want him?

*Why?*

I bang my fists against my head and close my eyes.

I need therapy. I start tapping on my cracked phone screen, looking for therapists. I need one. Bad. Like, right now. There's something wrong with me. Something truly dark and depraved about my sexual preferences and choices in men.

No. Not men.

*Man.* One man.

Just him. Just Tony. Why is he *here*?

He has had this hold on me since high school, for fuck's sake. I was only seventeen when we first got together. He, on the other hand, was twenty-two.

I should've known. I mean, I see it now. Why would a twenty-two-year-old man want a seventeen-year-old girl?

There is only one reason.

Control.

I wish I could say that first time was magical. Oh, I came. I came hard and fast. And then he made me come again. Several more times. But magical? No. It wasn't magical. It was hot, and sweaty, and *dark*.

We weren't even in a bed. We were in the dugouts of the baseball field at the high school. This happened outside, in the middle of the night, on a bench, while I was high and a little bit drunk too.

And then my whole fucking life got tipped upside down by this man. He was all I could think about. I almost didn't graduate! I was so obsessed with him. With the sex. With… all of it.

He took over my life.

For two years, he took over my life.

It was twenty-five months and seventeen days of yelling, and jealousy, and hate-fucks.

And even though I was unhappy, and filled with rage almost every second of the day, and sick with the thought of him walking away from me, I stayed in that relationship.

I lost so much weight. I went days without eating when he disappeared on the ocean in his boat. I stalked him. I used to sneak through Kraken Karen's backyard and stalk up to his house and peek in his fucking windows.

And it wasn't his house! The Dumas family didn't own the whole street back then. Tony lived at home. So I was peeking into his *parents' house.*

I was fucking sick over this man.

And then, slowly, we both moved on. The first year after we broke up for real was rough. I did a lot of graffiti painting back then. I got busted a few times, too. And when Tony found out I was in jail for the last bust, do you know what that asshole did?

He bailed me out. Got me a lawyer and everything. And that lawyer got me off with community service. That's when I got that first commission for the mural. A legit, public mural.

My first job as an artist.

But did Tony stick around? No. He didn't answer my calls. And all I wanted to do was say thank you. But did he pick up? No.

He disappeared again.

I couldn't eat. The whole sad mess started over from day one. And it took me an entire year after the bailout before I could think straight.

Tony Dumas *wrecked me.*

And now he's back to shatter all my pieces for good.

I grab the pillow and scream into it again.

**The next day** he's all I think about.

Tony. Tony. Tony.

I want to stab myself in the eyeball. At least then I'd be screaming in pain and not be muttering *Tony, Tony, Tony* inside my head on repeat.

But of course, when I walk in to the Fort Collins Theatre to get my noontime coffee, there he is.

I almost turn around and walk out.

Hell, who am I kidding? There's no chance in hell I could turn away from the heated glare he's sending me from across the coffee shop.

His eyes lock with mine. And this is when I realize—he really *is* stalking me. I come here for my noontime coffee every day before work. He has my schedule down. And he's gonna... what? Follow me around until I give in and let him hate-fuck me?

I don't think so.

And listen, I'm not saying no because I don't want to fuck him. Or let him fuck me. It has nothing to do with the fucking.

It's the principle of the thing, OK? He's not gonna sail into this town—*my* town—for one last forget-me-forever fuck and then go back home to his stupid little Key West life, OK? That's not going to happen.

Not on my watch.

This is *my* town. He and his family were the ones who chased me out of Key West eight years ago. I've settled in. I have friends.

Well, one friend. Well, sort of. Tara. *Why did you have to move away? We were a team! We were good together! We could've run this place!*

And now... now who am I stuck with?

Right on cue Vann Vaughn's truck pulls up in front of the theater coffee shop. He's talking on the phone, grinning. That boy is always grinning.

And even now, when he's on the other side of the window, still in his truck, almost twenty-five feet away—his eyes find mine. And then that grin is only for me.

Vann has a thing for me. It's a little bit sad the way he has a thing for me. Because it's all very one-sided.

I involuntarily glance over my shoulder at Tony and find him glaring at Vann.

Hmm. Now that's an option. I could use Vann to get rid of Tony. He'd do it. He'd do anything for me.

And it would work. Vann is kind of a catch. Sure, he's a player. And yes, he's one of those happy people. But he's a talented artist. He's very good and he's offered to tat me up on several occasions, but I've resisted. Getting a tattoo from a cute guy like Vann feels… personal. Especially when he's made it very clear he would like to date me.

It's my turn at the counter so I tell the pretty brunette with the bright blue eyes what I want. I don't know her personally, but she's very friendly with the Vaughn brothers, so when the little bell jingles and her eyes flick to the door and she beams a huge smile, I know Vann just came in.

The next thing I know his hand slips around my waist and he plants a kiss on my cheek. "I'll take what she's having," Vann tells the blue-eyed woman.

The girl laughs. "Is this your girlfriend, Vann?" She winks at me and then turns to get our coffee.

"Maybe," he says coyly.

"No," I say.

"She will be," Vann offers.

"Will not," I say. And then I look over my shoulder and find Tony standing up at his table, staring at us.

Glaring at us.

Vann looks too. "Hey, is that—"

"Yes," I hiss. "Don't show fear."

"Fear?" Vann laughs. "Hey! Tony!" Vann is yelling across the freaking room. He lets go of me and saunters off to greet my ex.

The brunette sets my coffee on the counter. "Don't worry. I'll put it on his tab."

"Thanks." I smile. But I take my coffee and turn away quickly, eyeing the door, wanting to escape, but unable to resist the magical polished-tiger's-eye pull of Tony Dumas without at least looking back at him one more time.

*Do not look back, Belinda. Don't do it.*

I look over my shoulder and find Vann trying to dap Tony's knuckles.

Tony is having none of it.

"Hey!" Vann calls across the room. Only this time he's talking to me. "Bring me my coffee, Belinda."

I make a face at him.

He begs with his hands. "Please."

All around me women are smirking and giggling at adorable Vann Vaughn. The state university is just a couple blocks down. So there are dozens of girls who would love to have the full attention of a Sick Boy.

Then all their eyes are on me.

I slink back to the counter, grab Vann's coffee, then make my way over to the other side of the room.

I want to come up with a logical reason for why I'm doing this, but there isn't one.

I just can't help myself.

Tony Dumas is like a magnet. He is gravity. And I am unable to resist his pull.

Of course, everything about this is a bad idea. Vann openly flirts with me every chance he gets. Tony is a jealous asshole.

Nothing good can come from my decision to make this a party of three.

But I do it anyway.

"Thanks, babe," Vann says, taking his coffee from my hand. Then he pulls out a chair. "Sit, Belinda. Take a load off and enjoy your coffee."

"Umm... I gotta get to work."

I turn to leave, but Vann grabs the sleeve of my hoodie and tugs me back. "Come on. It's Tony. Did you know he was in town? We need to catch up. And besides, we don't open up for hours. There's nothing to do at work."

I glance at Tony. His expression is flat. Almost unreadable. But I *can* read him. I don't need to notice the way he's working his jaw to understand what's going on inside that head of his.

"Yeah," Tony says. "Sit, Belinda. Enjoy your coffee."

Vann takes a seat, pulling me into the chair next to him. "When did you get into town, Tony? Let me guess, you came for a world-famous Sick Boyz tat. I saw some ink on you back in Florida. It's not bad"— Vann says this in a way that clearly indicates he's seen better—"but we can certainly fix you up with something spectacular." Vann looks at me. "We have room on my schedule today, right, Belinda? Fit Tony in."

"Uh..."

"Sure," Tony says. "Yeah. I'll take you up on that offer, Vann. Do I get a family discount?"

"Are you family?" Vann asks. His grin never falters. But it's very clear to anyone who knows Vann Vaughn that this statement is really a challenge.

"Close enough," Tony says. He nods his head to me. "Belinda and I go way back."

"I've heard," Vann says. "How long ago did you date the fisherman, Belinda?"

"Uh…"

"High school," Tony says. "We were high-school sweethearts."

"Really?" Vann says.

"That's not really accurate—"

"Well, that's too bad," Vann continues.

"Why's that?" Tony asks.

"You know, high-school sweethearts? That's just a practice run, right?"

I stand up. "OK. We have to go now." I pull on Vann's hoodie sleeve the way he was just pulling on mine. Thankfully he gets to his feet.

"We do. We have work," Vann says, contradicting himself from just a few moments earlier. "But you stop by this evening, Tony. I promise to *fix you up*."

And yup. There it is. The threat.

"Let's go, Vann. Now." I pull him and he comes along. But of course, that can't be the end of it. Not with two men involved.

Tony calls out, "I can't wait to see what you have to offer."

"Bye!" I call, trying to make sure that's the last word.

But Vann is walking backwards now, his hands out, his grin just as big as ever. "Trust me. My offer is a good one, *Tony*."

When we get outside he grabs the sleeve of my hoodie again, pushing me towards the passenger door of his truck. He opens it. "Get in."

"I'm just walking across the freaking street, Vann. I don't need a ride."

"Get. In."

I look up and find him glaring at me.

I get in. I'm certainly not going to have an argument with Vann in front of the theatre coffee shop for all to see.

He closes my door, walks around the front of his truck, and gets in too.

"What the hell was that?"

"I don't like him." He starts the truck and backs out onto College Avenue.

"I don't like him either."

"Then why is he here?"

"I don't know. You'll have to ask him when he comes in later for a tattoo. And hey"—I stare at the tattoo shop as we blow past it—"where are you going? I have work."

"You work for *me*, Belinda. Who cares about work? We don't even have appointments until four this afternoon."

I point at him. "I don't work for you. I work for your brother, Vic. And technically you have appointments at two. You Vaughn brothers just don't show up until four."

"Same thing." He takes a hard right and I lean into the door with the force of the turn.

"Where are we going?"

He looks straight ahead. "Where are we going? We're going on a date, that's where we're going."

"A date?"

"Do I stutter?"

I laugh. "You're being stupid."

"I don't like him. I don't want you with him. He's… bad for you. I can just tell."

"I'm not *with* him. He just showed up last night."

"Last night? You saw him last night?" Vann pulls his truck over to the curb and puts it in park.

"He just…" Shit. I should not have said that.

"He just what?"

"He followed me home from work last night."

"What? That fucking asshole. I will kill him."

"Your brothers walked home with me. Nothing happened."

Of course, that's not really true. He kissed me. I kissed him back. I spent all night obsessing over him.

"Why is he here?"

"I don't know."

"This is bad."

"Vann, I can handle him. It's fine. Besides, he's not like that."

"Not like what? Not like… a fucking criminal who smuggles people into the US?"

"Kids," I say. "They smuggle *kids*."

"I get it. It's a pretty little crime. Filled with bleeding-heart feelings and all that good shit. But it's still dangerous. The FBI still showed up. With helicopters. We had to enlist the entire marina into the Dumas family business to pull that last job off. There's no way any of us would've been forgiven if we'd gotten caught. And he got you involved."

"He didn't, actually. I got myself involved. And we didn't get caught, so it doesn't matter."

"I don't like him."

"You don't like him because… he's a bad guy? Because I don't like him either, Vann"— another lie—

"but he's not actually a bad guy. He's a little weird. Especially in the sex department. But—"

"What?" Vann is looking at me with an open mouth and wide eyes.

"Sorry. TMI. But... he's not dangerous. That's all I'm saying."

"Belinda," Vann says, taking one of my hands and holding it in his. "I don't think you understand. He's part of... you know." He waves his hand around in the air. "The witnesses."

The witnesses he's referring to are all the witness protection program people who live here in the Fort Collins area. There's an unnaturally high number of them. Like... more than two dozen in the same twenty-five-mile radius.

No one with a brain thinks this is just some coincidence, but purposefully planting your witnesses in one area doesn't have to lead to insidious government corruption or secret shadow government-type doomsday plans.

Unless you're Vann Vaughn, of course. He's into that shit.

"So what, Vann? I'm one of the witnesses too. There's nothing weird going on with us. I would know, wouldn't I? And the Dumas family were the ones who got me sent here."

"That's my point. He should not be there. The streams should not cross."

"Was that a *Ghostbusters* reference?"

"I'm pretty sure it's an evergreen expression these days, Belinda."

I laugh. "You're being ridiculous! And completely overreacting."

"Am I? Well, that's a relief." He's being sarcastic now. "This town is filled with rogue FBI agents and people in the federal witness protection program. We have enough going on without your stupid high-school sweetheart showing up for a reunion!"

"He's not here for the witnesses, trust me. He's here for me."

Vann's neck jerks back in response, his normal good-naturedness replaced with narrowed eyes that flash with anger. He points at me. "You're into him, aren't you?"

"I'm not *into* him." I'm not over him, either, but I keep that to myself. "It was just one kiss!"

"You *kissed* him? When?"

Ooops.

Vann is speechless. He looks away. Looks back at me. Starts to say something. Stops. Shoves the truck into gear and pulls away from the curb.

We drive east in silence for a few miles, going who the hell knows where. Then he's shaking his head as he mutters, "I cannot believe you kissed him."

"He kinda took me by surprise. It's not going to happen again."

"Right."

"You know what, Vann?" I point at him. "It's none of your business. We're friends. I like you. A lot. I wish I could like you more. I think you'd make a very fine boyfriend. And I think you're sexy. And kinda smart." He looks over at me and frowns. "And really fucking talented."

"But?"

"But..." I sigh. "I just don't have... you know. The feels."

His jaw clenches as he looks straight ahead. Then, in a very low voice, he says, "The *feels*."

"Look, I'm not trying to be mean, OK? It's just… you're good. You're so good."

"I'm good?" He side-eyes me. And it comes with a glare. "So good it puts you off, doesn't it? You're one of those girls who like the bad boys?" He scoffs. "That's so fucking predictable, Belinda. In fact, it's disappointing."

Now it's my turn to be angry. "I'm not here to impress you, Vann. I didn't even come here by choice. I got stuck here."

"You're not stuck here now. You can leave any time you want. But you stay."

"I've been here for eight years. Maybe I've settled in? Maybe I don't want to pack up my shit and move somewhere new again? Maybe I don't want to start all over? Ever think of that?"

"You could go *home*. Your best friend lives in your home town. But you're. Still. Here."

"You keep saying that."

He's silent for a few moments. I know what he's thinking. He's thinking I'm here for *him*.

And that's not true. I am not here for him. I'm here for me. I planted roots in this town. I have a job I look forward to, a cheap, cool apartment that doesn't eat up half my paycheck, and I hardly ever have to leave the old downtown so I don't even need a car.

I'm here for me.

I'm not saying I don't like Vann. I do. He's my friend. But that's all he'll ever be. Just a friend.

I know what it feels like to be in love with someone, and I do not have those feelings for Vann. I just don't feel that… that… *obsession*. I'm not obsessed with him. And maybe I'm romantically simple, or cliché, or possibly even stupid for craving this type of all-consuming, can't-eat-anything, sick-feeling-in-my-stomach kind of love, but... I *want* it. That's all I can say.

Except I don't say that. I don't say anything.

He glances at me again. This time the animosity has been dialed down a notch. "I'm just looking out for you, Belinda."

"I get it. I understand that. But Tony and I have... you know. History. And he came here for closure. That's all. I left Key West without saying goodbye and he's probably just trying to fit all the pieces together."

"Closure?" Vann laughs. "He didn't come here for closure, Belinda. He came here for you. I took one look at that dude and I saw it. I knew him for less than a minute and I understood. He's in love with you."

"He hates my guts. He admitted that he's only here to bang me so he can forget me."

Vann guffaws. "Harsh."

"Very."

"But you still want him. It's so fucking..." He grabs his hair. "Infuriating! Why do nice girls like you fall for assholes like him?"

"And not assholes like you?"

"You just called me a good guy."

"Yeah. And I think you are. But there are probably a hundred women in this town who would take exception to my opinion of you."

He huffs some air and blows the hair up that's covering his eyes, then looks straight ahead as we continue east, away from town.

I turn in my seat and study him for a moment.

Vann Vaughn is fucking hot. I'm not going to tell him that, but I'm not going to lie to myself, either. He's one of those people you just want to look at. His jaw is square, his eyes are blue, his hair is blond, his body is well-muscled, but still on the lean side. And he smiles a lot. These smiles are wide, and honest, and reveal dimples.

He has a friendly face, even though both his arms are well on their way to being full sleeves. His theme—all these Sick Boyz have a tat theme going—his theme is words. Paragraphs and paragraphs of words. Poems and passages from old books. Song lyrics and gravestone epitaphs. Vann Vaughn is in love with letters. Some of them are big and bold, like the giant double X's on each of his shoulders. And some of them are small and delicate like the list of his nieces' names down his left ribcage.

His blond, all-American looks and his ink are the definition of a contradiction.

Which just makes him… interesting. And, let's face it, sexy.

"Vann?"

"Hmm?" He continues looking straight ahead.

"You might be my best friend." He glances over at me, then back at the road. "I mean that. Tara's gone and you're all I have left. Please, please, *please*—I'm begging you. Don't ruin this."

"Don't ruin what, Belinda?"

"Us."

"I think you just made it perfectly clear that there's no us."

"Are you deaf?"

"I hear you." He sighs. "It's just… I like you, Belinda. A lot. I think we would be good together and you won't even give me a chance."

No. He's right. I'm not going to give him a chance. Ever. And now that I have articulated that in my head there is only one thing left to say and he needs to hear it.

I really don't want to say it.

But I have to.

"Like I said, Vann, you're sexy. And smart. And talented. And sweet. And charming. And basically all the things. But I'm looking for an obsession. I'm looking for an addiction. It might be sick and it might be ridiculous. But I don't care. I only get one life and I want all the feels before it's over. You're not that obsession, Vann. You're not that addiction. So if the only reason you're nice to me is so you can hang on to the idea that one day we might be a thing, then…" I throw up my hands. "Pull over and let me out here."

He pulls over.

And I get out.

## CHAPTER FIVE

***Anna Ameci's*** seems to be the go-to restaurant for dinner in this small section of old Fort Collins. But that's not why I decide to go inside and eat. I go inside and eat because I can see Sick Boyz tattoo shop if I get a table by the front window.

It's not quite dark, and the tattoo shop has their windows blacked out with some kind of translucent paint. So the shadow behind the counter who I know is Belinda isn't clearly outlined. But I fixate on that dark, grayish smudge behind the glass anyway.

She came in late today. Got dropped off by an Uber. Not sure why that happened, but I know it has something to do with Vann Vaughn. He didn't come in late. He was actually early.

This part of downtown is old-school. There's a strip of parking that runs down the middle of the street between the north and southbound lanes of College Avenue. So right now I'm looking at Vann Vaughn's giant black truck in one of those parking spots.

It's interesting that they left the coffee shop together but didn't show up to work at the same time.

"Did you make a decision yet?"

I look up to find a pretty waitress smiling down at me. She's sexy in a very traditional way. Hips, tits, ass. And dark red hair tied back in a ponytail that sets off her blazing green eyes.

"I think I'll just have a drink."

"Oh, come on," she says. "I can tell you're hungry."

"Can you?"

"Mmm-hmm." She slips into the seat across from me, leans her elbows on the table, and props her chin on her folded hands. "Want me to tell you what's good here?"

"You really want me to eat, don't you? Let me guess, this place has a profit-sharing plan."

She giggles. I would put her at about... twenty-five, maybe. She's cute, but in a dangerous sort of way. She's got a gleam in her eyes that says *Don't fuck with me* and *Fuck me* at the same time.

She leans back in her chair and grins. "Full disclosure. My family owns this place. So you're not far off."

"You're..." I glance at her name tag. "Soshee Ameci?"

She tips her chin up. "The one and only."

"What kind of name is Soshee?"

She extends her hand. "Hello there. I'm Soshee and you are...?"

"Oh." I stand up and take her hand, then lean over and bring her knuckles to my lips, kissing them. "Tony. Tony Dumas."

She holds on to my hand for two seconds too long. Long enough for me to make an observation about her skin—it's soft—and her grip—it's light. She blushes, lets go of me, and I sit back down.

She draws in a deep breath, pretends to fan herself, then chuckles. "It's a nickname. Short for Stacy."

I laugh. "I'm pretty sure it's not."

"Whatever. My older cousin couldn't say Stacy when I was born. So she called me Soshee. And it stuck."

"Well, I like it."

"Thank you. Me too." She looks out the window for a moment. Her smile falls just a little. Just enough for me to notice. "So why are *you* obsessed with them?" She nods her head in the direction of Sick Boyz.

"You say that like we have something in common."

"We do."

"Ah…" I laugh. "You like one of them. Let me guess. Vann?"

"Mmm-hmm." Her eyes are drawn to the tattoo shop. And there's a longing in them that makes me sad, for some reason. "But he's obsessed with his new flavor of the week at the moment."

"Ah, let me take another wild guess. Belinda Baker."

Her eyes dart to mine. "How do you know that?"

"I'm stalking her."

Soshee bursts out laughing. It's a loud laugh. Like the kind of laugh you long to hear on dark nights. The kind of laugh that lights up a room.

Everyone in the dining room takes notice.

They all look in our direction and an older woman at the cash register bar shoots Soshee a dirty look.

"Sorry," Soshee calls.

"Your mother?"

"Aunt. My mother is a fortune-teller down in Boulder."

I shake my head and stifle a chuckle. "No shit?"

"No fucking shit. We're the red-headed stepchildren of the family. Both literally and figuratively."

"So you take after her? Your wild, Bohemian mother?"

"One hundred percent."

"Do you tell fortunes too?"

She taps her head. "I see everything."

"Well, you do have a front-row view of this town." I nod to the window.

She giggles. "You don't miss anything, do you?"

"Not a single fucking thing."

"I like you, Tony Dumas. We should be friends."

"Friends as in we're gonna fuck tonight? Or friends as in friends?"

She laughs again. She's an easy laugh. I like that. It's a signal of sorts. The kind of signal that lets you know someone likes you. Which she just admitted, three minutes into our brand-new stranger relationship.

"That's exciting," she says. "And bold. And, I will confess, a very intriguing offer. But if you're stalking Belinda Baker, I'm gonna have to take a pass."

"You've already got your hands full with her?"

"Exactly." She huffs and her smile falters. "She's a very hard act to follow."

"That she is."

"Why though? Why is she so… interesting? I see the way people look at her. It's like… she's a magnet or something."

"Hmm. I feel that pull."

"Why though?"

I shrug. "I wish I knew, to be honest. I don't want to be here. She's been out of my life for ten years. Missing entirely for eight of those. But she shows up in my town a couple months ago out of the blue and suddenly I can't fucking think straight. The next thing I know I'm two thousand miles away. I have a short-term rental apartment, I left my business in the hands of my dipshit brother-in-law, and I'm starting to think I've lost my mind."

"Love has that power."

"I'm not in love with her."

"Of course not. And I'm not in love with Vann Vaughn, either."

"Touché. I actually do have business here. But it's not a short-term rental type of business. It's a quick look-see and then back on the plane to Key West. But I've been in town for four days now and I haven't even gotten started on it."

"Too busy stalking her?" Soshee says. And it's not an accusation, either. Just a fact.

I nod. Then sigh. "Yeah. There's something wrong with me. I'm sick, I think."

She nods in agreement as she purses her lips and stares across the street. "I get it." Then she turns to me and her bright green eyes meet mine. There are a few seconds of silence as we stare at each other and it becomes uncomfortably awkward. So I pick up the menu and start looking at the food, unsure where this goes next.

"The lasagna is so good, you'll want to cry when you take the last bite."

Interesting choice of words. Crying after it's over. That's why I'm here, right? I glance at Soshee over the menu. "Is that right?"

"Mm-hmm. And the Bolognese? I practically come before I take the first bite."

I lean back in my chair, surprised, my frown sliding up into a smile. Now we're talking about coming at the beginning. A switch-up. A very nice change, if I'm being honest. And an intriguing way to cement this new friendship. "Jesus Christ, Soshee. Now you've got me thinking about the way you bite and come."

She giggles again. Yeah. She's definitely an easy laugh. Certainly likeable. "I know," she says, still giggling. "TMI. But seriously, the food here is good. You should eat. And don't forget dessert. We have a bakery in the back…" She bites her lip and sighs, then looks around and whispers, "The cannolis?" She runs the tip of her tongue across the edge of her teeth. "Better than getting a blowjob in the alley."

I can't help it. I laugh. Loud.

"Shhh." We get another dirty look from the aunt across the room.

"Sorry," I say. "But—"

"So you'll take the lasagna?"

"Uh…"

She giggles again. Points at me. "Oh. You're dirty. Bolognese it is. I'm off work in ten minutes, so I'll bring two plates. That way we can come together."

Then she stands up, winks at me, and walks off towards the kitchen.

My mouth falls open. I'm stunned.

What the hell just happened?

I'll say one thing. For the first time in three months I'm thinking about a girl who is not named Belinda, or Rosalie, or Rosalinda.

**Soshee returns** twenty minutes later, sans traditional black and white Italian-restaurant waitress uniform. Instead she's wearing a short, flirty sage-green skirt and a very fluffy cropped tan sweater that shows off a cute bellybutton ring. Behind her comes a troop of servers.

She slides in across from me and leans back in her seat as plates are put in front of us. It's a lot of food. The spaghetti, of course. Plus a basket of bread, a bottle of wine, two green salads, and an almost overflowing charcuterie board.

She thanks her co-workers and then starts pouring us some wine.

"Well," I say, leaning back to get a look at the dinner, "you definitely know what you want."

"That I do," she says, handing me a glass of red wine. "This is our first date, Mr. Tony Dumas. We need to mark the occasion."

"Is it a date?"

"Friend date," she says, winking at me as she takes a sip of her own wine. "Don't worry. I'm not coming on to you. I just…" She sighs. Looks out the window at Sick Boyz. "Two AM is a long way off."

"Are we staying until they close?"

"That's what a proper stalker would do."

"Are we proper stalkers?"

"We are." She clinks her glass to mine. "We take our jobs very seriously."

"Well then." I clink my glass to hers this time. "Here's to our first date as stalker friends."

**Soshee Ameci** is good company. She talks a lot. But she doesn't overpower me. I'm a hard guy to overpower, actually. I hold my own. And she's funny. Even though I can tell this situation with Vann and Belinda makes her sad, she doesn't mope.

In fact, she rallies like a champion. "You know," I say, after our plates have been cleared and the table has been brushed clean with a small sweeper, "you're taking this all very well."

"This meaning Vann?"

"Yeah."

She shrugs, glances outside across the street. "I'm a good catch, Tony Dumas. I know my worth. And you can't make someone love you, but you can make them take notice. And that's what I aim to do. If he chooses Belinda over me, I will ensure that he regrets it one day. And I don't mean I'll ruin his life or anything so predictable as that. I mean…" She tilts her head up. "I will be the best me possible and make sure he understands what he walked away from."

"I'm starting to think he doesn't deserve you."

"Yeah. Maybe. My brain thinks that too. But my heart…" She places her hand over it. "It's sick at the thought that we're not meant for each other."

"Hmm."

"Is that how you feel about Belinda?"

"No." I shake my head. "No. It's more like… an obsession. One I lost control of without knowing it."

She points to me. "An addiction?"

"Yeah. Like that."

"So walk away."

"I don't think I can."

"But why?"

"Why can't you walk away from Vann?"

"Touché."

But it's a real question. And we both know this because we go quiet as we stare out the window. People are coming and going at the tattoo shop. This is a college town and that college is just a couple blocks down the street. So I'm guessing students wander in there all the time. To look, mostly. Dream. Maybe even some of them make appointments.

But you can tell the students from the actual customers without much effort. You know who's really getting work done just by their look.

They are serious tattoo fanatics. This shop is no joke. These brothers are the real deal.

And I hate that. Because Belinda is an artist. Even if tattoos were never part of her creative dream before she came to live in this town, there's no way she doesn't appreciate what goes on inside Sick Boyz Ink.

"Are we really going to stay here until they close?" I ask.

Soshee doesn't even look at me. Just nods her head. "I am."

"Will you follow him home?"

"Hmm." She drags her eyes off the shop and finds mine. "Will you follow *her* home?"

I nod.

"We can do that together. They live at the same place."

"I know. I hate that."

"Me too."

"I followed her last night."

"Vann didn't work last night."

"I know. But the two other brothers did. They walked her home."

"Fucked up your good time, huh?"

"Nah. I sneaked around the garage after they went inside. But she caught me. She was waiting for me."

"Did you guys…" Soshee waggles her eyebrows at me.

"No. I kissed her. And she kissed me back. For a second. Then she told me to stop." I sigh. "And I did. And she pushed me away and told me to get out of her life. That's pretty much where it ended."

Soshee is wincing.

"I know," I say. "I get it. I should go home. I have a business to run."

"But you're not going to, are you?"

I shake my head. "I think…" I look at the tattoo shop again. "If I could just fuck her one more time, ya know? I could put it behind me."

"You don't really believe that?"

"I do. I put her behind me before. For nearly ten years. I can do it again."

"Hmm. Well, how did you do it last time?"

I think I blush. Because Soshee laughs. "Oh, my God. What did you do?"

I shake my head. "I can't say it out loud."

"Yes, you can!" She reaches across the table and slaps me on the arm. "You can't leave me hanging like that. Tell me!"

"We... screamed at each other. Said every fucking insult you could think of. I'm talking some very mean shit. And then we fucked. Still insulting each other. Still raging. Still willing to display our hate. And then when it was over?" I shrug. "It felt... over."

"Hmm. The be-all-end-all ultimate rage-filled hate fuck. That's intriguing. So you're gonna try that again?"

I nod. "I think it'll work. I need to make this girl go away."

"Are you sure you're not in love with her?"

"No. No way. We're not meant to be together. This is some sick obsessions shit, Sosh. We are not soulmates, or lovers, or even frenemies. She is the one who *needed* to get away. What we had together wasn't blind love, it was sick rage. We were a match made in hell, it was hate at first sight, and when she walked away from me and never looked back it was a relief. It was bliss. I need to get that bliss back."

"Wow. I think that was the most thoughtful sentence you've said all night."

"I've been thinking about it for a while."

Soshee laughs. "So you simply need a hate fuck?"

"Yeah."

"And then you're out of here?"

"Yup. Gone."

"Well, I'm not going to lie. I'm really going to miss you when you go."

"We literally just met a few hours ago."

"So funny. Because right now, you feel like my best friend."

I hold up my nearly empty glass of wine. "Cheers, my new BFF."

She clinks me and smiles. "Cheers to us."

## CHAPTER SIX

**BELINDA**

**The anger I felt** when Vann drove off and left me on the side of Mulberry Street, a good three miles out of town... yeah. That's some rage right there.

Of course, the practical version of me knew I'd asked for it. I did. I said drop me off. I got out. He pulled away.

But what the actual fuckety-fuck?

It was fine. I walked off my rage for about a mile, then I called an Uber.

Vann was already at work when I arrived. In fact, he was in his studio and the buzzing of the tattoo machine was filtering down the hallway to the front seating area.

I did not go back there. I did not say one word to him. I just sat at the counter, greeted the people who came in—mostly to look at the ink displayed on the walls—and minded my business.

Fuming. Raging. Filled with heat and anger.

Eventually the other brothers arrived. Vic first. He's the oldest. Huge dude, tatted up from top to bottom. He grunted at me amicably when he came up to the front to check his schedule, nodded his head at the people in the waiting room, and then disappeared inside his studio.

Vonn and Vinn, the twins, showed up next. They did the same—but they always talk to me. So I pretended I wasn't about to murder their baby brother and smiled as they joked and clowned about tramp stamps with the sorority girls in the waiting room.

But eventually all the brothers were busy and I was left with my thoughts as everyone with appointments went back to get their work done and the lookie-loos wandered outside.

I asked Vann to drop me off. I can't be mad that he did that.

But I am.

He is all I think about.

I barely pay any attention to the customers who come and go. Or the schedule. So it's not until nearly dinnertime when I realize Vann didn't actually have an appointment this afternoon. In fact, he doesn't have an appointment until eight o'clock tonight.

So who the hell has he been working on all this time?

I'm not going to look. It's none of my business. I do not care.

I don't need Vann. Best friends are totally overrated.

Totally. Overrated.

Except when they're your only friends.

I need more friends. That's my mission this week. Get more friends. I'm gonna put myself out there and find a new BFF. I need to replace Tara. Vann is not going to be my default best friend. It's not going to happen. No way.

I'm mad at him. We're over. He can take his all-American good looks and that stupid perpetual charming grin and shove them all up his ass for all I care.

Done. That's what we are.

Over.

*A little after six* I weaken. It's pure and simple curiosity. I slip off my stool and walk down the hallway. But it's not for Vann. It's only to get everyone's dinner order.

Because that's my job.

Vic declines dinner. He has a case of protein bars in the break room and his current client has a huge back piece he's trying to finish, so he's not taking a dinner break. Vonn and Vinn want Anna Ameci's, because of course they do. My day would not be complete if I didn't have to run into bitchy Soshee Ameci at least once.

And Vann...

I stop in the doorway to his studio, confused. He's hunched over the back counter, a spotlight shining down on the space in front of him.

"What the hell are you doing?"

He doesn't turn around. Just keeps buzzing the machine.

"Are you tattooing yourself?"

He pauses the machine and growls, "What the fuck do you want?"

"It's dinner time. What do you want to eat? Your brothers want Anna Ameci's, so I'm gonna call the order in."

"I don't need you to get me dinner. I can get it myself."

"You're probably gonna run into Soshee," I say lightly, trying to joke about the fiery red-headed waitress who has feelings for him that aren't reciprocated.

His machine starts buzzing again. Clearly, he is ignoring me.

I don't like fighting with him. This is not what we do. I want us to go back to the way it's supposed to be. Where he smiles at me and I laugh at his grin and fun antics. We're a good team. A friendly team. We tease each other, and have deep serious conversations about bombpops verses creamsicles, and we're always on the same team when his twin brothers break out a Frisbee for an impromptu game.

We're friends, for fuck sake. Why does he have to complicate things with deep feelings?

His new anger is… intimidating. I don't think we've ever had a proper fight. Definitely not one where I tell him to drop me off three miles outside of town and he actually does it.

So I'm not used to this attitude of his. I feel a little unsure of myself as I wait in the doorway.

"What?" he snaps, pausing the machine. But he doesn't turn to look at me. Doesn't even glance over his shoulder.

"Look—"

"I'm over it, Belinda. OK? Just… go away."

He goes back to his ink.

"Fine," I say, turning on my heel and heading back to the front of the shop. But I mutter, "Fuck you, fuck you, fuck you," the whole way.

I order the food and then sit on my stool, tapping my fingernails on the glass counter as I wait for it to be ready for pickup.

This is not my fault. I did not lead Vann on. I tried to set him up with Tara, for fuck's sake. And we had a good time when we did the little road trip to Key West. We went to the beach and had a party with the freaking Dumas brothers. We slept in the same cottage, and drank, and had meals together, and… that was fun.

I mean, the whole going home thing was weird, and seeing Tony was unsettling, but the Vann and Belinda part? That was fun.

Why can't he see that we're good together as just friends?

Why must he push this thing we don't have between us?

It's not my fault I don't feel his pull, right?

I sit there for a few more minutes, then slip my jacket on and head out to pick up the food. Praying that Soshee isn't working the takeout counter.

She's not. Thank God for small miracles. Her younger cousin, Annabelle, is. She takes my money and tells me she'll be right back with the food without any animosity.

I like Annabelle. She's only about seventeen, but she's cute, and friendly, and doesn't hate me because Vann and I are BFFs.

Well, used to be. I guess that's over now.

I really hate him for ruining our good thing. I'm seriously pissed that he's fucking all this up.

But I take a deep breath and absently wander towards the edge of the dining room. And who the hell do I see?

Tony Dumas. Having… dinner? With Soshee Ameci.

"What the fuck?" I mutter.

They're both laughing. Staring into each other's eyes from across a table near the window. Two wine bottles and a dessert plate between them with remnants that look like they might've been the famous Ameci Chocolate Lava Cake.

Tony leans across the table and swipes his finger over Soshee's lip, like she had a drip of chocolate there, and then he licks his fingertip.

I gag and turn away.

Vann is wrong about Tony and me. We actually do hate each other. It's just… hate sex is… *hot.*

I'm not jealous of Soshee. I'm not. He can flirt with her all he wants. I do not care.

But the reason I don't care is because I know he wants to fuck me. He followed me home last night. He kissed me. And we would've fucked—right there, against the garage—if I hadn't stopped him.

And if I wanted to, I could walk over to that table and make Tony ignore Soshee Ameci.

The front door jingles and I turn to look.

Vann walks in.

"I thought you weren't hungry?" I ask.

But his eyes immediately dart to the table near the window where Tony sits with Soshee. He stares at them for a moment, frowning. And I can't tell if he's frowning about Soshee or Tony.

Then, for the first time since he dropped me off on Mulberry Street, he looks at me. "What the fuck is going on there?" He nods his head towards Tony and Soshee.

"Don't know, don't care," I say, turning my back to him and walking back to the takeout counter. "Why are you here, Vann?"

"Because I came out of the fucking shop and saw them staring at me through the window. I think she's trying to make me jealous."

I scoff. "You don't even like Soshee. What do you care?"

He doesn't answer me right away. So I turn back to him, trying to get a look at his arm, curious about the tattoo he's been working on all afternoon. But he's got the whole inside of his forearm covered in Saniderm and the edge of his long-sleeve thermal shirt has slid down to cover it.

He's not looking at Soshee and Tony anymore. He's looking right at me.

He says nothing. I say nothing. And the moment becomes awkward immediately.

"What?" I finally ask.

He glances at Tony and Soshee, who are now looking at us, then glances back at me with electric-blue eyes all lit up with... what? Anger? Excitement? Longing? "I think you two deserve each other," he says.

"Really? Why's that?"

"Because you both like to play games." Then he takes a step towards me. Several steps, actually. Until he's so close I have to tip my head up to keep our eyes locked. Suddenly his fingertips are threading through my hair, gently touching my scalp.

And then he leans down and kisses me. Right on the lips.

I'm stunned, and embarrassed, and unable to pull away.

So I kiss him back.

His mouth opens and I respond by opening mine. And the next thing I know our tongues are twisting together, and we are making out in the waiting area of Anna Ameci's Restaurant.

He pulls back first. Grins at me. Touches his lips with the tip of two fingers as he smiles.

"What the hell was that?" I whisper.

"You're gonna make a big mistake, Belinda." He whispers this back at me softly, no anger in his voice. "Very fucking soon. I just want to make sure you know what you passed up when that happens."

He turns away and walks out of the restaurant.

"Here we go!" Annabelle says, plopping a brown takeaway bag on the counter. "Sorry for the wait. You're all set, Belinda. I've put it on the Sick Boyz tab."

I look over at the dining room and see Tony glaring at me. He gets to his feet.

And I'm like... nope. No fucking way am I in the mood for the fight that's coming. I'm not able to process what just happened and if Tony Dumas thinks he can force me into some kind of public emotional outburst when he confronts me, he's mistaken.

I grab the bag and head for the door, calling out, "Thank you," to Annabelle as I push through it. And then I head across the street.

But there's a brand-new crowd of freaking college girls blocking the doorway, all of them gazing up at Vann Vaughn like he's some kind of hot Colorado tattoo god, so I head into the alley, walking fast, trying to buy myself some time to figure out what just happened.

I round the corner to the back alley and duck into the little alcove that houses the back door to Sick Boyz, press my back against the bricks and… *breathe*.

Wow. That kiss was…

Wow.

And that's when Tony Dumas comes into view. His mouth a flat, angry line. His eyes dark with heat. His chest heaving through his tight t-shirt as he breathes through whatever feelings are coursing through his blood. "What the fuck was that?"

"What are you doing here? Won't your new girlfriend wonder where you're at?"

"Is that jealousy I hear in your voice?"

I scoff. "You wish. I don't give one flying fuck about who you have dinner with, Tony."

"It wasn't dinner. It was lunch."

I scoff again.

"That's right," he says, coming into the alcove towards me, getting way too close to me. So close that I can smell the familiar, sexy scent of his body. "We spent the entire day together. Laughing and talking like normal people." He lowers his voice. "Flirting." He's so close now he reaches up and rests his hand against the side of my face. "She won't turn me away when I try to fuck her later."

"Good for you," I say, pushing him back. I clap my hands together. Slowly. Like he's special and deserves this mocking accolade. "She's in love with Vann, by the way. So whatever you get from her is just sloppy seconds."

"Hmm." He smiles at me with tight lips. "I'd believe that. If I thought he was fucking her. Which he isn't. So no, sorry. She appears to be all mine."

"You can have her. No one cares, Tony."

"Except you."

"No." I laugh. "I do not care who you fuck."

"No?" he says, once again taking a step forward. His fingertips reach for the edge of my t-shirt and he pulls me towards him until my breasts bump up against his chest.

"No," I whisper back. And it's the truth. I do not have room in my head for Tony right now. That's not what's on my mind in this moment. At all.

My thoughts are consumed by Vann.

But, for some reason I can't quite articulate, this time, when Tony kisses me on the mouth the way he did last night… this time I do *not* push him away.

## CHAPTER SEVEN

**TONY**

***Soshee is a love-game*** mastermind. I bow to her.

We get lost in conversation as we sit across the street from Sick Boyz Ink waiting for the night to be over so we can stalk our respective targets and bully them into something yet unknown.

I'm pretty sure she's picturing herself fucking Vann Vaughn tonight.

I know I'm picturing myself with Belinda. I want to do deliciously dirty things to her. Not romantic things. Nothing about what I'm doing here has anything to do with romance.

It's pure hate-fucking.

I want to put my hand up to her throat and feel her swallow.

I want to yank her jeans down to her knees and fuck her up against a brick wall.

I want to bite her lip when I kiss her and make her whine.

I want to bang her and then walk away, satisfied that I got what I came for.

And then I want to go home a free man. Forget all about Belinda Baker just like I forgot all about Rosalie Thompson ten years ago.

My obsession with Rosalinda will be over. Tonight. I'm going to make sure of it. And Soshee has agreed to help me.

So when we see Belinda come out of Sick Boyz and head towards Anna Ameci's we make a plan. I will confront Belinda as she waits to pick up her food. And then Soshee will slip across the street and confront Vann.

What we didn't expect was for Vann to follow Belinda over here.

And that kiss he gave her, in full view of both me and Soshee? We didn't see that one coming either.

My body is hot with rage and anger when he kisses Belinda. They share some kind of moment. Here, in front of everyone. Vann leaves. Belinda watches him… and the look on her face?

What the fuck is that look? What does it mean?

She glances at me and I get to my feet. But she's out the door before I can move.

"We're on," Soshee says. Then she points to the window and we both watch Belinda cross the street towards Sick Boyz. But Vann is standing out front of the tattoo shop with a group of college girls, so Belinda darts into the alley to avoid him.

"You take the back," Soshee says. "I'll take the front."

And like a dream team in the game of let's-use-each-other-to-get-what-we-want, Soshee and I exit Anna Ameci's and cross the street. Vann is inside now, and she follows him through the front doors, glancing over her shoulder at me just long enough to wink.

I slip in the alley, wondering if Sick Boyz locks the back door. Wondering if Belinda will be in the break room or already back at her station in the waiting area.

But I don't need to wonder long, because she's not inside when I round the corner to the back of the building.

She's leaning against the brick wall like... like she needs a moment to catch her breath.

Is she *swooning*?

I just stare at her, my body numb with feelings I'm currently unable to describe, but for some reason the word *unraveling* comes to mind.

I ravel back up and say, "What the fuck was that?"

Belinda shoots me a face of pure contempt. "What are you doing here? Won't your new girlfriend wonder where you're at?"

"Is that jealousy I hear in your voice?" I laugh.

She scoffs back at me. "You wish. I don't give one flying fuck about who you have dinner with, Tony."

"It wasn't dinner. It was lunch."

And even though she tries to play it off, she doesn't quite manage it.

"That's right," I say, walking forward into the little alcove. I get close to her. Way too close. So close I get the urge to lean in to her neck and smell the sweet scent of her botanical shampoo. But I'm not unraveling. I'm in control now. So I say, "We spent the entire day together. Laughing and talking like normal people." I lower my voice to a throaty growl. "Flirting." I'm so close now I can reach up and rest my hand against the side of her face. "She won't turn me away when I try to fuck her later."

"Good for you," Belinda says, pushing me back. And she starts to clap. Slowly. In a mocking way. "She's in love with Vann, by the way. So whatever you get from her is just sloppy seconds."

"Hmm." My lips press together as I force a smile. "I'd believe that. If I thought he was fucking her. Which he isn't. So no, sorry. She appears to be all mine."

"You can have her. No one cares, Tony."

"Except you."

"No," she huffs. "I do not care who you fuck."

"No?" I ask, getting even closer to her. My fingertips reach for the edge of her t-shirt and I pull her towards me until her breasts bump up against my chest.

"No," she whispers back.

And even though I am the one who commands her full attention right now, I can just tell her mind is on something else.

No. Not some*thing*. Some*one*.

She's thinking about *him*. That kiss. The way she... swooned. Because that's what I just caught her doing.

She didn't dart behind the building to avoid Vann at the front door to the shop. She went to the back door so she could have a moment to herself. To relive that kiss in her head before she shook it off and had to join the rest of us in the real world again.

I snap my fingers. "Eyes up here, Rosalie."

"Don't call me that." Her eyes blaze as she spits these words up at me.

I press my body against her with a little more force, grind my hips a little. "Changing your name won't change who you are, *Belinda*."

"I didn't just change my name. I changed my life, *Tony*."

"I don't really care what you call yourself. I'm happy to go along with the lie. But when I'm standing in front of you, I need your attention on me."

"What do you want? Do you even know why you're here? I didn't invite you. I didn't lead you on back in Key West, I didn't flirt with you, I didn't hang around like a lonely little puppy waiting for her master to take notice."

"No. You left."

"And that pisses you off, doesn't it?"

She's got me there.

"Hmm." She smiles, averting her eyes. As if not looking at me can hide the smirk.

I take a step back, let go of her shirt. She glances up at me with a tight frown. "OK," I say. "You want me to go home, Rosalie? I can do that."

"Oh, can you?" She scoffs. "If that were the case you wouldn't be here in the first place. If that were the case, you wouldn't be following me around like a creepy stalker. If that were the *case*—"

"So why don't you just let me fuck you, get it all out of my system, and I'll be on my way?"

"Oh." She laughs. "Oh." She points at me. "You are the biggest douchebag I've ever met."

"Then why are you still standing here? Hm? That bag of food is getting cold. Be a good Girl Friday and take it inside to your masters. Such a fucking amazing career you have going here. I'm so proud of you."

She slaps me. "Fuck you, Tony."

My hand comes up to my cheek to feel the heat and sting of the slap. I grin at her and she makes a face. But she doesn't push me away and she doesn't go inside. She stays right where she is.

So I step closer once again. My fingertips find the edge of her shirt. But this time, I don't hesitate. I palm the soft skin of her stomach and slide my hands up to her breasts, grabbing the edge of her bra and pulling it down so her tits bounce out.

She sucks in a breath. But that's the only signal she sends me.

It's enough. Practically a "yes." Pretty much a "keep going."

I lean in to her neck and whisper, "You like this, don't you?" Her shoulders bunch up like I just gave her a chill. "You like this sick game we play. You can't get enough, can you?" One hand slides down to lift the edge of her skirt. I pause for a moment, my fingertips caressing her thigh, my head slightly cocked so I can see the side of her face.

I wait for her to stop me before I move forward.

She doesn't stop me. She bites her lip and begins to breathe faster, staring straight ahead, eyes fixed on some unknown point across the alley.

"Mmm-hmm," I hum. "You like it."

"It's got nothing to do with 'like,' Tony. It's…" But she doesn't finish.

"It's OK," I say, nibbling on the edge of her ear. She bunches her shoulders up again. Shakes her head. "I feel it too. I'm not here because I want you, *Rosalinda*. I'm here because I need you. You're my sick obsession. I weaned myself off of you almost a decade ago. Had you sent away. Got over it. Forgot about you. Rosalie who?" I laugh a little and she turns her head away from me, exposing her neck. I kiss it. Softly. Tenderly. I can be that guy. But with this girl, it's just another trick I've learned over the years. "But then you came back. And it was like… taking that first drink after being sober and the addiction coming back unwanted. Trust me, I'm not here for you. I'm here for *me*."

Her jaw clenches as she takes in these words. She presses her lips together and inhales a breath through her nose. "So I'm your fix? Is that it?"

"That's it."

"And you're gonna... what? Fuck me right here? In the alley?"

"Well, I would've gotten over it last night in a more private place, but you stopped me."

"You're not going to leave me alone until you get what you came for?"

I kiss her neck again. This time she doesn't fight it. She drops her head to her opposite shoulder in an act of submission. I kiss my way down her neck until I reach her clavicle. I nip the tender skin and she hisses in a breath.

"Just give in completely," I whisper. "And then it will be over."

"You promise?" She turns her head to look at me. We're so close I can see the little swirls of green and gold in her hazel eyes. I lean in and kiss her mouth. It becomes soft and pliable immediately. A completely different reaction than the one she had last night.

I don't promise her anything. The time for talking is over now. We've gone past the point of no return.

My fingers leave her thigh and slip between her legs. I massage her pussy through her panties for a moment, getting them all wet.

She leans back into the brick wall of the alcove, closing her eyes and enjoying it.

I smile. *Got you.*

And then I push her panties aside and slip two fingers into her pussy. She arches her back and raises her chin like she's about to pray to some unknown god to make her come.

"Look at me, Belinda. I'm the god in control of your orgasm now."

She takes a deep breath. I continue to play between her legs. And then she opens her eyes and stares straight into mine, her hand in motion now too. Popping the button on my jeans and dragging the zipper down in two quick movements.

I laugh. I can't help it. I knew she wouldn't be able to resist me.

A moment later she's got my cock out, pumping it with a tight fist. I withdraw my fingers from her pussy and grab her ass, lifting her up and pressing her against the wall. Her legs wrap around mine immediately. Like they belong there. Like we've done this hundreds of times before.

We have.

I have always loved fucking her outside.

A moment later I'm inside her. Pressing my chest against her breasts and grinding against her hips. Her fingers thread into my hair. She fists it when I thrust into her, going deep. Deep enough to make her cry out. I pause our kiss to bite her lip, silencing her cries, but increasing her moans.

Her knees squeeze me, holding me close to her, locking us in place as we fuck.

We are short breaths and long sighs.

We are lovers, but not friends.

We are animals and this is nothing but instinct.

She comes, clenching the muscles of her pussy around my cock, squeezing it tight the way she did with her hand a few moments ago.

I want to come inside her, but I won't. I won't lose that much control. So when she's done, when she is slick with the cream of her release, I pull out and spill all over the inside of her leg.

We freeze the moment, neither of us daring to move as our hearts race and our breaths come out in gasps. I lean in to her neck, smiling.

And then... the doubt creeps in and I begin wondering if I just made a mistake.

I don't love her. She is just a planet orbiting in my zone. I pull her towards me and she responds because she has no choice.

Because these are the laws of physics.

We're not here in this alley, sweaty and calm, because we're meant to be together.

We're here because we're meant to be apart.

"Put me down," she says, pushing me back with a grip on the shoulders of my jacket.

I don't move for a moment.

"Tony." She growls my name and squirms in my arms, already regretting our desperate act. "Put me down."

I drop her legs and take a step back, tucking my dick away as I create distance. She sighs and looks down at her leg, then up at me, eyes flashing with anger.

I grin at her, the need gone now, my sanity firmly in place. But I'm not an animal. I slip my hoodie over my head and throw it at her. "Use that."

She catches it, wipes my come off the inside of her thigh, and throws it back. Then she points her finger at me. "Go home. You got what you came for and now you need to go home."

Then she picks up her bag of forgotten food, opens the back door to Sick Boyz Ink, and slips inside.

## CHAPTER EIGHT

**BELINDA**

*I go inside*, close the door, and lean against it.

What the hell did I just do?

"Oh, my God!" I whisper. What the fuck is wrong with me? I know better! I *know* better.

It took me so long to get over him. So many months of crying myself to sleep. So many months of that sick, gutted feeling in my stomach. So many months of utter despair and sadness.

And the worst of it wasn't that he got away—it was that I knew he was the wrong man for me. And yet I couldn't stop those feelings. I could not control my emotions.

He took me.

He took me, and he used me, and he threw me away.

And I knew he was doing it. He didn't even lie about it.

Just like he's not lying about it now. He came here to fuck me and throw me away once again.

And I just... *let him.*

I walk over to the breakroom table, set the food down, and then grip the edge and lean over, still breathing hard from the sex, my heart still hammering inside my chest from the lust.

I am sick. All over again. Because I already want him again.

And if he doesn't go home… if he doesn't leave town… we're going to do this forever. We will be stuck in this sick rut of obsession. We will use each other up until there's nothing left of either of us.

He will ruin me, and I will ruin him, and… and…

"What the fuck are you doing?"

I turn to see Vic Vaughn looming in the doorway, his massive six-foot-plus frame completely blocking the light from the hallway like some dark monster coming to expose my secrets.

"I…" I look at the door, then quickly avert my eyes and find the food on the table. "I got dinner." I point to the bag. "For Vonn and Vinn. They wanted meatballs from Anna Ameci's."

I can still feel the stickiness from Tony's come lingering on my inner thigh like evidence and I want nothing more than to go into the bathroom and wash it off.

Wash Tony Dumas off like the filth he is.

Vic just stares at me, his expression hard, like always, his blue eyes dark, like always. His tatted-up arms crossed over his chest and his expectations unclear, like always.

The random laughter and chatter of people fills the shop filtering in from the front. I hear all sorts of things in the moments of silence as I wait for Vic to say something.

The squeaking of wheeled stools as his brothers work. The buzzing of the tat machines as they ink art on skin. The low hum of the autoclave behind me. And the sick music of long-forgotten rockabilly coming from the sound system.

Vic. His real name is actually Vicious. Yes. His crazy tattoo-artist father and whoever their mother was actually named their baby boy Vicious.

When I first found that out, I imagined his parents having a Sex Pistol fascination, but knowing what I do now of good old Vic here, I seriously doubt that's where his name came from.

He *is* vicious.

Not at all good-natured and charming like Vann. Not at all fun and entertaining like the twins.

Vic Vaughn is serious to the $n^{th}$ degree. He is a cold man with an assassin's heart. An assassin who just happens to make art.

"What?" I say, unable to bear the silence another moment.

He narrows his eyes at me. "Get back to work, Belinda." And then he turns and walks back to his studio near the front of the shop.

I head for the breakroom bathroom reserved for employees. And I'm just about to pull the door open when I hear, "I *said*, get back to work."

I look over my shoulder and find Vic back in the doorway. For a moment I consider arguing with him. But then I just nod.

He turns away again and I follow him.

The hallway leading to the front is long and narrow. The right side, as I travel back to front, is just a wall filled with pictures of the ink this shop has created over the years. Those years add up to decades. This place has been a staple in the old Fort Collins downtown since the Fifties.

And on the left side of the hallway are the studios. Four in total. Each of them has a pocket door. Vic has the studio closest to the front, then Vonn, then Vinn, then Vann in the last one closest to the break room. When I first came to work here the father had the front studio and the twins shared one. Their sister used to work here too, but she has since retired to do face painting for kids. Didn't care for the blood. Has some weird obsession with germs or some shit.

Vic turns into his studio, satisfied that he's going to get his money's worth out of me tonight, and I slowly walk to the front. I pass Vann's room—his pocket door pulled closed now—and I'm just about to open Vonn's door to let him know his food is here when I hear laughter burble out from Vann's studio.

What the hell is going on in there?

I pause, curious. Because... that laugh.

Oh, no. It can't be. Vann doesn't let Soshee Ameci anywhere near his studio. He knows damn well she's in lust with him and he has insisted to me for more than six months now that it's over between them and he doesn't want to lead her on.

So that *cannot* be her.

I backtrack a little until I'm standing in front of Vann's door.

And then I hear more than just laughter. I hear *fucking*. I'm talking grunting, and moaning, and sighing, and skin slapping. God.

I quietly pull the door open a crack and immediately wish I hadn't. Because it *is* her.

Soshee Ameci is sitting on the counter, just to the left of Vann's neatly stacked and custom-curated ink assortment, with her legs open. Vann's hips are between those legs. He's thrusting into her with force.

She's got her eyes closed, her hands wrapped around his neck, fingertips playing with a curl of wild blond hair that is just long enough to touch his shoulders, mouth open as she pants out her lust. And he's got his hands flat against the upper cupboards on either side of her body like he needs the support, the muscles of his back clearly defined under the tight Sick Boyz t-shirt he's wearing.

I don't know what to do.

I understand what I *should* do.

I *should* close the door just as quietly as I opened it, walk up front, sit down on my fucking stool behind the glass counter filled with after-care products and piercing options, and mind my own fucking business.

And that's my plan when suddenly Soshee opens her eyes and our gazes lock.

She smiles at me. And then she starts moaning.

Not loud. Not loud enough to carry into other rooms over the din and clatter of people in the shop or the music coming from the ceiling.

Just loud enough for me to hear it.

"Oh, Vann," she says. "Oh, yes. You feel so good. Do I feel good?"

"Fucking A," Vann grumbles. "Your pussy is hot, Sosh. Squeeze my dick. Squeeze it hard, baby. I want to come—"

"Oh, Vann," Soshee says. "I'm coming, I'm coming—"

"Goddammit, Belinda!" Vic's voice booms down the hallway at me.

I glance at Vic, barreling towards me, fierce anger in his eyes. But then I look back at the spectacle of fucking in the studio and find Vann looking over his shoulder at me.

I blush. He backs away from Soshee, hurriedly tucking his dick away in his pants.

And then I bolt.

I run to the breakroom bathroom, fling open the door, slip inside, and then slam it closed behind me, locking it with a satisfying and much-needed *click*.

And then I hear Vic again, the anger in his voice very clear and apparent. "What the motherfucking fuck is going on in here, Vann?"

I plug my ears. I want to wash my eyes out with soap. I need to get that image of him fucking her out of my head.

But I can't.

I just see it. Over and over again.

His dick swinging out of her as he turned. Wet with her…

"Gross! Oh, my God, that's just so gross!" I lean against the wall and cover my eyes. Like either of these things will help erase the trembling in my legs and the image burned into my memory.

There is a fight going on in the breakroom. I hear Vann. I hear Soshee. I hear Vic. Something about dicks, and pussies, and professional behavior. But the music is extra loud in this bathroom. Men. This is really their bathroom. I normally use the one up front reserved for clients because… well, porn mags are everywhere in this one. "Gross, gross—"

Someone bangs on the door. "Belinda!"

It's Vann.

I just shake my head. I'm going to need to quit. I… I… there is no going back from this. I don't even understand why I'm so upset. I don't even like the guy. I literally just got fucked by my ex in the disgusting back alley.

But the next thing I know, I'm on my knees on the scuffed floor covered in muddy boot marks, leaning over the toilet, retching.

More pounding on the door. "Belinda!" It's still Vann.

"Go away," I say, wiping spit from my mouth. "Just... forget it. I quit. I'm done. I can't—"

But I stop. Because I don't even know what I'm saying. I'm just... confused, and sad, and broken, and ashamed. And almost none of that has anything to do with Vann.

And yet he's the one I can't face right now.

Who cares if he's fucking Soshee? Not me. I do not like that boy. I do not want him. I have never wanted him.

But that *kiss*...

He kissed me across the street just twenty minutes ago. A kiss so passionate and filled with longing, I couldn't think straight.

Maybe that's all he needed? Maybe he's just like Tony? He got it out of his system and now he's moving on. To Soshee!

"Belinda!" Vann pounds on the door. "It's not what it looked like!"

"Oh, really!" I laugh. Loudly. And get to my feet. I start grabbing paper towels from the dispenser—one, two, six, ten—until I have a whole wad of them. I get them wet under the tap and start wiping the dried come off the inside of my thigh.

And then I stop. Because I have a revelation.

I don't know who I am anymore. I seriously do not understand what just happened.

But here's what I do know: I need to get the fuck out of this town. Right now.

"Belinda." A calmer voice now. Deeper. More authoritative. Vic. He knocks, doesn't pound. "Open the door." He says it quietly because he is a man who almost never needs to raise his voice to make a point.

"No," I say, sucking in a deep breath. "I... I quit. Just... go back to work and I'll get my things and—"

"You do *not* quit. I don't hire *quitters*, Belinda. Now open the motherfucking door. Or I will break it down and come in anyway."

Again, all this comes out in a low, soft voice. Which is scarier than a yell, if I'm being honest. I prefer the bellow. The bellow says he's frustrated, not angry. The whisper says he's serious.

He rattles the knob and the whole door shakes as he makes his point.

I sigh, then reluctantly walk over to it, flip the lock, and step back.

Vic opens the door and I get a brief look of Vann peeking over his shoulder, trying to see past him. Vic steps in and closes the door behind him.

Suddenly this room is way too small. He towers over me. Like—this man is seriously big. A good foot taller than I am, for sure.

"Look," I say.

"No. You look," Vic says, cutting me off. "I didn't hire you because you're cute and fun to look at. I didn't hire you because you have pink hair and wear flirty skirts with cowboy boots. And I most certainly didn't hire you so Vann could weasel his way into your life and have fun flirting with you at work. I hired you because I think you have talent. I hired you because you show up every day without exception."

I hold up a finger. "Except for that time I disappeared to Key West."

He glares at me. I shut up. "I hired you because I think you're going to be an amazing tattoo artist one day."

I huff. "One day, huh?"

"Starting tonight."

"What?"

"I need some help with my client. He's in the army and he's shipping out on Monday. He needs a lot of filler to get this back piece done and a new design on his shoulder. He doesn't know when he'll be back and he wants it done before he leaves."

"So you want me to… what, do filler?"

He cocks his head at me. "Are you too good for filler?"

"No. I'm just confused. Why now?"

"Because Vann is stupid and young. He has a crush on you. And you, obviously, do not feel the same way. And…" Vic sighs. "I get it."

I squint my eyes at him. "You get… *what*?"

"It's a game, Belinda. I've played it myself a million times."

I try to picture Vic Vaughn having a crush on a girl who doesn't feel the same way back, and find I do not possess the kind of imagination this scenario requires.

"He's hurt. Your ex is in town—"

"He told you that?"

"I overheard him telling Vinn. Not the point. He's jealous so he figured he'd pay you back a little."

"First of all," I say, holding up a finger, "he didn't pay me back. I don't care who he fucks."

"Right."

"Second, you've been stringing me along for years, Vic. I can count the number of actual tattoos I've done here at this shop on my fingers and toes. And suddenly you want me to help you with a client? Why?"

"I'm not stringing you along. When you first got here the old man was still working. There are only four studios, Belinda. It's a numbers game. Then the old man left, Vann got his studio, and still there are only so many to go around. Vinn and Vonn shared a studio for years. They're not going to do it again. But… if you can find your own clients, and do some walk-ins, I'll let you use my studio on my days off."

I squint at him. "Because I have promise."

"Because you have talent. I've seen your sketches. And I'm not going to beg, OK? Do you have any idea how many applications I get a day for artists looking to do an apprenticeship? A lot. A dozen, at least. This isn't pity, this isn't me being nice. This is practical. This is business. Now do you want to fucking help me tonight or not?"

I don't want to smile. I really wish I could stop the smile. I even try biting my lip to make it go away.

But there is no hope of that at all.

I legit grin from ear to ear.

And then I giggle.

"I'll take that as a yes?"

I nod. "OK."

"Great. Now get your fucking ass out of the bathroom and help me." He opens the door. It swings wide too fast, banging against the wall. He steps out, passes Vann, who hovers near the table where Vinn and Vonn are now eating their meatballs.

"Belinda!" Vann says.

Vic turns on him. Points his finger in his little brother's face. "Shut the fuck up, Vann. No one wants to hear your pathetic excuses."

Then he looks at me and nods his head towards the door.

I walk down the hallway.

And massive, tatted-up Vic Vaughn follows me like he's my brand-new bodyguard.

## CHAPTER NINE

**TONY**

*I stick my hands* in my pockets as I make my way back up the alley to College Avenue. I don't smile. Not outwardly, anyway. But I can't help but feel satisfied that I got what I came for and now I can go home.

It wasn't an amazing fuck, as far as fucks go. But my goal has been met. And, for the moment, at least, I'm content.

Soshee is still inside the shop and I don't want to go home without talking with her, so I linger in the alley between Anna Ameci's and a candle shop and wait for her to appear.

It doesn't take long. And I wonder if she had as much luck with Vann as I did with Belinda.

She crosses the street, heading towards the theater coffee shop, but then spies me in the alley and heads my way, grinning.

"I take it you got lucky," I call to her once she's close enough to hear.

She runs to me, eyes bright and mouth smiling. She grabs the sleeve of my jacket and spins me around with her. "Oh, my God!" she yells. "I cannot believe that just happened!"

"What? What happened?" She's practically jumping up and down and her happiness is contagious, so I get caught up in her excitement.

She calms down a little and steps closer to me, still clutching my jacket. She looks over her shoulder with a gleam in her eye, then up at me. "He fucked me."

"Damn, girl. You have skills."

She giggles. "Right in his studio. And the best part? Oh, my God. The best part is that Belinda caught us."

"What?"

"Yeah. She came in just as we were finishing, and saw me come. I was looking right at her when it happened."

"Fuck. What did she do?"

"She bolted. I think she locked herself in the bathroom."

"Hmm."

"Did you get lucky?" She practically squeals these words.

"I did. I fucked her in the alley behind the shop. Came all over her leg."

Soshee slaps my arm playfully. "Gross!"

I narrow my eyes a little. "You didn't let Vann come inside you, did you?"

"He didn't get a chance!" I almost howl with laughter. "Vic caught us. And then… chaos. Vann pushed me out the front door and"—she shrugs with her hands—"here I am."

"So… this was good?" I ask.

"Good enough," she says. "I mean, fuck Belinda, right? I don't even care that she saw us. Vann wanted me. He was all talking dirty and enjoying himself. And it's kismet that you and I"—she points to herself, then me—"we're both getting a quickie from these two people at the same time."

"Kismet, huh?"

"Yes. Vann wants Belinda and she was with you. I think it's perfect."

"Hmm."

"What?"

"Do you really like him?"

"Are you kidding? He and I are soulmates. He just doesn't know it yet." She narrows her eyes at me. "Why?"

"I don't know. He doesn't seem like your type. And I'm not sure you're going about this the right way."

"What do you mean?"

"I mean, Vann? He's into big trucks with huge tires. Mirrored sunglasses and hoodies. I bet he snowboards, right?"

"Oh, hell yeah. Back in school he used to disappear all the time with his friends to hit Vail. They barely let him graduate he missed so many days."

"Do you snowboard?"

She laughs. "I don't even ski. I hate it. All those people… ugggh. Tourists? No, thank you. I can't deal with dumbasses."

"That's kind of my point. You're one of those free-thinking, go-with-the-flow girls. You're a local, I-eat-organic-and-my-mother's-a-fortune-teller kind of girl. He's… *not*."

"He is."

"He's so not. Vann Vaughn is all about appearances. He has no depth. He's a walking tattoo-artist cliché."

"You don't really know him, Tony."

"Like I said, I know his type. I've met hundreds of guys like Vann Vaughn back in Key West. Blond, tanned, built. Charming. But underneath it all, they're just douchebags looking to get laid."

"Like you?" She winks at me.

"Kinda like me. But I'm not actually a douche. I've got purpose."

She links her arm in mine and starts tugging me towards the coffee shop. "What purpose?"

"Just… you know. A long-term plan. And I do good works."

"You do?" She snorts. "Pardon me for saying so, but you don't come off as the good works kind of guy."

"No?"

"Not even a little bit."

"So how do I come off? From your stranger's perspective?"

"Are we still strangers?" Soshee cocks her head to the side as we walk across the street.

"Aren't we?"

She stops walking in front of the Fort Collins Theater and plants her hands on her hips. "Do you want to come up and eat dinner with me?"

"Up?"

"I live here." She nods her head to the old brick building that houses the theatre. "They have shitty lofts on the top floors. They're going to remodel the whole thing in a few months, so my time here is limited. But—"

"Wait." I hold up a hand to stop her so I can laugh. "I live here too."

"What?" She slaps my chest playfully. "No way!"

"I swear. I got one of those B&B things for the week. It's on the third floor."

She tsks her tongue. "That's one floor below me!" She slaps me again. "Now that is kismet, my friend!"

The next thing I know she's got me by the hand and she's dragging me into the theater. She weaves her way through the coffee shop towards the stairs and holds my hand the entire jog up to the fourth floor. Doesn't drop it until we're standing in front of an old, battered steel door.

She produces a set of keys from her bra—I die with delight when she does that—winks at me, and then throws the hulking door open, pulls me inside, and slams it closed behind us.

Soshee Ameci is, in a word, wonderful. And so is her place.

I look around and find that my eyes cannot stay in one spot for too long. There's so much to see. So many beautiful, interesting things in front of me.

I'm not any kind of expert in design, but I've seen this type of style before. Mostly in chic coffee houses on TV. She's got overstuffed velvet couches in a shade of blue that hints towards gray and mustard-colored throw pillows with blue paisley accents. The entire loft is surrounded in paned windows, but she doesn't have traditional curtains. She has strings of brightly colored blue and yellow beads hanging in front of the windows. And right now they catch the fading gold light of the sunset hovering over the mountains in the west and send sparkles twinkling on the high, pitched ceiling.

On the raw-edged wooden coffee table in front of the couch there sits a tea set. Like… a full-on fucking tea set. Cups and saucers. Two pots. Little spoons on a tray. And all the patterns on the china are mismatched. Not in a busy way though. In an eclectic way that conjures up feelings of home, even though my mother doesn't drink tea and I'm pretty sure she doesn't even own a tea pot. Still, I get this feeling of nostalgia and a vague, undefined longing for the good old days.

Sitting on top of a dresser with many drawers of different colors there is something that might be a... shrine? If one were praying to the Lord of Suns. Because she has a collection of round, glass orbs in every shade and tone of orange, yellow, and red you can image. Paperweights, maybe? Crystal balls? I'm not really sure. I don't really care. They are stunning. And behind them are candles in every variety. One very tall, elaborate candelabra that must hold more than a dozen candlesticks sits in the back, the Lord of Suns himself, presiding over his court of stars. And then lots of pillars, and tea lights, and votives scattered around the orbs.

I suddenly want it to be dark. I want her to light every single candle in this room just so I can stand in the middle of it and become part of the fantasy she has conjured up in my imagination.

I let out a breath, realizing I was holding it in. "Damn, woman. This place is kind of amazing."

"Really?"

I look over at her. She's got her head cocked at me in confusion. "Yeah. I fucking love it. My place at home is like... well." I chuckle. "The fucking rental downstairs."

"Boring?"

"Yes."

"Minimalistic?"

"Definitely. I'm not sure what that look is called, but it's certainly not *this*."

Soshee chuckles. "It's called..." She thinks for a moment. "Clean slate."

I laugh and agree with a nod. "Yeah. That about sums it up. But this place?" I look around again. "It's pretty spectacular."

"Most people tell me it's way over the top. And all of this stuff came from my mother." She huffs a laugh. "It's all second-hand. She used to have a consignment shop a couple years ago. Before she moved down to Boulder to tell fortunes full time."

"Well, that explains the vintage feeling of nostalgia."

Soshee laughs again. "Well..." She seems speechless. "Wow. I think I just fell in love with you, Tony Dumas. Thank you."

"People don't really think this is over the top, do they?"

She sighs. "They really do." Then she looks around at her home and her shoulders slump a little. "All the kids from high school?" She glances at me. "They used to call me the gypsy's daughter. And not in a good way. I made the mistake of bringing a friend home in seventh grade. My mother and I lived in this crappy trailer on the north edge of town back then. And even though she didn't say anything while she was there, the next day in school I got the nickname. Everyone made crosses with their fingers and spread rumors that we were Satan-worshippers. Most of this stuff is left over from that trailer. I couldn't afford all new furniture and anyway, I like my style. People can fuck off, ya know? But the nickname faded over the years, and I don't want to encourage a revival, so I don't usually bring people here."

"You brought me."

"Yeah, but you're just a visitor. You'll be here for a day or two more and then you'll go home and I'll probably never see you again. I guess I didn't really care what you thought."

I stare at her for a moment. Really *see* her.

She's pretty. Beautiful, actually. But in a way that says I-work-hard-for-this-look. Her eyes are dark with smoky makeup, her lips painted up a shade of red that accentuates her almost maroon hair, and her skin is smooth and pale, but still maintains a glow.

I find myself wondering what she looks like after a shower. After all the embellishments have been washed away and the only thing left is the real person underneath.

I bet she'd be more than beautiful like that. She would be stunning, I think.

"Well, those people are stupid," I say, realizing that I'm staring at her and she's starting to feel uncomfortable. "Your place is like a... a tribute to Pottery Barn back when Pottery Barn felt vintage and cool."

She laughs. Loudly. "Oh, my God. That's it. You're totally moving in with me. I need your kind words surrounding me at all times. You can be my very own walking, talking suit of armor, Tony."

"Hmm," I murmur, liking her description of me. When Belinda is around I lose sight of myself. She changes me into this... asshole I am right now. I put up walls, and morph into the angrier, darker boy I used to be.

I'm not really that guy. I was. Once. When I was young and stupid. When the weight of family expectations was first set upon my shoulders. But I haven't been that guy for a long time now. I'm fine with the secret things my brother and I do. I actually look forward to the sneaking, and plotting, and planning these days.

But when Belinda came back—Rosalie. No. Rosalinda. This weird amalgamation of the two girls. The one I once knew and the one I don't know at all—when she came back it was like all that long-forgotten rage came with her.

"Well… do you want a drink?"

I look over at Soshee and in that same moment I forget about Rosalinda. I almost forget how I got here. "Yeah. I think I do."

I join her in the kitchen as she pours us each a glass of wine. Soon we're chatting and talking like old friends instead of new ones. We order dinner from the theatre restaurant downstairs. And when the food comes, the sun has set, and I help Soshee light every single candle in her loft.

Then I just stand there, in the middle of the space, and let myself fall into the enchantment.

Forgetting all about a girl called Rosalie who is now called Belinda.

And remembering what it's like to fall for a stranger.

## CHAPTER TEN

# BELINDA

*At first, tattooing with Vic* is nerve-wracking on many levels. His client is a guy around my age with a lean, muscular body. He eyes me with fierce suspicion when Vic brings me into his studio and tells him I'll be helping out with filler on the right side of his back while Vic works on the new tattoo on his left shoulder.

I expect him to object. Not because of me, specifically. But because two artists working at once? On the same body? I'm not much of a tattoo collector myself, but I have a couple. And there is no way I'd let two people work on me at once.

But that's not his objection.

It really is *me.*

"I thought you said Vann could do it?" Army dude, who is called Trev, says.

"Vann has a client tonight. If you want this done before you leave, it's gotta be Belinda. She's my up-and-coming protégée. Trust me, she will amaze you."

I smile sheepishly at Trev. Vic is lying to him about all those things. Vann does have a client tonight, but that appointment isn't for a couple hours, at least. And the part about me being his protégée—I think I would know about that, if it were the case. Also, I'm fairly certain he doesn't think I'm about to amaze anyone. Vic thinks I have potential. But the last thing a person about to let you carve up their skin with ink wants to hear is that their artist has *potential*.

Vic pulls a stool out from under the counter and slides it over to my side of Trev's prone body in the chair. I glove up, listen as Vic explains the design to me. I'm doing some pretty typical filler. Flames and smoke and possibly—Vic says we'll see how things go—some hand lettering.

Then we settle in. Trev is a talker. He chats almost non-stop to Vic. I didn't check him in—I was getting food when he arrived. But I've seen his name on the schedule several times since I started working here. He's a regular, of sorts. And he and Vic seem to go back a long way.

I only half-listen to their conversation about parties, and girls, and motorcycles—hey, at least the elder Sick Boy is on theme, right? Instead, I concentrate on doing the best job I can on the filler flames. Vic's artistic style borders on photorealistic. So I take my time trying to make my flames match Vic's already present design.

It would be nice to be able to do my own style and my own designs, but this is not my client. And Vic's work on Trev's back is spectacular. The last thing I want to be known for is fucking it up with filler.

I'm facing the door—which is open—so it's hard not to notice Vann walking by every few minutes so he can look at me.

I'm not interested. I'm one hundred percent not going to talk to Vann ever again.

Not because he fucked Soshee Ameci in his studio and I caught them, either. That's so not why. It's because I'm totally embarrassed about how I reacted. Or… really… overreacted.

He probably thinks I'm jealous.

He probably thinks, *Ah ha! She does like me. And that little hysterical display after she caught me fucking another girl is proof!*

But it's not. I'm *not* jealous. I'm actually disgusted. In fact, Vann Vaughn is even less attractive to me right now than he was this morning when I considered him hot.

I don't think he's hot. Nope. His grin isn't charming. It's… ah… sleazy. Yeah. He's sleazy. Fucking random girls he doesn't even like in his studio with all kinds of people around.

What's wrong with him?

I get the irony. I'm a hypocrite. I just fucked Tony outside in the alley. But in my defense, there was almost a zero possibility of us being seen. And it was only to get Tony off my back and make him leave town.

Fucking Tony tonight was a joke, of sorts. Maybe even a necessary evil.

That's it.

Vann walks by. Again. And he looks right at me. Again. I pretend not to see him from behind my safety glasses. Anyway, it's a quick pass by. He's heading to the front to check people in.

A few minutes later I hear him laughing. Even over the music, and conversation between Vic and Trev, not to mention the giggling girls in the waiting room, I can hear that laugh.

OK. I will admit that Vann has a nice laugh. It's catchy. And easy. And light. Not a too-loud haha, but not a huffy chuckle either. It's deep and comes from his chest. It makes you want to smile.

"Follow me," I hear him say. "I'm in the back."

He walks by the room, and then a blonde girl— young, beautiful, sexy—hell, let's just call her look "porn-star cheerleader meets cliché stripper princess"—follows him. But she practically slides to a stop and backtracks.

I shoot her a weird look, momentarily pausing my work.

"Vicious Vaughn. I thought you were off tonight?" Slutty Princess leans against the doorjamb and grins at my boss.

Vic stops working too, and then pulls his facemask down and swivels in his chair. "Cherry! What's up?"

Cherry? Her name is *Cherry*? Gag.

"I would give you a hug, but—" He holds up his gloved hands.

"I'll take a raincheck," Cherry coos. "But I thought I was booked with Vann because you were off tonight."

"He came in for me," Trev mumbles.

"Hmm," Cherry hums.

"What, I'm not good enough for you, Cher?" Vann jokes.

Cherry turns to Vann and pats his cheek. "Oh, no. It's not that at all, sweet Vann."

Sweet Vann? Double gag.

"But this design tonight is… in a… how should I put it?" Cherry pokes her cheek, making a fake dimple, and pretends to think. "A delicate place."

I snort. Everyone looks at me. Even Trev lifts his head up from the face pillow. "What?"

"Yes, delicate," Cherry continues. "But you won't mind, right, Vann?"

Vann looks down at her... uh... yeah. *Not subtle, asshole.* And then his eyes shoot back up and over to me. "Wait. What?" he says. "You want a tattoo... there?"

Vic and Cherry laugh loudly. "You'll see, sweetie," Cherry says. She shoots Vic a look that says, *Your loss, buddy*, grabs Vann by the collar, and tugs him to the back, towards his studio.

"What the hell was that?" I ask.

"That was Cherry," Trev says. He and Vic both chuckle like I'm missing the inside joke.

"OK."

"She wants a cherry tattoo down on her—"

"Right," I say, putting up a hand. "I get it."

Vic and Trev chuckle some more.

"Belinda and Vann have a budding thing going," Vic says.

Trev lifts his head up again to look at me. "That right?"

"No," I spit. "No. Absolutely not."

"She caught him fucking Soshee just before I dragged her in here with me."

Trev laughs and puts his head back down. "Ah, this all makes sense now."

"What makes sense? And no one cares who Vann is fucking, Vic. Least of all me!"

Trev lifts his head again. "That was you throwing that tantrum earlier?"

"She was gonna quit over it."

"No one cares, Vic. Can we just get back to work? And you!" I point to Trev. "Stop moving around. Some of us are trying to work here."

Trev and Vic look at each other and guffaw.

I huff through my mask.

"OK, OK, OK," Vic says. "We'll get serious."

"Yeah," Trev mumbles. "Let's get back to the topic of Cherry's pussy tattoo!"

Which they do. They chat about Cherry's pussy—not her tattoo—since it seems that Vic and the girl who right now has her legs open for my Vann used to date once upon a time.

Wait.

Did I just call him mine?

I cringe, thankful for the facemask so Vic can't pick up on it. But he's too busy asking me if I've ever tattooed any private parts to even notice my internal conflict. "College girls," he explains in a mocking, serious, listen-to-me-grasshopper tone, "ask for all kinds of weird shit once they see who their artist will be. You know, because I'm hot." He winks at me and I roll my eyes. "And up until now, it's only been the girls coming in doing that shit. But you wait, Belinda. Once these college boys hear you're taking clients, I'm sure they'll all be lining up for dick art!"

Trev guffaws so hard, my needle slips on his side and my perfectly shaped tendril of smoke goes crooked.

"Funny," I say, wiping off my working area with more force than I need. "Haha."

"I'm kidding," Vic says. "No dude in his right mind wants a needle anywhere near his cock."

"Yeah," Trev says. "They'll go for the butt cheeks first. Then if they like you"—he actually sits up a little so he can see me—"then they'll want your opinion on the shaft tat. Just so they can whip it out and show it off."

"They'll ask for a snake that grows." Vic laughs.

"Meet my little friend," Trev says. "Who gets bigger as you watch!"

"Touch him, Belinda. He won't bite."

"Hold it tight, Belinda." Trev snorts. "He might get away!"

They fall into fits of laughter.

"Are you guys fucking thirteen years old in here, or what?"

All three of us look over at the door where Vann is standing. And boy, is he ever scowling at me. "Why are you looking at me?" I say. "I have no part in this!"

"This is like… sexual harassment, Vic. You're not allowed to say that shit to Belinda."

Vic looks at me. I look at Trev. And then all three of us guffaw.

"Fuck you guys," Vann spits. He disappears down the hallway.

"Fuck you, Vic," Vinn mocks from the studio next door. "You can't say that shit to Belinda!"

"Yeah, fuck you, Vic!" Vonn joins in from further down the hallway. "It's sexual harassment!"

I'm pretty sure even the customers in the waiting room are laughing now.

"Fuck all of you!" Vann yells. His door slams closed.

Vic puts up his gloved hand and I high-five him. Then he winks at me.

"Thank you," I say.

"You should be thanking me, Belinda," Trev says. "I'm the hottie making your night right now."

"Any time that brother of mine is an asshole to you, Belinda, you come to me. I'll handle it."

I nod, liking him a lot more than I did just a few hours earlier. He really did plan this whole night just to make me feel better. He didn't have to ask me to stay. He has all kinds of people interested in my shit job, after all. He could probably replace me in a day. And he didn't have to drag me in to his studio with him to take my mind off things, either. He definitely didn't have to share his client with me.

But he did all that. And he did it for a reason. Probably not to make Vann feel bad or even teach him a lesson. I think he just did it to be… nice.

Which is nice.

The three of us settle down and Vic and I get back to work. He and Trev are quiet now. Maybe thinking about things the way I am. Or hell, maybe they're still thinking about Cherry's pussy.

The point is, I don't care.

Because inside I'm smiling. Happy. Maybe even OK with the weirdness that has taken over my life for the first time ever.

I've felt like an outsider for eight years. I was forced into moving to this town because of the witness protection program. I have a fake name and a fake history. Everything about who I was was cleared away to make room for the new me.

And then Tony Dumas showed up to remind me that the new me isn't real.

I think that's what bothered me most about today. Rosalinda, he called me. Some weird Frankenstein's monster person who is not who she once was, nor who she was told to be.

Tony made me feel fake.

But nothing about the past few hours at work has felt fake.

It feels… right.
It feels like I just became a Sick Boy.

## CHAPTER ELEVEN

**"Did you rent this place** because you can see the front door of Sick Boyz from up here?"

Soshee and I are sitting at a two-seater, bar-height table looking out the window at the shop as I say this. Her loft is aglow with dozens of candles. They've been burning for hours and some of them have even gone out, their fuel supply exhausted.

"If I say yes, will it make me pathetic?"

"No." I smile at her. We're definitely a little buzzed after finishing off a second bottle of wine. That's a total of four bottles of wine between us today. "But you might be asking the wrong guy."

She laughs. "Right. Stalking your ex from a decade ago? Not the healthiest decision you've made recently."

"Tell me about it. It's weird, though. I don't even like her, Sosh."

She smiles when I use the familiar, shortened version of her name. "You have to like her some, though. Right? Or you wouldn't be here. And that would be super unfortunate, because then we wouldn't be friends."

"Truth."

"Which part?"

I shrug. I don't want to admit that Belinda—as Rosalie, anyway—was a weakness that almost broke me. But I'm not much of a liar. "Both. I did like her. Once upon a time. Or… I'm not even sure *like* was the word. It was more of a…"

"An obsession?"

I point to her. "Maybe?"

"I know that feeling. So the answer to your question is yes. At first I wanted it to spy on Vann. He's always out there on the street, either in front of the shop hanging out with his friends or random people— that guy makes friends with everyone, any time of day—or at the motorcycle shop his older sister owns with her husband." She points to a lit-up sign that says 'Shrike Bikes.' "The theater owners are friends of theirs. And my family as well. That's how I got this place. I begged and begged and begged them to rent me this loft space for half price. They only agreed because they're going to remodel in a few months and the tenant who lived up here before me got another place and moved out early."

"But now?"

"Hmm?"

"You said at first. At first you wanted this place so you could spy on Vann. But now? You feel different?"

She looks around, sighs. "I love this loft. It feels like home. I don't think I've felt that way about an apartment before. I do enjoy the view." She smiles down at College Avenue below. "And I still love it when I catch Vann down there. I feel like a voyeur, I guess. It's exciting to be able to watch him and he has no idea I'm doing it." She sighs again, heavier this time. "I'm really going to miss this place when I have to move next month and that feeling has nothing to do with Vann." She sits up straighter. "But I'm trying to appreciate it in the now, you know? Just be thankful I get to live here at all, even if it's just for a short period of time. So, the short answer to your question is yes and no."

We both laugh and she goes silent for a moment. Probably thinking about all the things she just said and how it's a little bit TMI to be saying all this to a guy she's known for less than a day.

I get lost in people-watching for a moment. Spy that yippy white dog again, this time not wearing the green and white CSU sweater and with a different person at the end of the leash. "Yeah, I get it," I finally say. "Not that I live in the past or anything." I turn my attention back to Soshee. "I'm usually a pretty grounded guy. I'm not a professional stalker. I swear to God I've never followed an ex two thousand miles across the country just so I could secretly plot a get-over-her scheme."

"Oh, now I really feel awkward. Because that's something I'd totally do and I wouldn't even feel guilty about it."

I laugh. "Yeah, but it's part of your charm."

"Am I charming?"

I look at her. Study her a little more closely than I have up until now. And my conclusion is that she is more than just charming. "Soshee Ameci. You are the most interesting girl I've met in a very long time."

"Since you first met Belinda, you mean?" She's got a gleam in her eye. Almost a twinkle. Like she's teasing me and testing me in the same moment.

"I'm not gonna lie to you. There's no point. Yeah. Rose—" I stop at the name slip-up. I'm really not in the mood to explain why the girl she only knows as

Belinda is known as Rosalie in other parts of the country. "Belinda is…" But I can't really find the right word for the energy Rosalinda radiates. "I don't know. She's just… different than most people. She gets to you. Gets under your skin and kinda makes herself at home. And then, even though you weren't planning it, you find that her presence in your life is a constant you can live with."

"And then you realize it's also a constant you can't live without?"

"Huh," I hum. "Yeah. That's kind of a good way to explain it."

"What about you?"

"What about me?"

"So you're here for her, and then what? You're gonna take her home with you when you leave?"

I can't tell if that's hope I hear in her voice, or the edge of disappointment. "I already told you no. My older brother actually sent me up here to check on some things."

"I hear you saying that, but it doesn't make much sense."

"I know." I sigh. "I get it. Trust me, it makes no sense to me either. I just… felt… compelled to check up on her. And I hate it." My voice rises in agitation. "I fucking hate that I'm here. I hate that I can't stop thinking about her."

"Hmm. The old enemies-to-lovers thing. It's hot, I guess."

"Is it? Or is it just sad?"

"Oh, I don't know. In the books it's hot."

"Books?" I laugh.

"You know. This is like… what do they call it?" She looks up at the ceiling as she thinks. "A theme, or whatever. A trope. Falling for the wrong guy?" She smirks at me. "Or girl. It's kind of classic."

"It might be classic. I get the attraction to someone who's totally different from you. You don't understand them yet. They have their own outlook on life. Maybe even a completely opposite worldview. And it's alluring for some people. I think falling for someone like that is kind of... mature."

"Mature?" She chuckles. "In what way?"

"You know. When you have this belief system and you're committed to it, right? It takes a lot of self-reflection to be able to look at things from another point of view. And then to like a person who believes the opposite of you? Yeah. That's maturity. It's... *wisdom*."

"Hmm. I guess I never thought of it that way. I've never personally had an enemies-to-lovers relationship. I don't hate Vann. I'm pretty sure he doesn't hate me, either. He might not be interested in me the way I am him, but he doesn't hate me."

"I don't have that kind of relationship with Belinda, either."

"No?" Soshee's eyebrows go up.

She thinks I'm lying. Or at the very least delusional.

"No. Not at all. It's not like we have two completely different outlooks on life. I think our personal belief systems probably line up quite well. Belinda is just... I don't know." I throw up my hands. "I seriously don't know why I'm here or what I think is going to happen before I leave."

"Your brother sent you on business." It takes a lot of self-control on Soshee's part not to laugh out those words.

"Right. Business. I haven't even started asking around about that."

"You wanted to fuck her."

"Yes." I sigh. "But... *why*?"

"She's pretty. You can't tell me you're not attracted to her. She's a little bit short, but that just makes her cute. And she has a style to her. Those short skirts and cowboy boots. That pink hair. Her career as a tattoo artist. That's kind of... fucking awesome. People are just naturally drawn to her." She huffs. "You are my exhibit A. She's like Vann in that respect. And she has an attitude." Soshee frowns. "I wish I was like her. She really is a badass girl."

"What the hell are you talking about, not like her? You're not short, but you're sexy runway-model tall. That's a big, fat check in the pro column as far as I'm concerned. And trust me, your legs look amazing in that short skirt of yours. And you've got red hair. Natural, right?"

She nods. "It's all me."

"Belinda dyes her hair. Trust me. That's not the real her down there. Not even close. If you knew what I knew about her, you'd see it my way. Besides, you're just... naturally you. Belinda is a construct. Plus, you *definitely* have an attitude."

"Yeah, I know. But Belinda has that cute I'm-a-little-firecracker kind of attitude. Mine is more of a Poison Ivy personality."

I guffaw at her. "Poison Ivy the superhero? Well, she's sexy. And she has red hair. So, yeah, I can see it."

"But she's a bad guy. No one wants to be friends with the villain in the story."

"Don't they? I think everyone loves the villain. Even when they hate them. And anyway, Poison Ivy is more of an anti-heroine. She's all about the ends justifying the means."

"Hmm. But Belinda has more of a don't-fuck-with-me-or-I'll-insult-you-with-cute-trendy-euphemisms kind of attitude. Mine is more along the lines of I-will-poison-you-in-your-sleep kind of attitude."

I laugh. Loudly. Then point to her. "People respect that kind of attitude, Soshee. Don't sell yourself short." And then a new idea kinda hits me. "You know what this is?"

"What?"

"It's very much a case of… not mistaken identity. But something like that."

"I don't understand."

"Well, you're falling for the wrong guy and I'm… not falling for the wrong girl. That probably makes no sense."

"Hmm. No. It sorta does. I get what you're saying. He's not right for me." She pouts her lips. "And Belinda isn't right for you."

"Exactly."

"That sucks though."

"Why? Because you've invested time and energy into stalking Vann? And now you might have to admit that it was a waste?"

She sighs. "Yeah. Definitely something to think about, I guess." She smiles weakly at me. Then her attention redirects to the street down below. "Well, there goes Vann."

I look down at College Avenue below, and sure enough, there's Vann coming out of the shop. He walks to his truck, gets in, then pulls out, takes a right on Mountain Avenue, and disappears from view.

"Closing time, finally. But at least he didn't leave with Belinda."

"There's Vonn and Vinn," Soshee says. "I guess everyone's done for the night."

We watch as one of the twins locks the front door to the shop and then the two custom motorcycles parked in front of the shop roar to life in the silence of downtown and they pull away and out of sight.

"No Belinda, though," I say.

"She probably went out the back."

"The lights are still on."

"That's probably Vic. It's pretty common for him to pull all-nighters. His clients are almost all out-of-towners. People come from all over the world to get ink from Vic so he does long sessions."

"Damn, woman. You're like a little fountain of information." Then I point to her. "No. A really tall, sexy, red-headed mountain of information."

She slaps my pointing finger away and laughs. "Stop it." But then she sighs heavily and stands up. She grabs the wine glasses and takes them into the kitchen. I grab the empty wine bottles and follow, handing them to her. She sets them on the counter and turns to me, leaning back against it. "Thank you for being my spy partner."

"It was my pleasure, Soshee Ameci." I take her hand and kiss her knuckles.

She smiles, but doesn't blush, and then pulls her hand away. I wasn't trying to make her blush, so that's a good sign that she isn't thinking I'm about to make a move on her. The whole jilted-lovers-find-each-other trope really is sad and not classically romantic.

"We should do it again sometime."

I point to the floor. "I'm right downstairs if you need me."

"How long are you staying?"

"Well... I dunno. I got what I came for, I guess. Well. Except for the actual reason I came here. Which was to check up on something for my brother."

It's really unfortunate that Alonzo sent me up here to get answers, because Vann is actually the guy I was gonna talk to. He's the one with the local info I need. But that's a complicated story and I'm not going to involve Soshee in this shit. That's how things with Rosalinda got all messed up.

"But after that?" I shrug. "No reason to stick around."

"You sure about that?"

"I'm not here to woo her, Sosh. I just needed to get her off my mind so I could get back to my life and put the whole thing behind me."

"If you say so."

"I do. But... I'll see you tomorrow though? Probably? I'll stay the weekend, I guess. I'm paid up until Monday. Maybe I'll go be a tourist for the rest of my trip. See Colorado."

"Sounds fun. And yeah, come in for breakfast at Ameci's tomorrow. I'm working the breakfast shift and the bakery is the hot spot around here on the weekends. You must try more of our baked goods."

"I hear they're better than getting a blowjob in the alley."

She smirks at me. Then giggles.

I point to her again. "Poison Ivy. There are worse things to be."

"Point."

"Good night, Soshee."

"Good night, Tony."

She walks me to the door and I take one last glance at her as I make my way towards the stairwell. She waves, then closes the door and disappears.

It was a nice night. It really was. She's a nice girl. And easy to talk to. And pretty. Very pretty. If I was in the market for a girlfriend, I might try to take her mind off Vann. But I'm not. I'm going home in a couple days and then I will put Rosalinda and Fort Collins, Colorado behind me.

But when I get to my door, I pause.

Rosalinda and Vann.

They live at the same house. Well, technically, she lives above the garage. But still. He has such... *access* to her. Access I do not have.

He's there right now. And so is she. They could be doing anything. Fine, so they didn't leave together. That doesn't mean anything. Soshee was right. Belinda probably went out the back. And she's probably home right now. And did I detect a little slump in Vann's walk as he got in his truck?

He fucked Soshee earlier today. He has to know she lives up here. Her apartment lights were on. One glance up and he would've seen us.

But he didn't look up. He was looking down, in fact.

He has no interest in Soshee Ameci. Which means he's very much stuck on Belinda Baker.

*Don't do it, Tony. Don't even think about it. Just stick your key in the lock, open the door to your rental, and go to sleep.*

*Put her out of your mind.*

*You got what you came for. It's over.*

But there is still that little nagging feeling that it's not.

And the next thing I know I'm hopping down the stairs to the ground floor and pushing my way through the back door of the theater that leads to the alley.

It's a fifteen-minute walk down Mountain Avenue to the ramshackle Vaughn family mansion. It's nearly four AM, but when I get there, there are several lights on inside.

When I creep up to the side window and look inside, I see Vonn and Vinn sitting at a small table, eating sandwiches.

But no Vann.

I look over my shoulder at the garage. I can't see if her apartment has lights on from here because there are no windows on this side. But I'm here. I came all the way over here. So I'm not leaving until I at least take a look.

I walk around the garage and I'm just turning the corner, ready to climb the stairs that lead to her door, when who do I see?

"What the fuck are you doing here?"

Vann. Fucking. Vaughn. Sitting on the top step and leaning against her front door.

"I could ask you the same question," I reply.

"I fucking live here."

"You live over there," I say, nodding my head towards his shitty house.

Vann gets to his feet. "Dude, I'm not gonna tell you this twice. So you better hear me, OK?"

I huff a laugh.

"Stay the fuck away from Belinda. She's not interested in you."

"Is that right?"

"Yeah. That's right."

"Then why did she let me fuck her in the alley outside your tattoo shop when she came back from getting dinner?"

His mouth drops open.

"Oh, she didn't tell you? Hmm. Interesting. I thought you two were friends? Funny though, Soshee told me that you fucked her right about the same time."

"What?"

"What? Was she lying?"

"What the hell is going on here?" I whirl around to find Belinda behind me. "Why are you here, Tony?"

I smirk up at Vann, then turn my attention to Belinda. "I think we have some unfinished business."

"Did you fuck him?" Vann asks.

Belinda's eyes go wide. Her mouth drops open too. "What the hell, Tony? You *told* him?"

"We were comparing notes." I chuckle. "Seems we all had a little booty call at the same time last night."

And that's when Rosalinda's fist hits me square in the mouth.

## CHAPTER TWELVE

# BELINDA

*"What the hell?"* Tony yells. "You're insane!"

My fist draws back and I'm just about to swing again when a large hand closes over it. I whirl to find Vann standing behind me, my fist in his grip.

He winks at me.

I squint back at him. "What are you doing?"

"I think you've made your point." He directs his attention to Tony, who, to my delight, is bleeding from the lip. "Go home, Tony. Because you do not want my angry asshole of a father to come out here with his shotgun to chase you away."

Tony scoffs.

I kick out at Tony, trying to hit him in the shins with the tip of my cowboy boot.

"That's enough, killer," Vann says, pulling me back. "He's leaving."

Tony straightens his jacket, then looks at me. "What the fuck, Belinda? You hit me in the mouth!" He dabs at his bleeding lip with a fingertip.

"You told him we—" But I can't even say it. I'm humiliated. Again. Because of these two men. I point my finger in Tony's face. "Get the fuck away from me! Go home! You got what you came for!"

His face falls. His mouth goes tight. "Rosalie—"

"Don't," I snap. "Don't you dare."

"I didn't come here to fight with you, OK? I just—"

"I don't know what you're doing or why you're here, Tony! But here is what I do know—this has nothing to do with me! This is all you. You're in some... some kind of *crisis* and you're using me as an excuse. Just... please! *Go! Away!*"

Tony throws up his hands. "Fuck it. Fine. I'm gone." And then he turns and walks around the corner of the garage, disappearing from view.

Vann follows him.

"Vann!"

He doesn't stop.

"Vann!"

"I'm just making sure he leaves," Vann replies. He stops at the far corner of the garage and stands there for a few moments. Then he turns back to me.

I shake my head.

"What?" he asks.

"You need to go home too."

"No," he says, quickly walking towards me.

His long legs cover the distance between us surprisingly fast. And the next thing I know he's right in front of me. I take a step back, hit the bottom step of the stairs, and then step up. This makes me taller. Not as tall at Vann, but taller. So I don't have to get a crick in my neck trying to meet his eyes.

"I need to explain. I didn't get a chance earlier and—"

"I don't require an explanation, Vann. We're not together. You can fuck anyone you want. Even if it's a girl you don't actually want." I shrug. "What do I care?"

He just stares at me.

"What?"

"Why *do* you care?"

"I don't!"

"Then why did you get all upset at work last night?"

"It wasn't about you. It was about Tony."

"Because he fucked you in the alley? Right before you saw me with Soshee?"

"Can we just… not talk about this?"

"Fuck that," he says. "Fuck. That. I'm tired of not talking about this. And I'm not leaving here until we do talk about this. I'm fucking sick of this shit."

"What shit? I'm not leading you on, so if you try to say I am, I'll—"

"Jesus fucking Christ, Belinda!"

"What?"

"Are you blind? Or deaf? Or dumb? Or what?"

I just stare at him.

He takes a step forward, forcing me to take a step back too. And my step is actually a step up. He points his finger at me. I swat it away.

"I'm gonna say this once, OK? Just once."

"Say whatever the fuck you want. I don't care what you do."

He climbs one step. And so do I. "I like you," he says, climbing another step. So I climb another step. "I like your filthy mouth, Belinda Baker. I like your stupid cowboy boots. I like your pink hair." He keeps climbing the steps, so I have to keep climbing the steps. "I like the way you road-trip."

"What?" I'm so confused.

He's still climbing the steps and now my back is against my front door. "I like the way you wear that glitter shit on your eyelids in the summer. And the way you wear fingerless gloves in the winter even though you complain, every single day, that your fucking hands are cold. I like the way your hair smells when you show up for work and it's still wet. I like the way you spin on your stupid stool in front of the shop cash register and glare at the giggly sorority girls like you can't wait for them to wake up sober tomorrow and realize they just paid a hundred bucks for a My Little Mermaid tramp stamp. I like the way you bite your lip when you're tattooing and the way you always have a smear of ink on the side of your face by the time you're done."

I reach up to touch my face.

"Yes, you have ink there, right now. And I love that. Because you don't even care enough to check the mirror after you're done with a client to notice that you *always* have ink smeared on your fucking face after you tattoo someone. I like the way you kick at stones when you walk down the street like you're some troubled teen with pregnancy issues."

"What?" I laugh.

"I like the way you bitch, and moan, and complain that no one takes you seriously. In fact, I *love* that no one takes you seriously, because then they'd figure out just how awesome you are, and I'm afraid you'll actually find someone else before I can convince you that I am *good* for you. I want to *date you*, Belinda Baker. And you know what really pissed me off tonight?"

He pauses.

I become uneasy. "Am I supposed to guess?"

"I'm not mad that you fucked Tony in the alley. OK? That's not it. I'm angry that you gave *him* the chance that *I deserve*."

My stomach… *falls*. I don't know of any other way to describe the feeling I get when I internalize those last few words of his. Except… falling. Like the world has just been yanked out from under me. Like I'm adrift in a sea of mistakes.

Because he's absolutely right.

"Vann—"

"No," he says, still seething. "No." He holds up one finger. "I'm not done. You don't get to talk yet. I've been holding this in all fucking night while you laughed and joked with my goddamned brother and his stupid yoked-out army friend. Who, by the way, was leering at you the entire time."

"He was not!"

"He so was!"

"He was lying face down, Vann!"

"I just want to say this." He pauses again and his chest is rising and falling very quickly, like he's really upset. And his lips are falling into a deep frown. And his face is becoming flushed with heat. "I have *earned* my chance, Belinda. I didn't become your friend because I wanted to get in your pants. I didn't get you the apprentice job because I thought we'd be good together. I didn't drive you and Tara two thousand miles to Key West because I thought maybe you'd finally see me for what I am. I did all those things because I *like* you. With no expectations whatsoever. I did all those things because I enjoy you. And when we're together, life is fun. Even when we're running from guys called Diablo, and smuggling people on boats, and especially when we're just hanging out doing nothing. Saying nothing. That's my favorite time with you. Because we're at that place now. That place where we're comfortable. And I keep waiting for you to see how *good* we are. And you just"—he shakes his head—"refuse! You just refuse to even consider me. But this asshole Tony Dumas shows up out of nowhere and you give him all the considerations. You say you don't like him—"

"I don't!"

"You say that, but then why, Belinda? Why do you give him all the chances he hasn't *earned*?"

Now my chest is rising and falling unusually fast. And my lips are falling into the deepest of frowns. And my face is becoming flushed with heat. And the worst thing is, my eyes are welling up with tears like I might even start crying.

"Just tell me why," Vann whispers. "Just tell me. Or hell, just tell me you love him and I'll go away."

"I *don't* love him. I don't want to be with him. I don't want him here. I want him to leave. I wish he had never come here in the first place."

"That's even worse. He's no one to you? And yet he gets all the chances?"

"I'm sorry," I whisper back.

"I'm not here for an apology, OK? I'm not here to make you feel bad. I'm not trying to guilt you into something you'll regret. I'm here because I can't fucking… I can't fucking *exist* like this anymore. I can't do it. I want to date you. Why can't you just take a chance on me? Are you just not attracted to me? Am I not ambitious enough? What? What is it? What do you see in me that makes you say no without any serious consideration?"

These are all good questions. He has every right to ask them.

But I don't know how to answer him.

Vann sighs. His shoulders slump. He turns away from me and runs his fingers through his hair as he stares off into the dark nothingness of the back yard. "You know," he says, still with his back to me, "I'm really happy that Vic finally gave you a real chance last night." He turns to face me, his frown still deep, his breathing still too fast. "I'm super proud of you. I want you to… do everything that makes you happy. And if that happiness doesn't include me"—he shrugs— "OK. I get it. I understand. But I'm never going to stop being there for you. Ever. If you tell me to leave the way you did Tony, I won't. If you clock me in the mouth, I still won't. I'm not walking away, Belinda. Even if you tell me right now that we have no future together, I'll still be your friend tomorrow. So give it to me straight, OK? I swear to God, I can take the truth. Is there any part of you that feels the way I do? Or should I just give up and move on?"

I take a deep breath and hold it. But when that breath comes out, the truth comes out with it. "Tara is gone. She was my best friend and now she's living two thousand miles away. I can't even see my mom until whatever weird shit that's going on with the FBI and the Dumas brothers is resolved. I'm all alone here."

"You're *not alone*," he says, clearly becoming even more frustrated with me.

"Let *me* finish now, OK?"

He nods. "OK. Keep going."

"I'm all alone except for you. You are all I have. We are perfect friends. And you're right. We know each other now. You know all those things about me, but let me tell you what I know about you, Vann Vaughn. You are the most charming asshole who ever walked this Earth." He tries not to smile, but he doesn't succeed. "And you're smiling right now because you know that was a compliment and not an insult. You are honest, you are genuine, and goodhearted. You are happy, and almost never down, and you're confident. You believe in yourself so much, it spills over into other people. Everything about you is golden sunshine. You are so bright, you light up all us little dark people from miles away. I have never met someone like you before. Not in my entire life. And now that we've known each other for a while, I'm quite certain that you are one of a kind. And if I fuck this up—"

"You won't!"

"—if I fuck this up, Vann. I'm never going to find another friend like you. Ever. I'm going to die alone if I fuck this up with you."

"Belinda, we're good together."

"I know that. But I'm afraid. Nothing lasts forever. We can't just say, 'Welp, we're soulmates now. I guess we're set for life!' That's not how it works. One day it's going to end. One day it will fall apart. And I can't even fucking comprehend the kind of sadness I will feel when that happens."

"I understand that, Belinda. But it's no different with Tony. It's no different."

"It's completely fucking different! I don't care what happens to Tony! He's going to walk out of my life in a day or two and I'm never going to think about him again. Don't you get it? He's not a risk! He's nothing! You—you, Vann—you are a million, billion, trillion risks all wrapped up into one perfect man. I'm going to die of a broken heart when we fall apart. And I've lived through that before. I don't know if I can live through it again."

"You lived through it with Tony?"

I nod. "Yes. But it's still not the same. So don't tell me it is. You are… you mean more to me than he could ever hope to. And trust me on this, OK? Because I know him. He's not here to tell me the things you just told me. He's not here to make some grand gesture and win my heart. He's here because he needed to fuck and forget me. That's it. That's the only reason he's here. He is no threat to you. Or us."

Vann looks at me for a long moment, his face still supremely sad. "It's not fair."

"I know. And I agree."

"So do something about it, Belinda."

"What do you want me to do? Tell me and I'll do it."

He draws in a deep breath. And when he lets it out he says, "One date. That's it. One date and at the end of the night if it's too scary, fine. If you're still too afraid of what might happen, then fine. We'll be friends forever. We won't ever talk about it again."

I think about this for a few moments.

"One date," he whispers. "I earned it. Just give me the chance I deserve."

"Vann, this might—"

"This might what? God, Belinda. Just fucking take a chance with me! Everything is a risk. For fuck's sake, we committed several dozen felonies together down in Key West when we joined the Dumas family smuggling ring!"

I smile and flutter a little as that sick, falling feeling begins to subside. "You have a point there."

"We could be in prison right now." He steps forward and places his hands on either side of my head. His fingers grip my hair as he stares down into my eyes.

"That was a risk," he whispers. "I'm not a risk. I'm a fucking promise."

I swallow hard and nod my head. "OK."

His deep frown disappears immediately.

"One date. But if it feels weird, or I get any suspicion that this is a bad idea, then…"

"Then we go back to friends."

It's never going to work. I think I just signed away our friendship by agreeing to this.

Sure, it could go right. It could go great. But even if it does, how long will it last?

And what if it doesn't go great? What if the whole thing turns into a disaster?

No one, not even perpetually optimistic Vann Vaughn, really believes that we'll just go back to the way things were.

This date is either the end of us—or the beginning of us.

Vann leans down and kisses me. And it's as heart-stopping as the one yesterday inside Anna Ameci's.

It doesn't linger. But this kiss gets its point across in less than a single moment.

This kiss is the stuff of fairytale fantasies.

It makes me want him, it makes me long for more, and it breaks my heart at the same time.

"I promise you," Vann says as he pulls away from me. "I promise you it will be good. And I will not waste this chance. You'll see," he says, and takes a step back towards the stairs. "I'm going to prove it to you. I'm going to prove that you and I were meant to walk this life together starting… *now*."

## CHAPTER THIRTEEN

*I hear every word* Vann Vaughn pours out to Belinda from the side of the garage. I wasn't going to spy—what I just overheard was a lesson in gut-wrenching, heart-crushing unrequited love. On Vann's part, of course. Not mine. But… there is still something about Belinda—Rosalie, whatever she wants to call herself these days—that prevents me from walking away.

I don't use the word *prevent* lightly.

I feel this tug. And I can't even begin to explain it because it makes absolutely no sense. I could never—would *never*—stand up in front of Belinda and say those words that Vann just said to her. Never in a million years would I be able to force those words out of my mouth and mean them.

But he meant them. That shit came from his heart.

Fine. You know what? He can have her. I don't even want her.

*Congratulations, Vann. You win. If that pathetic outpouring of emotion is what changes Rosalinda's mind—slow clap, my friend. Slow clap.*

But I'm certainly never going to grovel at her feet like that. I should just go back to my rental and pack up my shit. Hit the next flight out of Denver International and settle back into my amazing Key West life.

That's what I should do.

Hell, that's even what I want to do. So bad.

But... but... *but*... I can't. I don't know what it is about Rosalinda—I'm not sure if it's the memory of who Rosalie used to be or the revelation that Belinda is still her, still mine, and yet not her and not mine at the same time. Or if it's just some misplaced sense of obligation. I. Don't. Know.

I don't get it.

The only thing I do know right now is this: I will not be going back to the rental and packing my shit. I will not be in Key West by tomorrow. I will not be putting her behind me.

Why? Or better yet, how? How the fuck does this little pink-haired girl control me like this?

It's like she has this spell over me. I thought hate-fucking her was the answer. I really did.

I get what that says about me. I get it. I'm a douche. People should just start calling me Jesse Boston, that's how much of a douchebag move this whole thing is.

And that's fine. I'm not going to deny that I'm an asshole. I'm not even going to deny that I came here to use her to fix myself. I'm not like Alonzo in the girl department—who, for the record, is insane and possibly stupid for dating a girl online for two years and then pledging his undying love to her the first time they meet in person.

Unlike him, I get out. And I get around. I've dated a lot of tourists over the years. Not to mention Spring Breakers. But I don't get attached to people. I certainly never got attached to Belinda. Not even back when she was called Rosalie.

Even then it was just a slightly different version of what's happening between us right now. One that came with a lot more fucking, but still, it was the same. We fight like mortal enemies and then we fuck.

It was sick. It still is. I don't even *like* her!

She has always possessed this innate pull that kept me coming back. A sort of gravity. And I guess I had the same pull for her. Because she hung in there for years. She put up with me the same way I put up with her.

But this? What I'm doing right now? Spying like a creep in the bushes on the side of her garage apartment just so I could get inside information on the future relationship status of a girl I don't even want to be with and a guy who elicits a desire to smack him in the teeth every time he beams that stupid charming smile at me?

What the actual fuck am I doing?

Why can't I just walk away?

I have no answer to that question. I can't even make up a lie to tell myself, that's how illogical this whole trip is. So I just wait there on the back side of the garage, hidden in some overgrown hedges like a damn cat burglar, looking up at her window for many more minutes than I can reasonably pass off as a 'safe' amount of time before I start formulating a plan to sneak off the Vaughn property.

"Fuck it," I whisper, then stand up, pull myself together, and start creeping along the side of the garage towards the front of the house. The lights are still on inside the mansion, so I'm careful. The last thing I need is one of those crazy brothers to come out here with a shotgun.

I'm just about to step out of the shadows and make a run for the driveway when I hear a familiar yipping sound and freeze in place.

A few seconds later I see that same annoying little dog from yesterday, this time being walked by someone completely different. Not the girl, a guy. But not the same guy as last night, either. This one is wearing a suit.

I check my watch. It's four thirty-seven AM. What the hell is this guy doing? Walking this dog at this hour, in a suit?

I dunno. Maybe he works far away and this is his usual dog-walking time.

That could be right.

In fact, it probably is right.

But there's a little nagging feeling inside that. The kind of feeling that begs you to pay closer attention to things. Because something is off.

The man doesn't stop in front of the Vaughn house even though the little dog is resisting its early-morning walk. He tugs on the leash, making the dog yelp in surprise, then kinda drags it along until they both disappear on the other side of the front hedge.

I take one cautious look at the Vaughn house, then bolt for the driveway and hide behind the hedges until I see the man and the dog turn left at the next block.

I have learned to trust that gut feeling when it presents. I'm in the smuggling business. I risk serious prison time twice a year. And even though the FBI has been tentatively on our side and watching our back for over a dozen of those smuggling operations, coming out the other side clean depends on wits and a healthy dose of suspicion.

And my gut is telling me that this dog is a clue.

To what mystery? I'm not sure. I just know he is.

So I follow them. And where do these two end up at the end of that trail? The coffee shop next door to Sick Boyz.

They linger in the alley behind the building both establishments share. And the dude stops briefly in front of the Sick Boyz back door, even looks around shiftily for a few moments, like he's having some internal debate about breaking in.

I'm almost ready to step out of the shadows and ask him what the fuck he thinks he's doing. But that gut feeling is back, telling me to chill. Telling me stay quiet and still and just watch a little longer.

And almost in the same moment, the back door to the coffee shop opens and the girl who was walking the dog that first time I saw it peeks her head out.

"What the fuck are you doing?" she whisper-yells to him.

The dog begins to yap again, jumping in the air like a typical terrier maniac.

"We could go in there and—"

"We've talked about this, Matthew. We were told to observe. Nothing else. Now get that mongrel inside before it wakes up the entire neighborhood!"

I hang back in the shadows as they disappear inside and the back door closes with a heavy *thunk,* the town going silent and still.

What the hell was that about?

He really did want to break into Sick Boyz. But they are under some kind of orders to observe? Observe who? The Vaughn brothers?

I can get on board with that. Those boys all look like a bunch of thugs. They all look like they deserve some extra, unwanted FBI attention. Because that's definitely who these coffee shop people are. I've met my share of undercover agents. I can practically smell them coming by now.

But that gut feeling tells me they're not there for the Vaughn brothers.

They're there for Rosalinda.

She is the obvious target here. I mean, she is one of the witnesses.

I backtrack out of the alley and then head towards the Fort Collins Theater as I think about this.

Could this be the answer I came here for?

Could these coffee shop people be the clue I need?

Alonzo didn't give me any specific instructions when he sent me up here—just said that Vann's suspicions couldn't be dismissed until we checked it out because things didn't actually go to plan during that last smuggling mission.

The FBI are definitely thinking about ditching our little agreement. Especially after we gave them the slip and ruined their plans during that last job.

I didn't think too hard about Alonzo's directive because let's face it—my mind was overcrowded with this weird obsession I have with Rosalinda.

But I need to pull myself together and focus. Because all this shit is connected somehow.

All of it.

Me, my family, our smuggling, the Boston brothers, Rosalinda, Tara, and maybe even the Vaughn brothers too. Vann did say that his sister is involved with the custom bike-builder dude just down the street. And he did hint around that the guy and his friends had their own run-in with the FBI several years back.

Add in the fact that this town is some kind of haven for discarded 'witnesses' and we've got ourselves a proper mystery here.

I think about this as I go enter the stairwell to the theatre building apartments and climb the stairs. I hesitate on my landing, looking up at the fourth floor, wondering if I should wake up Soshee and ask her some questions.

But my watch says it's too early to wake her up with nothing more than a bunch of suspicious gut feelings. So I go inside my apartment instead. Undress and climb into bed.

I wish I could say I fell asleep, but sleep is not my friend these days.

And even though I've been up for more than twenty-four hours now, it still eludes me.

The past twenty-four hours have been pretty monumental. So it's not like I don't have a bunch of stuff to keep me awake.

But I'm not thinking about the day.

I'm thinking about Rosalinda.

Why?

Why am I so fucking obsessed with that woman?

I should be obsessing over Soshee. She's pretty, and funny, and interesting. And I get that she thinks she's in love with Vann, but even I can see, after just twenty-four hours, that they are not a thing. Never going to be a thing.

I want to think about Soshee. Maybe even dream up some possibilities with her. I could see her and me together. We'd make a really good couple.

But fucking *Rosalie*… dammit. She won't get out of my head.

It's not fair and I don't understand it.

It's like she's haunting me. Like those ghosts in A Christmas Carol. Like I owe her something.

And that's bullshit.

I don't owe her *anything*.

## CHAPTER FOURTEEN

# BELINDA

*It took me hours* to finally fall asleep last night. I paced the floor of my small studio apartment in the dark like a freak who has no idea what her mind wants, let alone her heart.

But I could not stop playing Vann's words back in my head.

His speech was the definition of grand gesture. A super-big, spectacular, heartfelt, amazingly romantic grand gesture. I've never had a man say things like that to me.

And he was right about the way I've been dismissing him, too. Tony *didn't* earn his chance. At all. Ever. Even back when we were younger, when this sick obsession was basically about sex, he never said things like that to me.

But… it's not even the things Vann said last night that are making me think twice about my opinion of him.

It was the way he made me *feel*.

I know I've said that I wasn't into the age difference. He's younger than me. I'm pushing thirty at this point and that feels like I'm about to hit the top of that hill while he's just barely starting that climb into his prime.

But sometimes age has nothing to do with maturity. Because the Vann Vaughn I met last night was someone… sure of himself. And sure of what he wanted. And he articulated his disappointment in a way that didn't insult me. Or make himself look good while turning me into a shrew.

He built me up the entire time. I can respect that.

I pick up my phone, hit Tara's contact, and let it ring. Because if ever there was a time when a girl needed her BFF, this is it. And I don't care if we're two thousand miles apart, she's not getting out of being my best friend that easy.

On the first ring, I miss her even more than I did two seconds ago. And I didn't think that was possible. "Hey, bitch!" she says. And oh, my God. I've missed her voice so much in these past couple months. "What are you doing? It's a little early on your side of the country, isn't it?"

"Tara?" I squeak.

"What? What's wrong? Oh, my God. Something's wrong. What happened now? Is the FBI back? Did you see Diablo? What's happening?"

"No. Nothing like that. But—"

"Holy shit. You're sick."

"Kinda?"

"Oh, my God. Oh, my God. Oh, my God. What do you have? Please, don't say anything bad. I can't take it. I won't be able to take it. Life just got good, Belinda! We made it! We're on the upswing!"

"Tara!"

"OK. I'm shutting up. I'm ready. Tell me."

"I think I… I think I'm falling for Vann?"

She laughs so hard on the other end of the line, I have to move the phone away from my ear. I stare at the screen, waiting for her to stop. But that guffaw continues for a few seconds too long.

I tsk my tongue. "Why are you laughing at me?"

She guffaws one more time. "Wait. What?"

"It's not funny. He came here last night—"

"Holy shit. You're fucking him. Well, good for you, Belinda. I'm happy about this. I like that boy."

"No, I'm not fucking him. And don't call him a boy."

"Sorry. Man. Guy. Whatever. He's not that young. I don't know why you've always been so hung up on his age."

"It's not his age."

"OK. So… what is it then?"

"That's the problem. I don't know. Tony is here and—"

"What? Stop. Back up. What the hell is going on? Did you just say Tony—as in my boyfriend's brother, Tony—is in Colorado with you?"

"Yes! He's been here… Oh, I don't know. A few days, at least. He just showed up out of nowhere and…" I sigh. "I told you how I get with him. He makes me crazy."

"Holy shit! You're with Tony! We can be sisters!"

"No! I mean, I did fuck him yesterday outside Sick Boyz—"

She guffaws again.

"Stop laughing! This is serious! Because while I was fucking Tony, Vann was fucking Soshee—"

"She's the moody one with red hair? Works at Anna Ameci's?"

"Yeah, that's her. And he didn't catch me with Tony, but I caught him with Soshee. Right?"

"OK?"

"And then I had this like… reaction?"

"Define that?"

"You know. I locked myself in the bathroom and puked and cried."

"OK. Keep going."

"And then Vic came and made me tattoo some hot army dude all night."

"Not sure that matters. But OK."

"And then I went home, and Tony and Vann were arguing outside my apartment. And I hit Tony in the mouth"—she laughs again—"and then he left and bitch, then… *then*… Vann starts pouring his heart out to me. I'm talking… like… serious fucking grand gesture-type things just flew out. Romantic things like he earned a chance, and he knows we'd be good together, and why do I give Tony all the chances when he didn't earn them? Vann practically called me his soulmate."

"Well, that's not a surprise, right?"

"Isn't it?"

"Belinda, that poor boy has been in love with you for more years than we've been friends."

"I know, but—"

"I am not surprised. I think he's your one."

"My *one*?"

"You know. The one. The one you're supposed to be with. Marriage, babies, dogs, house. That kind of thing."

"Are you sure?"

"Mmm. Yeah. I'm pretty sure."

"Because he asked me out on a date."

"Great! That's super awesome."

"I should go, right?"

"Absolutely. Vann…" She sighs. "I mean, he's such a good guy, ya know? Except for that time he ambushed me and told me the FBI was crawling all over Fort Collins and I was in the middle of some deep, dark secret shit. He showed his ruthless side during that meeting. But sometimes you need a ruthless guy."

"Yeah. Ruthless."

"So go on the date. Have fun. Kiss him, Belinda."

"He already kissed me. Twice."

"Was it amazing?"

I sigh. Smile. Sit down on the couch. Sink back into the cushions. Smile wider. "It was so amazing. It kinda made me feel weird though."

"Weird how?"

"Like… my head got all fuzzy. And my stomach was unsettled. And I couldn't think straight."

"You swooned."

"I what now?"

"You know, like in the movies. In the olden days. When the proper ladies would be kissed by the dashing hero and they'd faint?"

"I didn't faint. But then Tony appeared and that's when I let him fuck me."

"That doesn't count."

"No?"

"No. You were in the middle of swooning, Belinda. You can't be expected to make rational decisions in the afterglow of swooning."

"You're just saying that to make me feel better. It was a shitty thing to do."

"So Vann's pissed off about it?"

"No. Not really. I mean, probably. But no. He was fucking Soshee at the same time!"

"Wow. You guys are weird. But OK. And you're pissed off about that?"

"No. Not really. I mean, yeah. Little bit. But no. He doesn't like her that way. It was just…"

"Oh! He was swooning too!"

"Hmm. Maybe? So he's not responsible, is he?"

"Nope. I'm pretty sure all the blame falls on Soshee and Tony for taking advantage of the two of you."

"And our swooning over each other."

"And that."

I sigh.

"You good now?"

"I miss you so much."

"I miss you too. But hey, why is Tony there, anyway? Alonzo told me that Tony is on a Caribbean vacay."

"That's weird. But OK. Tony says he came here for me. To, and I quote, 'fuck me one last time and forget me.' Unquote."

"Yeah. That sounds like something Tony would say. So is he giving you trouble? Should I send Alonzo in to drag his ass back home?"

"No, I think he got the message. Besides, we did have the fuck. So he's maybe good now? I don't know. I don't care about him. All I can think about is Vann and how he proclaimed his undying love to me last night. Because what if we don't make it, Tara? And then I lose the only friend I have left?"

"Oh, sweetie."

"I know. It's stupid. But I need him, Tara. I really, really need him. I'm not even joking about this. I feel like every time I meet someone good they get dragged out of my life. And I can't afford to lose anyone else,

Tara. I'm down to the bare minimum of people who give a lot of fucks about me at the moment."

"Stop it. We're all still here."

"No. You're there. And my mom is somewhere else. And... and Vann is the only one I have left. Besides Tony, and he doesn't count. He's only here because he's got some weird hate-fuck obsession with me and that's just leftover junk from the old days. It's not even real. And I'm sure he's figured that out by now—"

"You did punch him in the mouth."

"I did. So. Yeah. He's gonna leave. Not that I'm going to pine over him or anything. I'm so over it. But... he was sort of on my side, you know? Kinda? And that's totally over."

"Mouth-punching usually leads to that."

"I know. And that would be fine. If I still had Vann. But if I go on this date, and we become a thing, and then... time goes by, and we stop being a thing, then I don't have anyone. And I need him, Tara. I really do."

"Well, it sounds like he needs you too. This is how love works, babe. It's scary. And messy. And even though the swooning is actually a good thing, it feels like it's not at times. Because you're invested, ya know? Really, *really* invested. So I understand, but you just have to put on the brave face and tell him all this. Did you tell him all this?"

"Some of it."

"Well... I think it's time for you to make your grand gesture."

"I have to make a grand gesture?"

"You don't *have* to. But if there's one guy on this earth who would appreciate a grand gesture, it would be Vann."

"It would, wouldn't it? He's sweet, isn't he?"

"He really is."

"But I'm not really sweet, Tara. I'm like... bitchy."

She laughs. "You are. But honey, trust me. Your bitchy side is endearing and lovable. I know this because that's how I fell in love with you too."

"Aww. I love you too."

"So you're good?"

"But what if things go wrong on the date? This is our one chance to see if it's going to work out. And what if—"

"Stop it. You can't live like that, Belinda. Think of it this way—if you two don't work out then at least you tried, right?"

"Yeah," I agree.

But I don't *really* agree. I need this date to be perfect. I need a sign from some higher power that Vann and I will make it. And that I won't lose the only friend I have left.

I don't want to keep saying this to Tara because I don't want her to feel like she abandoned me. And even though I kinda think she did, she deserves her own happiness. And that happiness now resides two thousand miles away on Key West with a man called Alonzo.

So I ravel myself back up and put on the brave face. Try to be as good a friend to her as she is to me. "You're right, Tare. And thank you for the talk. What are you up to today?"

"Oh, my God. I'm such a good fisherwoman these days. I go out with Alonzo on his charters now on the weekends. And last weekend I caught a sailfish! Do you have any idea how hard it is to reel in a sailfish? And I did it all by myself. The next time you see me, I'm gonna show off my biceps. They're cut from all my reeling."

I chuckle, picturing Tara deep-sea fishing in a pencil skirt.

"We have two charters today. And we're just about to leave—"

"I'll let you go."

"No, no. If you need to talk more, I'll stay behind. I'll spend the whole day with you instead."

"No. That's OK," I say. But actually, it sounds really nice. Her life sounds nice. And there's a part of me—maybe even a really big part of me—that wants to go home. That's the part of Tony that's confusing, I think. He's not my *one*, as Tara puts it. That very well could be Vann. But like it or not, Tony is part of home. And I miss it. I can tell myself that I don't, and that this life is just as good—better, even. But doesn't everyone always wish they could go home?

I would never admit this to Tara, but I'm jealous of her and Alonzo. Not because he's some great dude—he could be, but I never knew him well enough to have opinions on that.

I'm jealous of her because Alonzo comes with a team.

A whole family of people on his side. And that little street they all live on. It's like… being surrounded by love. And now she's a part of that. Hell, she's more a part of Tony now than I ever was. And again, I don't want Tony. I just want… what he represents.

Safety on all sides.

And she just walked into that by accident.

It's almost… not fair.

"What are you doing today?" Tara asks.

"Work later," I sigh. "Weekends are super busy. And Vic said I can use his studio for my own clients now. So he's off on Monday. I'm hoping I get some walk-ins so my life can finally move forward and I can stop feeling like I'll be sitting behind that cash register for ten more years."

"That's great!"

"Yeah. It kinda is. Vic was really cool last night. Actually, everyone at the shop was really cool last night. I really thought I was going to lose my shit, but they held on to me tight and kept me from unraveling."

"They're good people."

"They are."

"Those brothers would definitely make good in-laws."

"Oh, my God! I'm not capable of thinking about the M word at six AM, Tare!"

"Sorry." She snorts. "But it's true."

I catch the sound of Alonzo calling for Tara two thousand miles away and take a hint. She has to go. And I have to go too. "Thank you," I say. "I needed to hear your BFF advice this morning."

"Any time, Belinda. You know that. You can call me any time."

We say our goodbyes, promise to visit and talk more, and then end the call.

I sigh and walk over to the window. And then I run Vann's whole grand gesture back in my head once more time.

Maybe Tara was right. Maybe I need to find a way to make Vann feel the same things about me that I feel for him right now? I just don't know how to do that.

## CHAPTER FIFTEEN

*A pounding on my door* wakes me from a fitful, half-sleep dream world of chaotic visions leftover from a long ago time. I force one eye open, confused about where I am for a moment. Then yesterday comes rushing back and I smile lazily as the dreamy chaos is replaced with yesterday's crazy Soshee adventure.

Wow. What a girl. And what luck to meet her when I came here for…

Fuck.

Yeah. I would really like to forget all about Rosalinda, and Vann Vaughn, and the FBI, and the witness protection program, and that stupid yippy dog that seems to be everywhere I am.

More pounding from the direction of the door. I throw the covers off me, pull on yesterday's jeans, and then casually check my phone for the time.

Nine oh three AM.

I yawn as I open the door and then immediately cover my mouth and smile. Because my red-headed Poison Ivy siren is on the other side wearing a pleated white tennis skirt and a light green tank top that shows a lot of cleavage. "Soshee? What are you doing here?"

She holds up a white bakery bag in one hand and a coffee holder with two cups in the other. "I told you to come by this morning so I could feed you." She pouts her lips. "But you blew me off."

"I didn't," I say, taking the coffee from her outstretched hand. "I just... slept in, I guess."

Not true because I'm not sure I can call what I just did actual sleep.

"I was just dreaming about you though." Also, not entirely true. But if I could choose a girl to dream about, it would definitely be her.

Soshee comes inside, kicks the door closed with the back of her foot, and then saunters over to the little table near the kitchen to set down the pastry bag. "Mmm. You dreamt about me? That sounds very promising." She looks over her shoulder at me. "If that's even true."

"Should I tell you about the dream?"

"Is it a dirty dream?"

"Do you want it to be a dirty dream?"

She tries not to smile, fails, and then shrugs her shoulders as her eyes travel up and down my bare torso. When her eyes meet mine again, she's biting her lip. "Nice... tattoos."

I look down at my shoulders. "Well, I'm no Vann Vaughn. But they're not bad."

She turns around, presses her hands on the table and leans into it a little as she studies my upper body where my ink lives. "Sea monsters. Interesting theme."

"It fits, believe it or not."

"I'm gonna need that story, Tony."

"I'm happy to tell it, Soshee."

"But let's eat first. We need our energy for today."

I walk over to the table and set the coffee down just as she pulls out a little paper box and opens it up to reveal little sugared things.

"Frittelle," she says, smiling big as she presents the box to me. "Eat them. I made them fresh less than an hour ago."

I pick one up—it's still warm—and pop it into my mouth. "Damn, Sosh," I say, savoring the sweetness as she watches me with an expression of delight.

"Good?"

"Divine."

"Here. Have another one. And sit." She pulls out a chair, pushes me in that general direction, and then takes the seat on the opposite side of the table, propping her chin in her hands as she smiles at me.

"Aren't you going to have any?"

"Trust me." She laughs. "I ate my fill while I was baking this morning."

"Sounds like a pretty good way to make a living," I say, popping another frittelle in my mouth.

"I can't complain," she says, pointing to my coffee on the table. "I didn't know how you take your coffee, so you got a latte instead."

I point right back at her, still chewing. "You better be careful. I might whisk you off to Key West, lock you up in my cottage, and keep you forever if you keep spoiling me like this."

"Promises, promises."

We both laugh, and smile, and stare at each other for a long moment that feels very natural and right. Until it lasts a little too long and becomes awkward.

"So," we both say at the same time.

"You first," she says.

"Well," I say, twirling my cup of coffee in my hands for a moment, trying to gather my thoughts as I stare at it. Because this girl is… wow. I raise my eyes up and meet hers. Sunlight from outside is hitting them in just the right way, changing their naturally deep emerald color into something more of a sea green. "I…" I suddenly don't know what to say to her. But at the same time, I feel like telling her all the things. "I… I like this place," I finally stutter.

"Good," she says. "I think this place likes you too."

"And you've been quite the nice surprise."

"Back at ya." She grins.

"What are your plans for today? More spying on Vann?"

"Psshhhh." She waves a hand in the air. "Who?"

"Vann Vaughn? Remember him? Dude who works across the street. Tatted-up with long paragraphs of boring words instead of sea monsters?"

"Oh, him," she says, once again waving her hand through the air. "I'm so over him."

"You are?"

"Mmm-hmm."

"Well… that's news."

"What are *your* plans for today? Take another shot at hate-fucking your ex so you can move on with your life?"

"Psshhh. Who?"

"Belinda Baker? Cute girl who works across the street with sticky-sweet pink pigtails instead of seductive red tresses?"

"Oh, her." Soshee giggles as I play her game. I think I could fall in love with that giggle. "I'm so over her."

"You are?"

"Mmm-hmm."

"Well, that's news too."

I chew on my lip a little, not accustomed to flirting with girls. Not that I'm bad at it or anything. I just don't do a lot of flirting. I don't actually do a lot of anything with the girls I'm typically with. Mostly just let them flirt with me and then let them take me somewhere for a fast fuck so I can make a quick escape afterwards.

But I kinda like the flirting. Or maybe I just like the girl I'm doing it with?

"No plans for today, then?" I finally manage to say.

"Well, I wouldn't say that."

"No?"

"I'm here with you, aren't I?"

"So you've got plans with me today?"

She shrugs. "If you've got time for me."

"I've got all day. And you're already here. So... it would be stupid on my part if I didn't take advantage of that fact."

"Oh. I get it. You want to take advantage of me." She winks. "I like you, Tony."

"I like you too, Soshee. You're the best thing about this trip."

"I am, aren't I?"

I nod slowly. "You really are."

"So tell me about this dream."

"Dream?"

"You know. The one you were having about me when I woke you up."

"Oh. That dream. Well... we were..."

"You weren't dreaming about me, were you?"

"No." I laugh. "But I really wish I had been. I wasn't dreaming at all. I was just tired, I guess. I got in late."

She cocks her head at me. "Did you go somewhere when you left my apartment?"

I nod and purse my lips, wondering if I should tell her this part.

But before I can answer she says, "To see Belinda?"

"Yeah." I sigh. "But never mind that. I really am over it."

"What happened?"

"Are you sure you want to hear this?"

"I'm not jealous. Well"—she pauses—"OK. I'm jealous. But not in a bad way. I just don't get why everyone loves her."

"I guess the same reason everyone loves Vann. Fucking asshole."

"OK, what happened?"

"He... he like... proclaimed his fucking love for her. I'm talking grand gesture kind of fucking proclamation, Soshee. I really hope you are over him, because she's falling for it. I can tell."

"Does that make you sad?"

"No! Not at all. I mean, I'm not lying. I didn't come here to win her back. I came here to hate-fuck her out of my head."

"And you did that."

"I did."

"And you're just... done now?"

"After she punched me in the mouth last night?"

"Oh, is that what that is?" she says, leaning over the table to touch my busted lip. "I wasn't going to say anything. But OK. She punched you."

I take her hand before she can pull away and just hold it for a moment. "She did."

"Because you... tried to kiss her?"

I'm still holding her hand. And she's not trying to pull away. "No. Because I told Vann I fucked her in the alley behind Sick Boyz and she... well, she didn't like that."

"What did Vann say?"

"You know." I wave my free hand in the air. "He was all understanding and shit. Since he was busy fucking you inside Sick Boyz at the very same moment."

"Oh." Soshee laughs and covers her mouth with her free hand. And is it weird that we're still holding hands? "Well, then." She shrugs. "I guess it's all out in the open."

"I guess it is."

"And you're what, done with Fort Collins? Gonna go home now?"

"Not now. Now, I'm gonna put it all behind me and... I don't know. I'm kinda hoping I can spend the day with you."

"With me?" She brightens. And I have to admit, I love her brightness. "What should we do?"

"I don't know. Whatever you want. What do you usually do on Saturday mornings?"

"Hmm. My regularly scheduled Saturday mornings might not work."

"You stalk him, don't you?"

She winces. "If I say yes, does that make me totally pathetic?"

"A little?" I laugh.

"OK, then. My answer is no. I usually spend Saturday mornings with hot guys from Key West."

"Really?"

"Truly."

"Guys like me?"

"Guys just like you."

"And what do you do with them?"

"You know. Little bit of this, little bit of that."

I fold my other hand over hers and squeeze it a little. She looks at her hand. Then her eyes track up to mine. "You want to have a date today, Soshee? Put the past behind us and like… move on and shit?"

"Only if you'll agree to be my trophy boy and let me parade you all over town and make all the local tramps jealous."

I guffaw. "Deal."

"Deal?"

"Such a deal." And then… then… I don't know what comes over me, but I bring her hand up to my lips and I kiss her fingertips. All of them. One at a time. So they each get their own well-deserved attention.

She stares at me as I do this, unblinking and still. I let go of her hand and wait for her reaction, my stomach going a little wild and crazy with the anticipation.

"OK," she says, a little bit breathless from my cool, flirty romantic gesture.

I stand up and wink at her. "I'm just gonna jump in the shower real fast and then we'll get this date started."

She places both hands in her lap and bunches her shoulders up to her ears. "I can't wait."

**Soshee talks to me** the entire time I'm in the shower and even though I'm not a talkative guy—like at all—and even though I can't really understand a word she says over the sound of the water, I kinda like her constant chatter.

It's something new for me. I've lived alone in my cottage on the same street I grew up on since I was twenty-five. I have never lived with a girl. Other than my sister, of course. And she left home at eighteen for college and never moved back, so she hardly counts.

I rarely let girls sleep at my place. In fact, I rarely bring them back to my place at all. I do hookups. And I don't really care where those hookups happen. So there is almost never a discussion between the girls I 'date'—if you can call it that—about coming back to my place.

So I smile the entire time I'm washing up, picturing Soshee out there in the rental apartment, helping herself to—well, whatever the fuck she wants. It's not like anything in this place is mine. I have one suitcase and that's it. So what do I care if she wanders around while I'm not looking?

I linger in the shower, enjoying the hot water pouring down my back. I didn't get much sleep last night—maybe two hours? But that's nothing new. I haven't slept more than two hours a night in months. Not since Rosalinda came back into my life and tipped me sideways on my axis. Whatever the actual number is, it wasn't enough and I should be exhausted. I should feel heavy from all the weird shit that happened yesterday.

But I don't. I feel refreshed and ready to spend a whole day with this red-headed siren. A whole day that has nothing do with stalking our exes.

I shut the water off, reach for a towel, and wrap it around my waist as I step out of the shower and head towards the bedroom where Soshee is still chattering away, her back to me as she riffles through my suitcase.

I chuckle. I can't help it. The one thing that's mine here, and she's got her little hands all over it.

"What are you doing?"

She whirls around, surprised, holding up a t-shirt that says 'Dumas Romantic Boat Tours.' "Stalking you." Then her eyes travel down my bare chest to the edge of the towel that dips just below the cut muscles of my hips. They pause there, then travel back up and meet mine.

I wait for the blush that never materializes.

This girl is *confident.*

Instead she smirks at me. "Damn, Tony. What did you say you did again? Because"—she points a polished red fingertip up and down my body—"that is quite the physique you have. And this shirt here is a tantalizing clue to a most delicious mystery that needs solving immediately."

Her eyes dance with delight as she says all that. And her little tennis skirt swishes as she cocks a hip.

I'm the one who blushes. Maybe. No, I take it back. I don't blush. But... yeah. Soshee Ameci is fucking sexy. Vann Vaughn is a dick. A blind one, at that. "I own a romantic sailing charter service down in Key West."

"I'm sorry. A what?" She appears thoroughly confused.

"You know, like... fucking sunsets on the water and shit."

She giggles. But it only takes another second for that giggle to turn into a guffaw. "Hold on," she says, placing a hand over her heart and catching her breath. "Let me get this straight. You, Tony Dumas, own what? A… sailboat? And you charter couples around the tropics looking for romantic sunset moments?"

I shrug. "Yeah. Pretty much."

"How the hell does that happen?"

"My parents, I guess?"

"No," she says, shaking her head. "Nope. That's not enough. Explain this properly because I don't think I'll be able to concentrate on our date if I don't get this story." She walks over to me, takes me by the hand, leads me to the bed, sits down, and pats the space next to her. "Sit. And spill."

I sit. Mostly because I just want to sit next to her and not because I enjoy talking about myself. But being close to Soshee like this… it makes my brain spin a little more than usual.

"I'm waiting!" Soshee says. "Start talking."

"OK. Fine." I sigh and lie back on the bed so I can stare up at the ceiling and give myself a moment to try to put my very complicated life into something that resembles a neat little box.

Because I like this Poison Ivy girl. A lot. She's smart. And interesting. And very sexy, of course. Plus, she's a little bit sneaky. I like that about her. I could totally picture her as my new partner in crime. I think we'd make a very good team.

Which is ridiculous. I've known her one day.

Vann Vaughn is a dumbass. He has no idea what he's missing. Soshee Ameci is fucking amazing. So I turn my head a little and look at her with a crooked grin. She's positioned herself sideways, one leg bent at the knee, her knee touching my thigh.

I can feel that touch through the towel and it kinda… turns me on.

"Have you ever heard of Bright Berry Beach Cosmetics?"

She tilts her head at me like a confused puppy. "Yeah. I love their lotion. I wish we had a shop here in FoCo. But the closest one is down in Boulder."

"Near your mom?" I ask.

"Yeah." She laughs. "It's like right down the street from her shop."

"Hmm." It's kinda cool that I knew that. About her mom, I mean. "Anyway. My sister is part owner of that company and—"

"Wait! What?"

"Yeah. My fucking sister…" I sigh. "She's a freaking billionaire. Owns one-fourth of that company. The point is, she's rich, right? And my parents own this dive shop."

"Like… SCUBA diving?"

"Exactly. So we came into some money just as my sister's company was getting off the ground—"

"'Came into some money?'" Soshee makes air quotes.

"Exactly," I say. But I eye her cautiously to see if she'll say anything about what that implies.

"Got it. Keep going. This story is getting better and better by the second."

I cock my head at her. "You're not gonna ask questions about that?"

"About what? That you just admitted you're kinda Mob? Pshhh. My last name is Ameci, OK? I know what's up."

"You don't. But… we'll get to that later. Maybe. So anyway, we get this money and started buying up houses on our little street in Key West. We started a vacation cottage business. And then Emma, my sister, she started sending us money once she had a few extra million and my brothers and I all started our own companion businesses near the dive shop. So I run the romantic sailboat shit. It's mostly honeymooners. And my older brother, Alonzo, he runs the deep-sea fishing boat. And my little brother, Luke, he sells these water adventure packages. Waterskiing. Speedboats. Parasailing. Shit like that."

"So how did you get stuck with the romantic sailing idea?" She laughs again, like she can't believe that's what I do for a living.

"Well, my first choice was the fishing. But Alonzo isn't the type of brother you argue with and he got his shit together first. And I'm not into the adventure water sports. So"—I shrug—"honeymoon sailboat charters was all I could think of."

She sighs. Heavily. Mockingly. And places a hand over her heart. "You're so romantic."

I laugh and then turn my head into the sun. It feels good on my face. I kinda miss Key West. Colorado has been sunny too, but it's not nearly as warm. "You can laugh all you want," I say, keeping my eyes closed. "But no one complains after they get off my yacht. I have customers who have been booking packages with me every year, without fail, for almost a decade."

She flops back on the bed next to me, so close our upper arms press against each other. "I'm not laughing at you, Tony. I'm appreciating the complexity of what's beneath your surface."

I snap my fingers, turn my head, and open one eye to peek at her. "Like the hull of a yacht. You only see the top part. But down below there's like… a fucking dining room and shit."

She turns her head and lets out another laugh. "Exactly like the hull of a yacht." She flops over on her stomach and presses her face into the soft comforter. "You're kind of a catch, Mr. Dumas."

I nod my head and close my eye. "I really am."

"So how come you're not hitched?"

"Hitched?" I ask, keeping my eyes closed. I could fall asleep right now, that's how relaxed I am. A real sleep. Not just a nap. With her next to me. I would like to spend this whole day in bed with her, actually. Maybe fuck her. But maybe not? Maybe just… enjoy her. "Hitched as in… married?"

"Or at least dating. Someone who is not Belinda Baker, that is."

I open both eyes and turn my head to stare at her. "I guess I just haven't met the right girl yet."

Soshee smiles at me, looking pretty relaxed and lazy too. "What's she look like?"

"The right girl?" I pause for a moment, then smile and close my eyes again, feeling very, *very* comfortable. "Well… you," I mumble. "Maybe."

"Hmm. You have my mind spinning."

"Good," I say. "Misery loves company."

"What?"

I sigh. "My mind has been spinning for months. I can't fucking sleep. I haven't slept more than two hours a night for months."

"Because of Belinda Baker?"

I nod, but say nothing. Because after all the chaos of the past couple months, suddenly my mind feels… still.

Soshee sighs. "Well, she's a lucky girl."

"Why?"

"Because she has your full attention."

"Not anymore," I say. I reluctantly open my eyes to look at her.

"I hear you saying that, but there's more to it."

"More? Like what?"

"I don't know. You tell me."

"I wish I could, Soshee. I really do. It's not... romantic. I swear to God, it's not. I just... have these lingering feelings about her. And I don't understand them. I'm not in love with her. And I'm not jealous of Vann, either. That's not it. I'm just... really confused about her."

"Why?"

"I don't know. I wish I did. Because if I knew what was causing this renewed obsession with her, I'd do something to fix it. Ya know? And move on. Go home. Get back to work."

Soshee changes position so she's on her side. She leans on her elbow and props her head in her hand. "Am I just a distraction to you and this little obsession problem you're having?"

"No."

"Just no? That's it?"

"I know you don't believe me. I get it. Everything about what I'm doing points to me repressing... something. And maybe that's the case. But some secret hidden love for her? That's just not it. I don't see myself with her. I'm not picturing a future with her. I just need her to go away. And she won't. She won't get the fuck out of my head."

Soshee stares at me, her green eyes bright and sparkly, like she slept like a baby last night after I left. "I don't mind, you know."

"You don't mind what?"

"If you're just using me."

"What?"

"I get it. This is fun. But we're strangers. And you're going home very soon. Possibly tomorrow."

"Not tomorrow."

"Then Monday."

"I don't know."

"All I'm saying is… I'm no stranger to a one-night stand."

"This isn't a one-night stand. It's not even night. We're not drunk or even looking to get laid."

"I'm just saying I understand, that's all. One date. That's probably all we're gonna get, right?"

"What are you talking about, one date? This isn't our first date."

She laughs. "It definitely is."

"No. We had our first date yesterday at lunch. And our second date last night. So this is our third date."

"We can't be on our third date when we've only known each other two days! And anyway, I don't think stalking our exes over food counts as a date."

"Why not?"

She slaps my arm. "Because. It just doesn't."

"We spent time together. We ate food. And drank wine. And talked. They all sound like dates to me."

"Um… I think you're conveniently forgetting how in between dates one and two we took time off to go fuck our exes."

I laugh, then point at her. "OK. That's maybe a little weird."

"Maybe?"

"Fine. It's unconventional. But I'm still counting them as dates."

"Why? Because that makes this date three? And date three is the official 'fuck date'?"

"Is date three the official fuck date?"

"It's in the rule book."

"I don't think I play by those rules."

"So you're not going to fuck me?"

I stare at her. No. I gaze into her brilliant green eyes and get lost for a few thousand eternities before I pull myself back to reality and find the right words that need to come next.

"I'm not going to disappoint you, Soshee. Trust me on that."

She gets up and extends her hand to me. "Trust you, huh?"

I take her hand and let her pull me to my feet. And when I'm standing I realize that we're very close.

Only inches apart.

I also realize I'm only wearing a towel.

I look down into her green eyes. Picturing myself kissing those cherry-red lips as I slip my hand up her flirty little tennis skirt. Imagine her moaning into my mouth when I do that.

"Yeah. Trust me."

"Hmm. So are you going to kiss me now?"

"Now? No."

"No!" She laughs. "What the hell! Why not? I'm sending all the right signals. Aren't I?"

She looks a little bit vulnerable when she asks me this question. A little bit of the tough Italian Mob girl disappears. But only a little.

"I want to. Don't get me wrong. But not now. That comes at the end of the third date. Your rules, remember?"

"Thought you didn't play by them?"

"Eh. They're growing on me."

"Fine." She sighs. "I can wait. But I'm going to leave you in charge of the date. And I'm not sure you're up to the challenge."

"Are you a challenge then?"

"Very challenging. I expect... mystery, mister. And intrigue. And maybe a little danger."

"Well, you are Poison Ivy."

She giggles. "That I am."

"Oh," I say, snapping my fingers. "Holy fuck. I almost forgot what I saw this morning while I was walking home from Vann's house."

"Wow. It must've been exciting to get you all perked up like this. I can't wait to hear all about it. Tell me everything."

I wince.

"What?" she asks.

"It's not exactly romantic. But it is a mystery."

"Just spill. I'll deal with the date disappointment."

I lean in to her. Put my lips right up to her ear until she shrugs up her shoulders from the chill I send through her body. "It's a mystery, Soshee Ameci. It's a dangerously intriguing mystery."

She turns her head until our lips are just a few inches apart. I look down at hers. All red and glossy and... kissable.

I want to kiss her. Badly. Hell, I want to throw her down on that bed behind us and fuck her into Sunday.

But not yet.

*Not yet, Tony.*

She's not a distraction.

She's a full-blown attraction.

And I want to do this right.

"Let me get dressed," I say. "And then I'll tell you everything while we have our third date, Soshee. I'll spill all my dirty secrets."

I will prove it to her.

I'll prove that even though this started out as something totally fake it's going to turn into something real.

## CHAPTER SIXTEEN

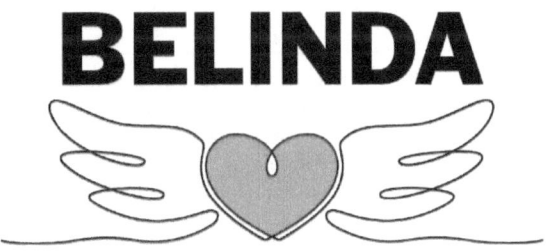

# BELINDA

*My dearest Vann. You are my best friend. You are my rock...*

Oh, this is stupid. I've been trying to write some kind of big grand-gesture speech like the one he spewed out at me last night (that came from his heart and wasn't planned out in advance), and I can't think of what to say.

Do I love him? Yeah, but... it's not like... *love* love.

I can't explain it. I don't understand my feelings for him.

It's more than love, but less than love. And saying that to him sounds like one big brush-off. So I'm not going to say that to him.

The problem is, I don't understand my love for Vann Vaughn.

He's definitely my best friend. That's not even up for debate. Even before Tara left, Vann and I were very close. We spent a lot of time together because of work. And I like our time together. That's why I don't want to fuck it up with this dating experiment. We know each other well enough that we have inside jokes. I know what he likes to eat when I grab lunch for everyone. I know how he takes his coffee. He doesn't need to write it down for me. I could pick his favorite t-shirt out of his closet. If I had ever seen his closet, which I haven't. I've been inside the Vaughn house millions of times, but never been upstairs.

Still, the point is, I *know* him.

And this knowledge of him came naturally. We grew from strangers to acquaintances to friends.

And this friendship is good. It's perfect.

But if he's so frustrated about me not giving him a chance to move on to the next step that he might not want to be my friend anymore, then I have a serious problem that deserves a thoughtful solution.

What will my life look like without Vann?

I'm suddenly sad. Because this is the real reason I can't come to terms with his request.

Either way, whether I date him or not, this... *love*... we have, it's over.

It either dissolves completely when we fail at being a real couple, or it fades away because I refuse to give him a chance.

I sigh. And then the sound of motorcycles filters in from outside.

It's going to be a nice day, I guess. Every spring there is a Saturday when the Vaughn brothers get their bikes out and the ride season begins.

Today must be that Saturday.

And then I smile. Because I know all the Vaughn brothers now, don't I?

I know what Vic and Vonn and Vinn get for lunch too. I know how they take their coffee as well. Maybe I don't know what Vic's favorite t-shirt is, but I could take a good guess and probably come very close.

It's very comforting to be inside their circle. Especially after all the turmoil that came before being allowed in. It's like a stillness. A sweet, slow stillness that people look for their whole lives and almost none of them find it.

This stillness, it's better than money. It's a feeling of belonging, and acceptance, and… love.

Just… not *that* love.

"Fuck it." I throw the pen and paper across the room.

I can't win.

Nothing ever stays the same. That's the only thing I know to be true. And this is why I'm so hesitant to date Vann. Change is coming. This stillness will be interrupted.

And there's nothing I can do to stop it.

So maybe I should just get on the ride and go where it takes me?

I get dressed, grab my purse, and go outside. It's still early. Barely nine-thirty in the morning. Way too early to show up for work. Because if the boys took their bikes out they will probably be gone for a while. Probably even show up late for work today and I'll have to manage all the waiting customers when that happens.

I sigh as I hop down my steps and walk around the side of the garage. And then I see Vann sitting on the front porch of the house, leaning against the railing with his knees bent and a helmet in his hands.

"What are you doing?" I call out as I make my way towards him. "I thought you'd be out on your bike with your brothers."

"Waiting for you."

"Me?" I point to myself.

He tosses his helmet up in the air and catches it. "You wanna go for a ride with me?"

That's when I notice there's a second helmet sitting on the porch beside him. "You waited for me?"

"That's what I just said, isn't it?"

His response is not facetious. It's very matter-of-fact. "Where are we going?"

"Mmm." He tilts his head back and forth like he's thinking. Then he gets to his feet, grabs the second helmet, tosses it to me—I catch it—and says, "Get on my ride and see."

He nods his head towards his bike. All the Vaughn brothers have very nice bikes. They are all custom. Their brother-in-law is Spencer Shrike, after all, who might be the most famous person in this whole town. But they didn't let Spencer build these bikes. They built them themselves. Spencer's shop just does the paint.

It occurs to me that knowing this about them is also part of that special love I can't seem to describe.

I start to slide the helmet on, but Vaughn crosses the distance between us and puts a hand on my shoulder. "Hold on. You can't go like that."

"Like what?" I look down at myself. "I have jeans on. I should be fine."

"No, Belinda. Your hair. You have to tie it up or it's gonna get all tangled."

"Oh. Right."

"You don't know that because we've never been on a ride together before."

"Hmm. I guess I never thought about it before."

He reaches into his pocket and pulls out a hair tie. "Come and sit on the porch."

I cock my hip and tilt my head. Trying to hide a smile. "Why?"

"You'll see." He takes my free hand and leads me over to the porch. "You sit there." He points to the bottom step.

I sit. And then he sits on the step directly behind me and starts gathering up my hair.

"What the hell are you doing?" I laugh.

"Tying up your hair."

I bite my lip. Probably blush, too. And then his fingers are dividing my hair up into sections and it feels so—different? Good? Both?—I almost want to close my eyes.

Then I realize what he's doing. "Are you... braiding it?" I laugh. "Where the hell did you learn to do that?"

"I have nieces, remember? Rory used to make me play hair salon with her before Ariel was old enough to take my place. She taught me all the skills."

I giggle like an idiot as I picture Vann dutifully playing hair salon with his niece. But then the sensation of him doing my hair—the spring air, the warm sun, the upcoming ride on his bike—it's all so delicious, I settle in and just enjoy it.

This could be the last time I have him this way.

We will date. I realize that now. There's no other way forward, except for me to move out of their garage and start all over again. And I'm not fool enough to do that. So we *will* date.

And who knows what happens after that?

It could all explode tomorrow.

It's not even up to me. Saying I will date him isn't the solution. Just because we date doesn't mean we fall in love. The future doesn't come with a guarantee.

Well. Maybe one guarantee.

Nothing will ever be the same again. That's the only thing I know for sure.

So I enjoy this. I enjoy every moment of it.

He takes his time braiding my hair. Like he's enjoying this just as much as I am. And when he's done, he fastens the elastic band and pulls a ribbon out of his pocket, showing it to me in the palm of his hand. It's black satin and has little skulls printed down the length of it.

I recognize it because we sell them in the shop.

"Can I use this as the finishing touch, Belinda?"

I turn my head and look over my shoulder at him. "No?"

"Yes," I say.

"Yes," he repeats, smiling. And then he ties the skull ribbon on the end of my braid.

I stand up and turn around, my hand automatically reaching for the long braid behind my back and pulling it over my shoulder so I can see the bow he tied.

I look at him. And when our eyes meet, I think I blush seventeen shades of scarlet.

"Ready?" he asks, getting to his feet. He's wearing light blue jeans with a few rips along his upper right thigh. There's an old grease stain on the other leg, faded now from being bleached out. And if a stranger were looking at it, they wouldn't know it was grease.

But I know it's grease. Because these are his favorite jeans. And that t-shirt he's wearing, the white one with the black Shrike Bikes raven and skull logo on the front, that's his favorite shirt too. And the boots on his feet—not the typical black ones he wears every day, but the old, scuffed-up brown ones he reserves only for bike rides—those are his favorite boots.

His blond hair is tousled and just a tiny bit too long. He has an appointment to get it cut next week. I know this. I know this because I made that appointment for him. So right now his hair is just the right length. The way it hangs over his face just enough to make his blue eyes a little darker than they really are takes his charming good looks to a slightly more mysterious level.

I nod. And that's all I'm able to do. Because I am suddenly at a loss for words.

He nods back, slips his matte-black helmet over his head and points to mine. Which I have been holding this entire time.

I slip it over my head and he adjusts my chin strap. Then he walks over to his bike, straddles it, kicks back the stand, and kicks it until the engine roars. Filling the quiet, quaint Mountain Avenue neighborhood with the promise of danger.

He waits for me on the idling bike, looking at me with… I don't know what that look is.

Longing?

Desire?

Love?

All of the above?

His shoulders look a little bit tense. Like he's waiting for something bad to happen. Waiting for me to change my mind, maybe?

But it's too late for that.

And when I swing my leg over the back end of the seat and settle up against his back, he reaches around, grabs my hands, and clasps them together over the tight muscles of his stomach.

I grab fistfuls of his t-shirt as he eases the bike down the driveway and his shoulders relax in the knowledge that he *finally* has my full attention.

## CHAPTER SEVENTEEN

**TONY**

*Soshee Ameci drives* a ten-year-old white Toyota Corolla. A true piece of shit. And I can't explain it, but her car choice makes me kinda love her.

Back home I drive a 1969 notchback Corvette Stingray in Le Mans blue. It's a nice fucking car. My rental is nothing special, though. Just a standard sedan in gold.

So when we're standing in the parking lot in the back of the theatre and she asks me if I want to drive, I tell her no.

She makes a face at her car, then looks back at me. "Are you sure? My car might break down. It's been known to do that."

I chuckle. "Yeah. I'm sure. Your car looks like it's up for an adventure."

"Hmm." She smiles at me. "Are you up for an adventure, Tony Dumas?"

I nod. "One hundred percent invested in this adventure. Nothing's gonna go wrong. Trust me."

She giggles and waggles a warning finger at me. "You're just tempting fate now, buddy."

"Bring it, Fate. I'm ready."

"You say that now, but my gas gauge doesn't even work."

"Soshee, if we run out of gas and get stranded on the side of the road, my life will be complete."

"OK," she says, sliding into the driver's seat. "But don't say I didn't warn you when the engine overheats and some random farmer has to give us a lift to a gas station in Berthoud on the back of his tractor so we can get a tow truck."

I get in the passenger side. "God, I really hope that happens."

She laughs and inserts her key. It takes three good tries before the car actually starts. And when she backs out of the parking space, it backfires.

She shoots me a dubious look.

I smile back at her and slide my sunglasses down my face. "Let's do it."

**When I told her** I wanted to get our fortunes told for our third date, she guffawed. Loudly.

"Why?" she exclaimed.

"That's my proof."

"Your proof of what, exactly?"

"That this is real."

"Hold on," she said. "You're gonna rely on my sketchy fortune-telling mother to confirm that we're over the exes and ready for something new?"

"You got it in one."

"This is such a bad idea."

But she's wrong. I can feel it. I don't even care if her mother's a fake. This is going to be the most mysterious, intriguing, and slightly dangerous date ever.

Mostly because her mother really could ruin everything. But also because I promised to tell her my truth.

And I fully intend on keeping that promise.

**We're quiet as we make** our way west towards the highway that leads down to Boulder from Fort Collins. But once we leave the city limits there's a lot of empty space and the silence that was comfortable turns into an air of expectation.

"OK, I'm ready," she says once she gets her old car into the last gear and there are no more traffic lights in our way. "I want to hear all about what you saw on your way home this morning." She points a red-tipped fingernail at me. "And don't leave out the dirty secrets. I'm dying to see more of your dirty side."

I grin at her. And maybe... possibly... fall a little in love with her. I just dig this girl. There is absolutely nothing about her to hate. She's the exact opposite of Rosalinda in every way possible.

She makes me feel like everything is going to be OK.

When I look at Rosalinda, I feel like the whole world has gone wrong. I get a heavy pain in my chest. The blue sky is suddenly filled with gray clouds. And there's dread. So much dread when I think about Belinda. Rosalie. Whoever the fuck she is.

But with Soshee I feel like the world has gone right. Like the sun is so bright, it forces the clouds to part. Like there's hope.

"Come on, come on. Don't keep me waiting."

"OK. But I have to start with the dirty parts. That's the only way this story makes sense."

"Oh, my," she says. "You really know how to get a girl excited. Spill."

I take a deep breath, consider how bad of an idea it is to say anything about my dirty secrets to a girl I just met yesterday, then let that feeling of hope take over and throw away the dread for good. I'm done with it. "OK. Let me talk and get out the first part. Then you can ask questions."

"You're pretty confident I'll have questions."

"Oh, you will. Trust me. So… first of all I would like to prelude this convo with the disclaimer that I'm a good dude."

She laughs. "Noted."

"And that sometimes doing the right thing involves breaking the law."

"Hmm. OK."

"My father started this little mission we're on a long time ago. Decades ago. So it wasn't our idea. It was just something my brother Alonzo and I grew up with."

"Like being in a Mob family." She winks at me.

"Kinda. Sure."

"Just tell me what you guys do, Tony. Trust me when I say that no matter what it is, I've seen worse."

I point at her. "You're not going to get out of explaining that."

"I don't plan on it."

"OK. Fine. We smuggle people into the US. Kids, mostly. But sometimes younger women too. Especially pregnant ones. And we're not sleazy sex-traffickers, either. We're just trying to make a difference in the lives of less fortunate kids. Most of them are orphans from different Central American countries. But we do a lot of runs from Haiti and every now and then Cuba too. We pick them up in the ocean and take them to safe houses along the East Coast and get them fake papers."

"Wow. That's... lofty. And impressive. And... wow, Tony." She makes a pouty face. "You have a secret squishy side."

"I do," I say. "But it's not all sunshine and roses. See, for a long time we've had this deal with the FBI. They cover for us. They kinda had our backs. But this last mission, just a few months ago, it became very apparent that the FBI wasn't really covering for us. They were up to something else and they were using us to hide that."

"Damn. Fuck. What were they up to?"

"We're not one hundred percent sure, but it's also probably smuggling kids. Just... not for the same reasons."

"Shit."

"It's hard to tell though, because we've done dozens of these missions over the years. And only two of them went sideways."

"What's that mean?"

"The FBI only cared about two of these missions. Two missions that were smuggling in little girls."

"Oh, no."

"No. It's not what you think. They weren't meant for sex trafficking either."

"How do you know?"

"Because these are very special little girls."

"Special how?"

"They're assassins."

"What?" She laughs. Loudly. "Say that again."

"They're assassins, Soshee. I am not fucking around. I met one of these girls a few months ago. Her name is Wendy. And Wendy is the creepiest teenage girl you've ever seen in your life. Oh, she's beautiful. Don't get me wrong. She's all blonde hair and blue eyes. Perfect, angelic face. But she's a cold-blooded killer."

"Are you fucking with me right now?"

"No." I pause to stare at her. "I swear on my sweet mother's life, I am not fucking with you. The FBI is collecting these girls."

"OK," she says. But I can hear the healthy dose of suspicion in her voice. "Keep going."

"And both times the FBI interfered with our missions so they could intercept these little girls, they failed. The first time—well, this is where you guys come in."

"Wait. Which guys?"

"Vann. Fort Collins. Belinda. All the other witnesses." Soshee looks at me with utter confusion before looking back at the highway. "She wasn't always Belinda. She was Rosalie back then."

"What?" Soshee makes a face. "What are you talking about? I don't understand. What does that mean? Belinda had a different name?"

"Umm." I run a hand down my face and realize I haven't shaved in a couple days. "Yeah. Kinda. Well… she saw the operation go down when the FBI swooped in and tried to take one of the kids in our shipment from the Caribbean. And they were pissed. Rosalie—

Belinda—I just call her Rosalinda to keep it straight—
she saw this by accident. And she and I were already
done, right? It was over. So I agreed to have her put
into the witness protection program and sent up here
to Fort Collins."

"She's… in the witness protection program?"

"Maybe?"

"I don't understand."

"I don't either. I mean, we all thought she was
being protected all these years. But then, on the last
mission, the same thing happened. The FBI came in
and told us they were going to take a girl off our
shipment. And we teamed up with the Boston
brothers—"

"Whoa. Hold up." She pulls the car over to the
side of the road, puts it in park, and turns in her seat to
look at me. "*The* Boston Brothers? As in… *Jesse*
Boston?"

"He's my brother-in-law. Married my sister last
Christmas Eve."

"Your brother-in-law is Jesse Boston?"

"Yeah. And I don't know how much you know
about them, but—"

"Know about them? Are you fucking with me
right now?"

"No. I swear. This is all true."

"I'm *related* to them."

"What?" I laugh, even though this isn't funny. Not
one bit. "That can't be. Those guys have no family. Just
each other. I know this. Their father and uncle—"

"Were killed. I know. Trust me, I've heard that
story a million times growing up. 'Keep your mouth
shut, Soshee. Don't tell anyone, Soshee. Or your mom,
or your sister or your little cousins will all be next.'

Because that uncle of theirs who was killed? He was my *father*, Tony!"

"What? You're Zach Boston's *sister*?"

She closes her eyes and turns her head away to stare out the window. "Oh. My. Fucking God. This cannot be happening."

"You're really Zach's sister?"

"Half-sister. We had different mothers. But yeah. Basically. I'm his sister. He got the cushy city life and my mother and I were sent here to Fort Collins to live with her side of the family after it happened. That's how I got here. And now you're telling me... what? That Belinda is part of this too? That you... we're all... connected to something dangerous?"

I wince and shrug. "You did want a mysterious, intriguing, slightly dangerous date, didn't you?"

"Oh, my God, Tony. This isn't funny. This is all bad. They know! They have to know who I am! And that means none of us are safe!"

"I... hate to say this, Soshee, but this is just backstory. I haven't even gotten to the real problem yet."

"What?" She looks like she might start crying.

"I'm sorry. Fuck. Maybe I should go home. Not tell you any more. Keep you safe."

"Are you fucking insane?" Any previous sign of upcoming tears disappears immediately and she becomes all business. "Start talking. Now. I want to know everything. Does this have anything to do with Tara disappearing? I've asked Vann like a hundred times what happened to her. I know they all went on some road trip, but then Vann and Belinda came back and Tara didn't."

"She didn't disappear. She's living with my brother, Alonzo."

"The fisherman?"

"Yeah." I smile. Because she was paying attention earlier. "Tara is fine."

"I don't know if I would call her fine. She was weird too. I could never put my finger on it, but she always came across as... fake. For some reason. Not that she wasn't a nice girl. I liked her. But there was just something off about her."

"Yeah, that's because she's one of the witnesses."

"OK, you've said that twice now. What's it *mean*?"

"This is where Vann comes in. Because he was the one who noticed that this Fort Collins place is crawling with... witnesses. People who saw something they shouldn't have. And they all got sent here. And my brother sent me here—I mean, I did come to figure out why I couldn't get Rosalinda off my mind, but I was actually sent here by Alonzo. To hit up Vann and figure out what he knows. Because we're pretty sure that the FBI people we've been working with aren't... like... on the up and up."

"They're dirty."

"Yeah. We think so."

"And now you're caught up in their dirty plans?"

"Yeah." I sigh. "We think that too. And it doesn't take a genius to see where this is going, does it?"

"Prison. All of you."

"Or death," I add. I don't want to admit that, but... it's so obvious. It would be dishonest to leave that possibility out.

Soshee swallows hard and takes a deep breath. "OK. So... let me get this straight. Tara and Belinda both saw something you Dumas people did—"

"No, Tara was in LA. I don't know what her other name was before she became Tara. I kinda zoned out during that part of the meeting—"

"Tony!"

"What?"

"Oh, my God. What meeting? And how did Tara see something you guys did in Key West if she was in LA?"

"She didn't. She saw something else. Maybe related? Maybe not? I don't know. None of us knows. All we know is what Vann told us. He's the one with the missing information. And now that I know you're actually related to the Boston family…"

"Now that you know that what? You're done with me?"

"What? No, Soshee. Not at all. I was going to say now that I know that you're involved… well, I'm not leaving this town until I figure the whole thing out. I'm not leaving until you're safe. And if that means I have to take you with me when I go home, so be it. I will not abandon you. Do you hear me? I mean it. I will not."

She sits in silence for a few moments, the car shaking a little as other cars whiz by on the highway, thinking about how I just turned her whole world upside down in the span of ten minutes.

I'm good at that now, I guess. Turning people's lives upside down seems to be a bad habit of mine.

"OK," she finally says. "What does this have to do with what you saw this morning on your way home from Vann's house?"

"Are you sure you want to hear it?"

She nods. "I'm sure. I feel like my mother and I have been running from this truth my whole life. And

I guess we have. Two thirds of it, anyway. I'm done, Tony. Whatever it is you guys are planning, I'm in. I'm all in. So tell me what you saw."

I do my best to explain the yippy dog and the various people I've seen walking him over the past few days. And then how I followed them back to the coffee shop next door to Sick Boyz. "The walker was thinking about breaking in to the shop," I say. "Like maybe the Vaughn brothers have something to do with all this too?"

"Or maybe they thought Belinda was hiding something in there?"

"She's not."

"How do you know?"

"Because she understands even less then I do. I've been thinking about this and it only makes sense. All Belinda knows is that she witnessed our illegal smuggling eight years ago and all she got for her trouble was a fucked-up second chance. I think it's Vann they're after. They must know that he's on to them."

"Oh," she breathes. "Oh, no." She looks at me. "We have to go tell him. Both of them."

"What about your mom?"

"Shit."

"Your mom comes first. Vann Vaughn can take care of himself. And I don't mean that facetiously. I mean they're the fucking Vaughn brothers, OK? People have his back. We're on our own here, Sosh. My team is back in Key West. So we go to your mom's first, then we take this back to Belinda and Vann."

I say this with a finality she doesn't even bother to fight. She just puts her crappy car into gear and pulls back on to the highway.

And even though I've got a million terrible things on my mind, my mind is slightly distracted by the fact that I'm going to meet Soshee's mother.

Who is a fortune-teller.

And that might make me even more nervous than the FBI problem back in Fort Collins.

She could see a terrible future for us.

Or… see past my charming side and find the darkness underneath.

## CHAPTER EIGHTEEN

# BELINDA

*I lean against Vann's* back and hold him tight around the waist as we ride north of Fort Collins. Not because I like the smell of his leather, or because I'm enjoying the feel of his hard abs—well, OK, maybe both of those things too—but the main reason is that he's a pretty great windbreak.

*Mmm-hmm*, my inner voice is saying. *Riiiight, Belinda. He's a good* windbreak.

I've been trying to ignore that inner voice since Vann left my apartment last night but it's fairly persistent on insisting that I might, in fact, be falling for a man I swore I had no feelings for.

I have insisted, hundreds of times, that I have no feelings for him. So many times, in fact, it's more like an automatic mantra these days than a well-thought-out decision. And, to be perfectly honest, *I'm* not even buying it anymore, so it's no wonder that my inner voice is gloating.

I like him.

Of course I like him. I have always liked him. Anyone who doesn't fall for the charms of Vann Vaughn is just a liar. They might not want to be his best friend—or girlfriend, as was my case—but he's an easy person to like.

You just want to look at him. He smiles when he talks. Almost always, without fail. And that smile comes with flashing dimples and bright sky-blue eyes. He has classic good looks. Square jaw, perfectly symmetrical face, tall, lean body that has well-defined muscles, but not the kind his brother Vic is sporting. I have never seen Vann work out and I've lived above his garage for several years now.

They have a gym downstairs. The garage houses all their bikes—even their gramps has a bike, though he doesn't ride it anymore. He rides in their father Vern's sidecar when they all go out for a family ride. So there's a bunch of bikes and a whole mess of gym machines. They're in there almost every day at some point. All of them, even Gramps.

Except Vann. So Vann's muscles aren't bulky. They're just genetically perfect.

I've seen him with his shirt off millions of times. These Vaughn men don't wear shirts at home once the weather turns nice. Of course they don't. They want to show off their ink. They are like walking billboards for Sick Boyz.

And yes, I can appreciate the sexiness of all the Vaughn brothers. But up until last night I looked at them like... an observer. Not one directly involved with their lives, but on the sidelines.

Now?

Well, I think this ride counts as my very first official date with Vann.

And when we turn onto a road called Bombs-A-Way and stop at a driveway gate announcing our entrance to a place called Shrike Ranch and Vann presses in the code to open the gate and allow us to enter the driveway, I realize what's really happening here.

He's taking me to his sister Veronica's house.

The older sister. It's a roadblock for a potential girlfriend wanting to date a baby brother much like a mother-in-law can be a roadblock when you want to marry a man.

There is no mother at the Vaughn house. At least that's what I thought. But once we make it down the long driveway and the huge farmhouse comes into view, I realize my mistake.

There is a mother here. And her name is Veronica.

Vann eases the bike up next to Spencer Shrike's personal ride and cuts the engine. We get off the bike and as soon as Vann gets the strap of his helmet unfastened, he is practically tackled by a gang of little girls.

His nieces, plus a few visiting friends, start jumping up and down tugging on his hands, and his jacket, and one very small one is trying to climb his leg like a tree.

I cover my mouth with my hand to hide my smile.

Vann takes it all in stride, grabbing a child in each arm and swinging them around until they scream.

A loud, shrill whistle pierces the air and suddenly everyone stops to look at the blonde bombshell standing on the porch, baby on her hip. "Get your little firecracker butts in here! I called you for brunch five minutes ago!" She waves a wooden spoon at them with her free hand. "And I do not want to hear one peep about cold eggs, you tiny heathens! Now go wash up!"

All the girls say, "Awwww," but they don't dare talk back. Or dawdle.

There is a whoosh of shirts and a scuffle of sneakers as the gang of girls abandon Vann for cold eggs and disappears inside the house. The porch door closes with a smack and Veronica wipes the back of her hand across her forehead as she comes down the porch steps bouncing her baby. "What are you doing here?"

"Just came by for a visit," Vann says. "It's a nice day. Wanted to take Belinda here for a ride. But we have work later, so can't go too far. Figured I'd come hang with my favorite sister."

"I'm your only sister," Veronica says, whacking him playfully with her wooden spoon.

Veronica Vaughn. She is younger than all her other brothers, save Vann. Also known as Ron the Bomb, Bombshell, Ronnie, and I've heard her brothers jokingly call her Momshell more than once.

Veronica used to work at Sick Boyz as an artist. Vann inks in her old studio now. But she retired to this expansive farm about twenty miles north of Fort Collins to raise a family with her hot bike-builder husband, Spencer Shrike.

"Hi, Belinda," Ronnie says. "Have you taken over Sick Boyz yet?"

"Not quite." I laugh. "But Vic did let me help him do filler last night."

She rolls her eyes and switches the baby to her other hip. "He's so magnanimous."

"I'm not complaining," I say. "And he said I could use his studio on his days off now."

"Really?" Ronnie's eyes shoot up. "Well, that's an offer he never made me before I had a studio to myself."

We both look at Vann, who is smiling that I'm-a-happy-guy smile at both of us. "Belinda and I are dating now."

"Is that so?" Ronnie smirks at me.

"Well, I get one date," Vann explains. "To prove myself."

Ronnie points her spoon at me. "Good thinking. Gotta take them out for a test drive before you commit." Then she looks at Vann. "But seriously, I'm glad you're here. Because I need a babysitter—"

"No!" Vann says, putting his hands up. "No way."

"Just pick the little monsters up from school on Monday. That's all I'm asking. It's your day off."

Vann is still shaking his head.

"It's my car pool day, Vann. And Spencer is having this big bike reveal that afternoon. The press is gonna be there, and we're getting special photographs in the morning for billboards, and this might be my last chance to take part in an event like this before I'm too squishy and mommed out to do the body-paint modeling."

Vann groans. "Why can't one of the other moms pick them up?"

"They're busy! Why would I be asking you if the other moms were available? You don't even have to watch the baby. She's part of the shoot."

"They're all babies, Ron. They need parental supervision at all times or one of them gets a crazy idea and the next thing you know they've opened up a fake tattoo shop in City Park called Sick Kidz and have already made thirty bucks when the cops show up to shut it down."

Veronica points her spoon at him. "That only happened once. And it was Five's fault. Not Rory's. You've met Five, haven't you, Belinda?"

I hold out my hand about shoulder height. "Boy genius about this high? Fastidious about his school uniform? Wears it on the weekends?"

Veronica chuckles. "That's him." She turns to Vann. "It's always him. And he won't be there."

Vann points back at her. "You lying little momshell! He's part of the car pool! If I pick them up, he is not staying at our house after school. He has to go home."

"Deal," Veronica says. And then she winks at me.

"And you have to feed us brunch," Vann adds.

Veronica smirks. "How would you like your eggs, little brother?"


Brunch at the Shrike Ranch is no small thing. They eat in the dining room, at a table that seats twelve—every chair filled—and is overflowing with a big country feast. Eggs are just the beginning. There are pancakes, and bacon, and sausage, and even a quiche. Veronica's husband, Spencer, talks to Vann non-stop over the chatter of ten females.

It's a nice family, I realize. Not that the Vaughn brothers aren't a nice family. They are. They're just... a whole lot of men in that house. You can practically feel the masculinity oozing out the front door.

This house is homey. Not perfectly designed, or particularly tidy, or even opulently upscale, even though you can tell this place cost a bundle. It's just very... lived-in, filled with love, and contains mostly girls.

It's a nice break from my normal routine. Which is mostly being alone.

And I realize that if Vann and I do become a thing, and it works—then I will inherit all these people. All those brothers at the Vaughn house. Veronica and Spencer and their pack of girls. Even though I have written off Veronica's pack of girlfriends as BFF material, they would make a nice backup.

The whole thing kind of sounds nice and by the time Vann and I are heading back down the Shrike driveway, I'm already well on my way to dreaming about a life filled with these people.

Vann doesn't take us home. Instead he pulls his bike up in front of Sick Boyz because it's well after noon now, and there are people hanging out in the front waiting for their appointment.

He smiles at me and takes my helmet, then fastens both of them to the sissy bar. "That wasn't my date," he says, like this topic has been on his mind the whole ride back to town.

"No?"

"Well, not all of it. Obviously."

"It was a good start."

"My sister didn't scare you away?"

"No." I sigh. "She actually earned you points."

"Points? Are we on a point system?"

"Mmm-hmm." I smile.

"What's my running total?"

"Well, I would give you five points for surprising me with the bike ride and braiding my hair on the porch."

"OK."

"And twenty points just for the bike."

He looks down at his bike and grins. He built this bike with his own hands, so this is a compliment he can get on board with. "It's the art on the tank, right?"

The art on the tank is a homage to classic tattoos. Brightly colored pin-up girls in vintage sexy bikinis, anchors, and swallows, cherries, roses, and hearts. And, of course, the obligatory heart with arrow and a mom banner flying across the front. It's sick in a Sick Boyz way.

"Yup, it was the art," I agree.

"Is that it then? Twenty-five points?"

"No, I give you five hundred points for your sister's farmhouse." He chuckles. "And a bonus point because they had ponies in the corral by the barn. And the brunch is worth… mmm… thirteen."

"So I'm up to five hundred and thirty-nine. What is this out of? Because if it's five hundred, then I'm in A-plus-plus territory. But if it's a thousand, then I have to up my game."

"Hold on. I'm still tallying."

Vann sits down on the seat of his bike and crosses his arms, grinning at me like a boy falling in love.

"I give you a thousand points for agreeing to babysit."

He blushes and looks down at his boots.

"And two points for dropping me off at work."

"So… one thousand, five hundred and forty points. I need the denominator, toots. I need to know how high I should aim."

"You lose ten points for calling me toots."

He laughs. "That's not fair. I really like calling you toots. I'll tell you what. I'll give you all the points if you let me call you toots."

"I'm not the one earning points today."

He cocks his head at me. "You sure about that?"

I tsk my tongue. "Anyway. Veronica pushed me over the edge no matter what. She likes me."

"Just let me call you toots. I have to call you something."

"You can call me Belinda."

"I do call you Belinda. But…" He leans forward so none of the people on the sidewalk can hear him, and he whispers, "That's not even your real name. So what do you care if I call you toots?"

Hmm. He's got a point there. "Fine. You can call me toots. Just don't call me Rosalinda."

"Ew. That's a deal."

"Tony calls me Rosalinda," I say. "I hate it."

"Because it's his nickname for you?" Vann asks. "Or because it's confusing?"

"It's not confusing."

"No?"

"No. It's just… stupid."

"OK." He puts up both hands in surrender. Then a wild grin fills his face. "I win. So I'm done arguing. So the tally? I'm up to one thousand five hundred and forty. Did I pass the threshold yet? At least tell me if I'm getting close."

"You're close. But not there yet." I try not to smile at him. Or blush. But I don't succeed in either of those areas. "Let's call it out of eighteen hundred."

"So I'm a solid B-plus at the moment."

"A solid B-plus. For sure."

He reaches for me, takes both my hands, and then gently urges me to take a few steps forward until my body is positioned between his legs. He lets go of my hands and slides his hands onto my hips, hooking them through my belt loops. Even though he's sitting, we're almost eye level and I can't stop myself from gazing into his eyes.

He sighs. "Well." Pauses. "I give you all the points, Belinda Baker. Plus a cherry on top for being spontaneous with me this morning and extra credit for agreeing to babysit with me on Monday."

"Hey!" I laugh. "I never agreed to that!"

His hands come up to my face and he holds them there against my cheeks, his blue eyes hooded now as he gazes back at me. I can see a reflection of myself in his dark pupils. He leans forward, like he's going to kiss me, but then stops short just before our lips touch.

I erase that small distance between us and kiss him.

There's no tongue. There's no moaning or anything like that.

It's just a sweet, sweet kiss from a boy who finally got his chance.

I pull away first and find him grinning at me. "I'm going to make some beautiful ink art today, Belinda. And you know why?"

"Why?" I whisper.

"Because all I'm going to be thinking about is the way you wrapped your arms around me on the ride today. And the way you smiled at my nieces. And the way your hair felt in my fingertips when you let me braid it. And how tonight, after we leave work, I'm not going to let you go up to that garage apartment."

"No?"

"No." He shakes his head. "You're coming home with me."

He nudges me backwards so he can stand up. Then he takes my hand and leads me through the small crowd of loitering college kids. And then we walk into Sick Boyz together.

## CHAPTER NINETEEN

**OK. Let me set the scene** here at Madam Ameci's House of Fortunes. That's the name on the small shingle sign swaying outside the small garden-level storefront tucked away down a flight of nearly hidden stairs on the outside corner of the Pearl Street Pedestrian mall in Boulder.

First of all… finding the hidden half-flight of stairs that leads to the entrance is kind of like looking for that Harry Potter train stop in London. You have to walk down four steps then duck under a curtain of fake plastic ivy and turn a corner before you finally see the lacquered red Dutch door built into the side of a brick wall.

The shingle hangs outside and I'm beyond bewildered at how anyone finds this place if you can't see it from the street, but when we pass through the door and jingle a set of small bells that announce our arrival, half a dozen faces of various ages turn to look at us as soothing meditation music flows down from speakers in the ceiling.

Soshee smiles at them and takes my hand, leads me across the teeny-tiny waiting room to a beaded curtain—now I know where she steals her home décor accessories—and creates a little entrance for me. "She's back here," Soshee whispers.

"Should we wait?" I ask. "Until… you know, she's done with her client?"

"Oh, we'll wait in the break room."

I shrug and duck through the beads, then wait for Soshee to slip past me and lead the way down the dark hallway lit up with a long shelf of flickering votive candles.

I can hear whispering from behind a silk curtain as we pass, but once we enter the break room and Soshee closes the door, the whole mystic vibe disappears. It's a white room with a single lightbulb hanging from the ceiling and a small, old-school TV playing black and white movies on silent.

Soshee points to one of four chairs around a vintage red dinette table. "Sit. She'll come in when she's done."

"Don't we have to tell her we're here?"

"Well, she *is* psychic."

"Right." I laugh.

"Kidding. I mean, she *is* psychic. I suppose. But she's got a security feed on the wall in her office, so she saw us come in."

"Doesn't hurt to stack the deck."

"Never hurts to stack the deck." I sit and she takes the seat across from me. "She's going to flip out when I tell her about you."

"Because Zach Boston is my sort-of cousin-in-law?"

"That. And"—Soshee cocks her head at me—"well, she's gonna know."

"Know what?"

"That you and I are now… you know."

"We're... what?"

She shrugs. "Connected."

"By Zach?"

"No. Just connected. In her mind, this is all fate."

"Well, it could be fate. Or it could be a sequence of events that led to this moment. Rosalinda saw something she shouldn't have. The dirty FBI has, for whatever reason, made Fort Collins their home base. Rosalinda got sent there. Tara got sent there. Vann is one of those people who pays attention and they all ended up on my family street in Key West because the past finally caught up with everyone and bam. Here we are."

She winces. "That's a pretty long sequence."

"Yeah," I say, leaning back in my chair. "It kind of is." I sigh. "So then. We're connected."

"I don't mind being connected."

"Well, I don't mind either. I'm cool with our connection."

"It did get us to a third date."

I smile, then maybe blush a little. "That it did."

"Are you worried about the third date?"

"Why would I be worried?"

"Because third date... that's when... you know. Things get serious."

"Serious as in..."

"Meeting my mother." She smiles innocently. "Of course."

I nod and grin. "Of course."

The breakroom door opens dramatically and a woman in a long, red, paisley—robe? Shift? Mumu?—walks in, mid-conversation. "—is still hot. I was expecting you earlier, but you know how it is. Predictions are all about degrees of accuracy." She stops just a few feet away from me and stares at Soshee. "Well. What are you waiting for?"

"Um…" Soshee shrugs. "I didn't catch that first part, Mom. You started that convo out in the hallway."

"Tea! Tea! Pour the tea! I left my client in the room to meditate. I only have about six point two minutes before she falls asleep on me and I have to get back." She claps her hands as she talks. "Let's get this show on the road!"

Soshee jumps up and walks over to a little kitchenette where a tea pot is sitting on a hot plate. An empty cup is waiting on the counter—tea strainer filled with leaves already positioned over the top—and Soshee pours the hot water over them.

"Don't stir!" Madam Ameci orders. "He needs to do the stirring!"

"I know. I know," Sosh says. She brings the cup over to me, hands me a tiny silver spoon, and says, "Stir it."

"Ahh… why?" I ask, looking between the two of them.

There is a striking resemblance. Madam Ameci's hair isn't a deep scarlet red. There are streaks of light that might be blonde or gray. But you can tell it was long and wild, just like Soshee's, back in her younger days. They have the same face too. I try and find a little bit of Boston in Soshee, but nope. She and Zach share almost no characteristics. She is the spitting image of her mother.

Which—can I just say?—is sorta comforting. Because Madam Ameci is still kinda sexy for being a fifty-something. Even with the paisley robe-shift-mumu thing covering her up from head to toe.

"That's how I get your vibe," Madam explains. Soshee tries to retake her seat across from me, but Madam snaps her fingers and points to the chair to my left. "That one."

"Fine," Soshee says, and slips into the chair to my left.

"Now you stir the tea."

"Don't you want to know who he is, Mom?"

Madam Ameci looks me straight on and purses her lips as her eyes narrow down into thin slits. "I know who he is."

My eyebrows go up. Maybe she really is psychic?

"You're the new boyfriend."

"Ehhhh," I say, bobbing my head. "I was expecting a little more than that."

Soshee covers her mouth to stifle a giggle. This earns her a heated glare from her mother. But that only lasts a second. The heated glare darts right back to me. "Do not get smart with me, Tony Dumas."

My eyebrows go up again.

"I texted her while you were getting dressed earlier," Soshee says. "She's cheating right now."

Madam Ameci stands up straight and gets a little haughty. "I don't need to cheat."

"I'm gonna stop you there, Mom. Because what we're about to tell you is gonna blow your mind."

Soshee's mother's eyes are still locked with mine. "He knows your brother."

"Yeah," Soshee breathes. "How did you know?"

Her mother shoots her a look that says, *Please. I'm a psychic.* But that fades quickly and she sighs as she pulls out the chair across from me and sinks down in to it. "I knew this day would come eventually. And I didn't need to use any psychic powers to predict it. I, along with the rest of the world, read the special wedding edition of that magazine with the photos of your sister and Jesse Boston. I'm actually surprised it took you boys this long to start figuring things out."

"There are a lot of moving parts," I say.

"That there are."

"You knew about the witnesses?" Soshee says. "And you didn't warn me? I literally just found out about them on the drive down. I've come here to bitch about Belinda Baker like six dozen times over the past couple years and you never said a word!"

"Warnings do no good, Soshee. You know that. Everyone needs to see the truth on their own timeline. And Belinda isn't part of your story. He is. If you had come here bitching about Mr. Dumas, I would've calmed you down and set you straight. But you didn't. You came bitching about Belinda. She has her own part to play and it has nothing to do with you. Now. Stir the freaking tea, Mr. Dumas. I'm on a tight schedule here."

"But if you already know why we're here, then why do I need a tea reading?"

"Silly boy." She tsks her tongue. "You're not here for that. You're here for you."

"Am I?"

"Stir. The tea."

"Whatever," I mumble. And stir the tea.

"Now drink it."

I stare at the tea and make a face. It smells horrible. And it looks like red mud. "Is that really necessary?"

"Drink the freaking tea."

"Fine." I lift the cup to my lips and take a sip.

"All of it. In one gulp, please."

I look at Soshee for help. "Just do it," she says. "The quicker you let her read them, the quicker we can get the hell out of here."

"Nice," Madam says to her daughter.

I force myself to gulp it. Because Soshee is right. I've had about enough of her mother for one day, thank you. Then I set the cup down. Madam Ameci scoops the cup up almost before it hits the table. She peers down at the leaves and nods.

"What? What's it say?" I can't believe I even said that. All those years I made fun of Alonzo's fascination with mermaids and sirens are now coming back to haunt me. He can't ever know about this or he will never let me live it down.

"Just as I thought."

"Jesus Christ, Mother. Just tell us."

"It's not what *has* been said, Mr. Dumas," Madam Ameci replies, looking only at me. "It's what *hasn't* been said. Chew on that, mister. Now," she says, standing up and straightening her robe-shift-mumu thing, "I have to go. Mrs. Chase is probably snoring by now. See you kids later!"

She makes a little hand wave gesture and then throws the breakroom door open and whooshes through it, disappearing as quickly as she came.

I look at Soshee. "What the ever-loving fuck was that?"

She laughs. "That was my mother. Aren't you glad you met her?"

I pick up the cup and peer down at the remnant tea leaves. "But what does it say? She didn't tell me."

"She spoke in code."

"Code? That was vaguebooking at its best."

"Welcome to the world of professional psychics. Where specifics are overrated and your success depends on how much information you already possess."

"OK. Whatever. But she's clearly not very concerned that we all might be caught in some kind of dirty FBI net. This whole trip was a waste."

Soshee's face falls a little.

"No. I didn't mean it that way." I take her hand in mine. "I'm really glad I got to meet her. I swear."

"Liar." She laughs. "I'm not taking it personally. Trust me. My mom is just… weird. I've learned to live with it."

I squeeze her hand a little before I realize what I'm doing. And when she looks up at me, I can tell she's holding her breath.

Is she hoping for a kiss?

I'm pretty sure I want to kiss this girl. Also very certain I don't want to do it here. "It wasn't a waste, Sosh. I could learn to like your mom."

She stifles a laugh. "I'm sorry she didn't give you any big revelations."

"I wasn't expecting any. Trust me."

"And I'm sorry that she was so apathetic about our amazing cross-continent connection."

"It is a pretty amazing connection, isn't it?"

"Are you kidding me? Bright Berry Beach has a boutique two blocks from here. That can't be a coincidence."

"It can't be," I agree.

"We would've met eventually. Even if you didn't come looking for Belinda."

"I didn't really—"

"It's fine," she says, placing a hand on my chest. I suck in a breath when she does that. Because she places the flat of her palm right over my heart. And I'm pretty sure she didn't mean to turn that instinctive gesture into something more meaningful, but I stop breathing as the heat from her hand passes through my t-shirt and into my heart. "I'm not jealous of her."

"Soshee." I laugh. "You literally told me you were jealous of her yesterday."

"Yeah. But that was when things were all about Vann."

"And today things are not about Vann?"

She keeps her hand over my heart and it responds by beating a little faster. "No." She says this simply and seriously. "They're about you. Of course."

"I see."

She takes her hand away but the heat from her touch remains. I linger in that heat and then make a decision. "Soshee?"

"Hmm?"

We are standing too close. She is two steps away, if that. Her head is tilted up, her eyes locked with mine, her mouth slightly open and her chest rising and falling underneath her tank top . "Can we end this date now?"

Her chin juts back in surprise. "You want to end this date?"

I nod my head slowly. "Yeah," I whisper. "Because I'm ready for date four."

She looks down to hide her smile, but quickly looks back up again. "You're trying to get out of how date three ends, aren't you?"

"No," I say, taking her hand. "I'm just trying to put it behind us so we can start something new. Because I feel like... like... everything that came before now was about the past. And I want this day to be about the future."

She points at me. "Good answer."

"It was, wasn't it?"

She laughs. "OK. Date four it is. What should we do?"

There's a back door in the breakroom. I have no idea where it leads, but I don't really care at the moment. I just need to get her out of here and into someplace else. So I take her over to the door. I open it up and when we walk out into the late morning sunshine, it really does feel like a new beginning.

I start heading in the general direction of the car, still holding her hand.

"Are we going home?" Soshee asks.

"Home," I repeat absently. We come to the edge of the alley and I look around, trying to figure out where the car is. I see it in the parking lot across the street and start heading that way. "Yeah. We're going home."

"You're sure? I mean, we're already in Boulder. I can think of a lot of unique ways to spend date four right here."

"Such as?"

"We could go to the park and make fun of the hippies. Or stand in front of a random Subaru Outback and pretend we're the cool outdoorsy cats who own it. Oooh, I know. We could get drunk on a craft brewery tour. Or maybe buy some pot, smoke out, and then crash a chemistry lecture at the university and giggle like idiots until we get kicked out."

I look at her and shake my head. Because I could totally picture her doing all those things. "Now who's trying to get out of the end of date three?"

"Me?" She points to herself as we stop in front of her crappy Corolla. "Why would I want to get out of the end of date three? You were wearing nothing but a towel two hours ago, mister. I was ready to end date three before it even started. Now we're an hour away from a decent place to fuck, probably gonna run out of gas on the way home, have to hitch a ride into Berthoud on a tractor, and fuck in a gas station bathroom as we wait for the tow truck to drop the car because we won't be able to stand the sexual tension for one moment longer."

I toss my head back and laugh. She laughs too. But then I get serious and place my hands on her hips and press my chest up to her breasts. I lean into her ear and whisper, "I'm only going to warn you once, Soshee Ameci. If you talk dirty to me like that again, I won't be responsible for what happens next."

"Mmm," she hums. "Now I'm intrigued. What would happen next?"

"I'll throw you down on the hood of this car, hike that cute tennis skirt up to your hips, and fuck you into oblivion in front of this whole town."

She hisses out a chuckle and pushes me backwards. "Get in the car, before I decide that sounds like a pretty good time."

God, this woman. I like her. A lot.

But as fun as the whole public fuck thing sounds, that's something I would do with Rosalinda back in the day. And I'm done with her. One hundred percent done with her. So done with her that I want everything I do with Soshee from this moment on to be the exact opposite of how I've handled things in the past.

So I get in the car and we leave Boulder and her crazy tea-reading mother behind.

**Soshee talks the whole** way home. Just like she did while I was in the shower earlier. It's a habit of hers that I could get used to. She has baggage. Everyone has baggage. But she's not one of those girls who dwells on it. She's always in the present. Not looking back or forward. Just enjoying the moment.

She articulated this philosophy of hers last night when she was talking about her apartment. She knew it was temporary but she was going to enjoy every second of her experience there until it ended.

I heard her. And I believed her. Didn't have a reason not to. But I didn't really think about what that meant.

She is comfortable in her skin. That's what it means.

It's a skill I've never really mastered. I've spent most of my life thinking about the past and how it relates to the future. Soshee Ameci is a breath of fresh air.

When she finally pulls her car into the parking lot behind the Fort Collins Theater, it's a little after noon. She turns the engine off and turns in her seat to look at me.

"So," she says.

"Here we are," I say.

"Mmm-hmm."

"Are we going to sit in the car?"

"No. We're getting out. But I have one question."

"You want to know my intentions with you before I take you upstairs and fuck you into Sunday?"

She points at me. "Sure. That's good too. But no. My question is… should we go and tell Belinda and Vann what we know first?"

I look in the direction of Sick Boyz. I can't see it from here because the theater building is in the way. But I can picture it just fine all the same.

The thought of seeing and talking to them right now… well, that's just a great big no. Actually, it's not Vann who bothers me. It's Rosalinda. Every time I think about her I get that sick feeling. For some reason I still don't understand, Rosalinda feels like a crisis waiting to happen and I'd actually like to pretend she doesn't exist anymore.

I open my door, get out, walk around the car, and open up Soshee's door. Then I extend my hand to her and say, "I have no idea who you're talking about."

She smiles and shakes her head.

"Come on," I say, beckoning her by wiggling my fingertips. "Sunday isn't going to wait forever."

"What?"

"For me to fuck you into it."

"Oh, my God."

I take her hand and pull her out of the car, kick the door closed with my foot, and then start leading her toward the apartments.

But just as we're about to walk inside, the loud rumble of a motorcycle makes us both look towards the street. The bike pulls up in front of Sick Boyz and the engine cuts off.

"Well," Soshee says, "I don't know what to think of their timing."

Their timing is a reference to the riders of said bike.

Vann and Belinda.

I look at Soshee, searching her face for torment over the fact that her guy was never hers to begin with.

But there's no torment there. Just a wide grin. "Hello? Sunday called. Said time's a-wasting."

I decide to learn a lesson today about living in the moment.

I grab the door and hold it open for the only girl who matters. "We don't want to disappoint Sunday."

She walks through and I follow her. I hold her hand all the way up to the fourth floor.

There is no discussion about whether we're going to my place or hers. My rental was never even a possibility, let alone a question.

And when she finally opens the door and waves me inside, I step across her threshold like a man entering a new life. Like a guy who finally understands the meaning of home.

And really, it's not about her apartment—even though it's the warmest, most welcoming space I've ever been in. We're not staying here. This place is just where we've landed in this moment. Whatever happens in the weeks and months to come, it's not going to happen here.

This is the first step towards a new day.

She closes the door quietly and suddenly there's a lot of emptiness in the room.

No words. No noise seems to leak in from the city down below. No music or even the sound of our own breathing.

I walk over to her massive wall of windows and even though looking down would be natural, I don't look down. Looking down is like looking back. Instead I look at the rays of sunshine filtering their way around and through the amber beads of her Bohemian curtains.

She walks up behind me. Stops and stays still and quiet. And when I turn to face her, she lets out a breath.

I study her for a moment. The way her long legs disappear inside the pleats of her short skirt. The way her t-shirt hugs her breasts and reveals the thin outline of her bra underneath. Her long, scarlet hair and her wide green eyes glisten in the bright light of day.

She reminds me of fire.

Not the heat or even the color of fire. The draw of it. The beauty. The *pull*.

I'm familiar with that pull, but this is different.

Soshee Ameci was right about her self-assessment. She is a lovely little bottle of poison. She holds something inside herself that is uniquely hers. Something powerful and dangerous. Something mysterious and mystical.

Not the way her mother is mystical. Not something ethereal. Something much more real than that. Something almost… tangible.

She is the villain in the story.

But so am I.

And I think that makes us a pretty good team.

I reach for her and pull her towards me, a new desire building inside me. A new willingness too. "I'm not good with words. I don't have a name for this. No label or description. I don't really understand how we even got here when two days ago I didn't even know you existed. But when I'm with you I feel like a totally different person. When you talk I want to listen. When you lead I want to follow. I like you, Soshee. I need you to know that before we get any further into our fourth date in two days. I like you. I'm here for *you*."

She inhales slowly and holds her breath for a moment, her eyes searching mine for a few brief seconds. "I like you too, Tony."

I want to say more. I suddenly wish I had taken notes last night when I was eavesdropping in on Vann's big speech. Because I feel different and I don't think what I just said is enough. I wish I could pull all the confusing, conflicting feelings out of my heart and turn them into words.

I'm about to give it a try when Soshee's fingertip gently presses against my lip. "It's OK. I get it."

And then she kisses me.

Just like that. She just… takes over. Takes charge and kisses me. She ends forty-eight hours of mystery and intrigue and turns it into reality.

My hands come up to her face and I hold her as I kiss her back. Her lips are soft and she tastes like sweet, refreshing oranges on a bright spring day. I slide one hand into her long, thick mane while the other one travels down the side of her body and lands on her hip.

She's lifting my shirt up, her long red-tipped fingernails gently brushing against the tanned-brown skin of my waist.

"I have a sudden urge to do very dirty things with you," I say.

She responds by reaching for the button of my jeans and popping it open. There is no hesitation. No second-guessing. Her hand slips down inside my jeans and when she takes my already growing shaft in the palm of her hand and squeezes it, I suddenly feel like this was the point.

*This* was the point.

Her. Me. Us. *This.*

My hand slides under her skirt. Right between her legs. No hesitation on my part either.

She pushes me backwards, still holding my cock in her hand, until my lower back hits the window ledge. I open my legs wide enough to let her slip her hips between them. My fingers ease past her panties and slide right up into a delicious pool of wetness.

And then her mouth is on mine, her tongue dancing past my lips as she tugs my pants down just enough to free my cock and then, before I even know what's happening, she's looking me in the eyes as she squats down and takes her kisses with her.

The moment her lips touch the tip of my cock I suck in a deep breath and want to close my eyes.

But I don't close my eyes. I don't want to miss a single second of this new beginning.

I wish I could play with her pussy as she teases me with her tongue, licking my head and swirling it around the tip like she's about to devour something delicious. But then she opens her legs and adjusts her skirt so I have the perfect view as she begins to tease herself too.

"Fuck, Soshee," I moan.

She grins at me, winks, and then opens her mouth and places my cock on her tongue.

My fingers thread through her hair and then I fist it, holding her tight. She stares up at me. Daring me to take control.

But I wait. I wait her out because I like her power. She makes a little noise that might be a giggle and then wraps her lips around my shaft and sucks me off.

I grip her hair, fighting an almost uncontrollable urge to force my dick down her throat. It's a pointless battle because she eases forward until I feel the back of her throat, like she can read my mind and my wish is her command. She holds it there like she's testing herself or maybe rising to a challenge.

"Soshee," I murmur. "Oh, my God, that feels amazing."

She pulls back, letting my cock fall out of her mouth. But she wraps both hands around it and begins massaging it, pumping her fists up and down my shaft in slow, even strokes.

My eyelids are suddenly very heavy. She watches me the whole time during the hand job. Grinning like a girl with a secret. Attentive like she knows exactly what I need.

And she must. Because everything about her is perfect.

But enough. *Enough, Tony. This isn't all about you.* I place my hand over hers and grip it, then guide her up so she's standing again.

She opens her mouth to say something—maybe something cute, maybe a little joke about what we'll do next—but I kiss her before she can talk. And then I lift her up with both hands, turn us around, and set her down on the window ledge. This time she's the one opening her legs and I'm the one easing between them. My fingers automatically slip inside her. She is dripping wet with anticipation. So, *so* ready for me.

Her hands are still massaging my cock. Up and down my shaft. Squeezing and turning.

I push my fingers deeper inside her and she pauses her motion for a moment to moan my name. "Tony," she says, her breath ragged and deep.

I bite her lip and kiss her on the mouth, my tongue picking up the dance she started earlier. I push my hips forward, still playing with her pussy, my thumb rubbing small circles over her clit as I grind against her open thighs.

She guides my cock to her entrance and it slips inside as I withdraw my fingers. "Holy fuck," she whines. "Oh, my God," she hisses as my cock fills her up and goes in deep.

I press forward, forcing her to lean back against the window. Sunlight is pouring in through the glass, highlighting her deep red hair with bits of fiery gold. I grab it with both hands and hold her steady as I pull out and thrust forward again. Then do it again. And again.

She moans each time. And each time I push a little further up inside her until she gasps and her body goes stiff.

"Everything OK?" I ask, my own words also surprisingly deep and throaty.

She grips my shoulders in response, her fingernails digging into the hard round muscles so hard they sting. I punish her a little for that and thrust hard. She gasps again. But when I ease back to give her some relief, she pulls me forward again. Trying to get me closer. Trying to press our bodies together so tight, we stop being two people and just become one.

"Fuck me," she moans. "Just... fuck me. Right now."

She says this with eyes wide open. The little flecks of gold around the edge of her irises catch the halo of light from her hair, making her look surreal and mystical.

But I can feel her. Inside and out.

She's not a dream. She's real.

And this... this slow, careful, easy fuck belongs to us now.

This is how we do it.

This is our new beginning.

I let go of her hair and brace both hands on the warm panes of glass on either side of her body and then bury my head in her neck as I move my hips and she lifts up her knees and opens her legs.

And then I say, "Come for me, Sosh. Come all over my cock."

Even though that never works, like ever works, it works.

She comes. She moans and writhes, and wiggles against me as she pants in my ear, dirty words spilling out of her mouth like water running down a mountain. "Oh, fuck yeah. Your cock is so big. This feel so good. Don't stop, don't stop, don't you *dare*... fucking... *stop*!"

The heat of her passion coats my cock and the muscles of her pussy clamp down on it like a vice. And that's it. Date three, four... one... whatever this is... it's over.

I pull out and come on the inside of her leg as I kiss her mouth like I just found my perfect supervillain partner.

## CHAPTER TWENTY

**BELINDA**

*I can't quite decide* what I'm feeling as I work the front counter at Sick Boyz.

Is it... the elation of a new relationship? Or the anxiety of a new relationship? Is it hope? Or fear? Or both?

I can't tell.

Here is what I do know:

Every time Vann comes up front to get a client the first thing he does when he appears from the hallway is smile at me. He's looking for me before I even come into view. Sometimes that smile comes with a wink. And I find myself straining to hear snippets of his conversations in the back.

I can't hear much. His studio is too far down the hall and there are three busy, buzzing studios in between us. But every now and then I'll catch a laugh. Or a few words being said loudly.

When he walks his clients up to the front for payment, he lingers for a few seconds even though the waiting room tonight is packed with hopeful walk-ins. He leans against the glass counter and watches me ring them up. He explains aftercare instructions—not in back, like usual, but at the counter. Like he's trying to find excuses to spend a few extra moments with me.

And even though I don't want to feel giddy over this possibility, I feel giddy. My stomach actually has butterflies when I know his session is coming to an end. I anticipate his arrival from the hallway.

Thankfully, I don't have much of a chance to think about this over the course of the evening because all the boys are booked solid from the walk-in appointments. But eventually two AM rolls around and even though we hardly ever close on time because you can't really rush a tattoo appointment and the boys don't like to split walk-ins into two sessions if they can help it, this night is different. I find myself with a long stretch of minutes where there is no one waiting for an appointment and Vann is the only brother left with a client.

Vinn and Vonn leave by the front door, flipping the closed sign over as they go through. And then Vic pokes his head up and says goodbye, leaving through the back.

This is when I start chewing on my nails. I'm not a nail-biter so it's a true sign of anxiety.

What will happen now?

I mean, Vann pretty much spelled it out before work. He said, "You're coming home with me."

But what does that mean?

I literally live on his property. So does it mean he's giving me a ride home? Does it mean he's coming up to my place? Does it mean he's taking me up to his bedroom? What? What does it mean?

"OK, Robbie," Vann says, coming around the hallway with his last client. "You're all set, man."

I glance up and once again find Vann's eyes locked on mine as these words come out. He gives me the invoice and chats up Robbie about aftercare, and then slaps the counter twice and says, "I'll be right back, Belinda. Don't go anywhere," and leaves to clean up his room and put shit away.

I ring up Robbie, make polite chit-chat until he leaves, and then start totaling up the receipts for the night. There isn't much cash. Everyone pays digitally these days. So I just put the cash in the safe in the back room and then linger there, listening as Vann wipes down his studio.

He comes out, looks at me. Smiles. Then enters the breakroom with me.

I don't know what I expect. For him to kiss me? Push me backwards and fuck me on the table? Lean into my ear and whisper dirty things? I don't know.

But all he does is flip off the music and lock the back door. Then he turns to me. "You ready?"

"For what?" I say.

He laughs. "To go home?"

"Right. Yup. Let's go home."

He flips off the lights and for a moment I'm stunned by the near-total darkness all around me. Then suddenly he's next to me, reaching for my hand and pulling me down the hallway that is only lit up by the pink neon that filters through the blacked-out windows from the sign over the door.

His keys jingle in his hand as he opens the door, pulls me through, and then turns to lock it up. He still has my hand.

This is really happening. Vann Vaughn and I are… *in a thing.*

At least for tonight.

He turns to me and grins. And wow. I might've taken that grin for granted over the past several years. He lights up the night with that smile. "Are you ready?" he asks.

I take a breath and let it out. "I think so. But… what am I getting ready for?"

His only answer is a soft chuckle. He takes me over to his bike, unhooks the helmets, and we put them on. It's chilly out. Probably a little too cold to be riding. But home is very close and when I get on behind him and wrap my arms around his middle, he's luxuriously warm.

I lean my face into his back, my head pressed against the leather of his jacket. He kicks the engine and slowly backs up, the roar of his bike filling the relative quiet of downtown. There are only a few people about, but every single one of them turns to look at us as we head towards Mountain Avenue and then make a right.

My stomach flutters again. Because I am literally two minutes away from what comes next and I don't have any idea of what that might be.

*Well. Come on now, Belinda. You know what that means.* We are going to have sex. The hand-holding is over. The first kiss is over. And if I'm being honest, if we don't have sex, I'll probably be disappointed.

What if he wants to take it slow?

I don't think I can do slow. Not now. Not after everything that's happened today.

Which is… weird. Since this morning I had absolutely no plans on fucking this man and now it's all I can think about.

Yes. I might not have realized that's what I was obsessing over this whole night at work, but that's what I was obsessing over.

And I'm nervous.

When was the last time I was nervous about being with a man?

I was never nervous with Tony. With Tony, I was always angry. It was a totally different kind of heat. Not a pleasant one, either. Even when I look back on the few good times, I don't get a sense of longing or nostalgia.

My feelings for Vann are nothing like my feelings for Tony and that is a very good way to start a new *thing*.

Too soon we are pulling into the driveway. Vann parks his bike at the side of the garage closest to the house and we get off. I take my helmet and just kinda stand there, unsure what to do next.

"Now what?" I say, looking up at him.

He takes my helmet from me with one hand and laces the fingertips of his other one into mine. Then we're walking towards his porch.

He says nothing. He doesn't pause to ask me if I want to come inside when we get to the front door, just maneuvers the handle with his arm, opens the door, and walks me inside.

He kicks the door closed with his foot, drops the helmets onto a bench where half a dozen other helmets live, and then we're walking towards the expansive staircase that leads upstairs.

I have been inside the Vaughn mansion many times. I have been in the front room, I have used the bathroom, I have eaten in the dining room, and I've probably hung out in the kitchen with them hundreds of times.

But I have never been upstairs.

Crossing the front room takes a few moments because it's large. Larger than the family room on the east side of the house or the formal living room on the west side, behind the staircase. And it doubles as a dining room, so we have to weave our way around the immense table. And that means I have time to wonder if I'm doing the right thing.

But those moments pass without me actually coming to any sort of conclusion and then we're climbing the old, wooden stairs, him one step ahead of me, our footsteps creaking loudly. Loud enough that I worry one of the other Vaughn men will hear us and create an awkward moment filled with questions I have no answers for.

But then Vann looks over his shoulder at me and grins. "You're nervous."

"No," I lie.

"You lie, Belinda Baker. I know you're nervous because I'm nervous too."

"Why are you nervous?" I whisper. "This was your idea."

He stops at the top of the stairs and turns to look at me. "Because I like you. You know this. I have liked you since I first saw you eight years ago."

I huff at that. Eight years ago he was in high school. I was only twenty-one, but still. He didn't have a chance in hell of dating me. You don't date a high-school boy when you're twenty-one, no matter how cute and charming he is.

"And I don't want to fuck it up by going too fast, but…" He pauses. "I'm willing to risk it at this point.

Because it took me eight years to make you *see me*, Belinda. And if you change your mind tomorrow, there's not much I can do about that. It's your mind and your decision. So if, tonight, you're gonna let me take you upstairs and show you what you're missing, I'm gonna do that."

"I don't know what to say."

"Say yes. Or say no." He shrugs. "Or say nothing."

We stare at each other for a moment. And then he turns and leads me around the stairs to another flight of steps I didn't even realize existed.

I guess I knew there was a third floor. I can see the windows from outside. But it never occurred to me that he lived up here.

He doesn't stop at the door. Just pushes it open and I follow him into the darkness.

He lets go of my hand and for a moment I feel adrift in the blackness. Then a small light clicks on in the corner and the room appears before me.

Never mind the room. Vann appears before me.

I catch him in the act of taking off his shirt. He lifts it over his head and I find his eyes locked on mine as he drops it to the floor where his leather jacket already lies in a heap.

His fingers drop to his belt and before I can even make sense of the fact that things have started, he's got it undone. He pauses here just for a moment to search my eyes. Maybe looking for hints that I want him to stop. That I might turn around and walk out.

But I don't. I unzip my jacket and let it slip down my arms. Starting my own heap of clothing at my feet.

He grins and his blue eyes shine with mischief. "Yes?" he says.

"Yeah," I reply.

He shoots me a lopsided grin. "You're sure? Because once you get a taste of this"—he pans his hand down his body—"I'm gonna ruin you for other men."

I grin back at him. Allow his joking to ease my anxiety. "I'll take my chances."

And then he's across the room, his hands on my hips, tugging on my belt loops and pulling me over to his bed. He sits down on the mattress and slides his hands around to my ass, giving each cheek a squeeze as his teeth drag my shirt up, exposing the bare skin of my stomach. He kisses me, tugging me towards him, and an ache begins to build between my legs.

My hands drop to his head as I close my eyes and let the warmth of his breath wash over me. I grip his hair and he lets go of my ass and pops the button on my jeans, tugging them down enough to expose the top of my hip bones.

Then he stops and I open my eyes to find him looking up at me. Not smiling. No readable expression at all. Just... staring at me.

I get it though. And my hands drop down to his and I help him by sliding my pants down a little further.

His thumbs push my shirt up and I reach for it, tugging it over my head. I throw it to the side and stand there in front of him in my bra. He reaches for my breasts, squeezing them through the lace.

Then he's kissing his way up my stomach and I feel my knees become weak and the muscles in my legs tremble with anticipation.

I bite my lip, trying to picture what comes next, and then pushing any and all expectations out of my mind so I can just relish what's happening.

I don't know how we got here. But I'm suddenly glad we've finally arrived.

This is our night.

And just as I think that his thumb is playing with my pussy through my jeans.

The building ache instantly changes to an insistent tingle. And then his kisses drop down again until I can feel his lips through the very top of my silky panties.

My hands find their way to the curve of his hard shoulders and my eyes follow my fingertips. Taking notice of the thick, dark double X's inked there. There is a circle of words around each double X. He has this design on the top of both shoulders and I've seen them hundreds of times, but have never been close enough to read the intricate calligraphy.

I bend down a little to see it better.

"What are you doing?"

"I'm trying to read the circle words." He grins at me when my eyes slide to the left. "The letters are really small and these giant X's never made sense to me. What are they?"

"Well." He sighs. Then turns his head to look down at his shoulder. "They mark the spot. Like a treasure map. X is also number ten. So two of them are double. It's the unknown number in an equation and they signify a cross in religion. But mine are just kisses."

I smile and then giggle. "Like XOXO. That's it? Kisses?"

He shrugs. "That's it. Just kisses. But the cool part is the circle quote around the X's."

I expect him to keep going but he falls silent. "Well? Are you going to tell me? Or do I have to hunt down a magnifying glass and read them myself?"

"It's a snippet of a poem by John Keats."

My eyebrows lift up in surprise.

"I'm a romantic, Belinda Baker. I thought you'd have figured that out by now."

"Just tell me what they say."

"They both say the same thing. 'And now a soft kiss—Aye, by that kiss, I vow an endless bliss.'"

"Endless. Bliss. That's your promise?"

He looks up at me with straight lips and a serious face. "Not just one promise. Two. Double X's, remember?"

"Four then. A quadruple promise because you've got two on each side."

"And four makes a box," he says, his lips lifting up into a smirky smile. "Surrounded by kisses on all sides."

I pause here and give myself a moment to take it all in. "For a handful of X's and some too-tiny words, that's kinda deep, Vann."

"It kinda is."

I look at all the other words on his body. I never thought much about them, but now... I guess I see them in a new light. "Are they all deep and poetic like that?"

"No. There's a grocery list here." He twists and points at the words inked down his right ribcage. "Milk. Eggs. Cheese—"

"What the—"

"My grandpa did that on my twenty-first birthday after I passed out drunk." Vann shakes his head. "For an old dude, he's kind of incorrigible. No wonder this town thinks we're crazy."

I laugh, picturing this.

"So then"—he twists again and points to his left ribcage—"I started another list on this side with the names of Ronnie's little girls." He shrugs. "I'm into symmetry."

But that's when I notice the new tattoo on the inside of his arm. The one he was inking yesterday after our fight.

The clear bandage has been removed but it's still shiny with this morning's application of antibacterial ointment. I reach for his arm and turn it a little, so I can read the words. "'Being deeply loved by someone gives you strength. But loving someone deeply gives you courage.'"

When I stop reading, I realize he's gone perfectly still. He tilts his head up at me, blue eyes searching mine.

"You inked this yesterday."

He nods.

"After our fight."

He makes a little motion with his head. A very small shrug. "I don't know why I love you, Belinda. I just do. I dropped you off yesterday because I was angry that you were being honest. You have always been honest about it. You have never led me on."

"Vann—"

"No. Just listen. I love you. It's not the kind of love that comes and goes. It's not lust, either. We can stop right here, and you can go home alone, and I'll be fine. You can make me wait another eight years for another chance, and I'll be fine. This love I have for you… it's the kind that lasts *through* things. *Past* thing. Into new things." He shrugs again, presses his lips together and sighs. "I'm here. I'm not going anywhere.

You're not going to lose me. It's just not that kind of love, Belinda."

I hold my breath, and then suddenly it comes spilling out and I push him back on the bed. It's not about the tattoo. Although I love the tattoo.

It's about him.

It's about me.

It's about us.

I kick my shoes off, slide my jeans down my legs, and climb on top of him, straddling his hips with my legs. And then I cup his face, lean down, and kiss him. Hard.

I kiss him like he kissed me yesterday in the lobby of Anna Ameci's. Like he's my best friend and my lost lover. I kiss Vann Vaughn like he's cool, clear water and I'm dying of thirst.

And he kisses me back like a man who is seen for the very first time.

Like a man who is appreciated when before he wasn't.

Like a man kissing a woman who finally realized his worth.

He pulls back. Just a little. Just enough so our noses are touching and our foreheads are bumping. And then his eyes lift up to mine and I feel like I need to hold my breath.

"Thank you," he whispers.

That's it. Just, *Thank you*. No explanation. But I don't need an explanation. I know why he's thanking me. I'm still holding his face when I sigh, "I have always seen you, Vann. But up until today, I just didn't see you with me. And I'm sorry for that. I can't even tell you how sorry I am for that. I feel like an idiot for not realizing that we're good together before now. I feel like I've wasted so much time and—"

"Shh," he says, cutting me off. And then he pulls the elastic out of my braid and his fingertips begin unraveling my hair.

He does this in complete silence, looking me in the eyes. And it feels like a metaphor. It feels like he's unraveling me as well as my braid. And when he's done and my kinked-up pink hair is free, he arranges it so that it spills over my shoulders and contrasts against the black lace of my bra.

"Belinda," he finally says. "I would wait until the end of time for you to see me. I would walk a thousand miles if you needed me. And maybe you don't realize this yet, but this isn't our first date."

"No?" I ask.

"No. Our life together started eight years ago when you showed up at this very house looking to rent the apartment over the garage. I remember it—not like it was yesterday. Because for me, from the moment I first saw you, yesterday ceased to exist. From that second on, there was only the future of you and me. That's it. That's all that mattered. And I don't even care that it took eight years to get here." He shakes his head a little. "Why would I care? I spent the entire time with you sleeping thirty yards away every night. I spent the entire time walking you to and from work at least a couple times a week. I have spent countless days with you at my side. I don't give a single fuck that we weren't lovers through all that. That's not what I was after. That was never the goal. I'm not thinking about missed opportunities. I'm not sorry that it took this long. I'm happy with who we are and how we got here. And maybe I got a little frustrated with you yesterday, but I didn't lose faith in what I knew we had. That's why I inked this tat on my arm. It was a declaration to myself that I would not give up. That I would keep going. That I would give you as much time as you needed. That I would be there through anything. As long as you let me, I will be here."

I realize I've been holding my breath and I let it out in a soft huff of air.

I don't deserve him.

I don't deserve his love, or his loyalty, or his faith and dedication.

"Shh," he says again. "Stop it. Stop thinking about the past. There is no yesterday, remember? There is only now."

I lean into him and press my lips against his. But I don't kiss him and he doesn't kiss me, either.

We just stay like that for a moment.

And then, with no words at all, we become something else.

Something new.

I place my hands on his shoulders and gently urge him to lie back. He smirks at me as he gives in, his hands sliding up to fondle my breasts. I lean down and my hair drags across his chest as I scoot back and kiss my way down his stomach as my hands trail behind. I stop and look up at him when I get to his zipper.

His expression is something between heated lust and unbelievable luck.

"Why are you looking at me that way?"

He reaches for the long strands of pink hair hovering over his stomach, playing with them. "You know why," he says.

"Because you've been dreaming about this day for eight years"—he chuckles—"and now you're not sure if this is real, or the ultimate sexual fantasy?"

"Yeah, that's it." He says this through a smile.

"Well, let me clear it up for you, Vann Vaughn. This is real. This is going to be your ultimate sexual fantasy come true."

I sit up and swing one leg over the side, then pull his jeans and briefs down until his cock springs out. I take it in my palm, wrapping my hand around it, my eyes locked on his until he closes them and his whole body relaxes. I kiss the tip of his cock and chills explode on his body. I open my mouth, ease my head down over his cock, and seal my lips against his shaft.

He grips my hair and lifts his hips up slightly. I bob down, flattening my tongue against his shaft and pressing my lips tight as I lift back up.

"Jesus, Belinda," Vann moans.

I do it again. Then again. And again. Each time going a little bit faster, taking him a little bit deeper in my throat. All the while I keep my eyes locked on his face, just staring at his perfect manly beauty.

He opens them suddenly, but his lids are heavy with desire, his mouth pressed into a flat line of concentration as he watches me.

That turns me on. And I let one hand slip between my legs so I can play with myself.

"Ah, no," he whispers in a husky, throaty voice. "That won't do."

His leg comes up, hooking around my hip, and the next thing I know his cock has slipped out of my mouth and I'm on my back.

I squeal and begin scooting up the bed. He places his body over mine, grabbing my knees and spreading them wide open just as I hit the backboard. He grabs my thighs, pulls me towards him so I'm nearly flat again, and then he reaches for my hand and places my fingertips over my pussy.

"If you're gonna do that," he says, "I'm gonna watch properly."

I begin massaging my clit. And for a moment his eyes linger on mine. But only a moment. He glances down, watching as I play with myself. I feel a little blush of embarrassment. I have never done something like this with a man before. At least not with the lights on and not with a partner paying such close attention.

So. Yeah. It's a little weird. But I don't care. The tingle that started a few minutes ago is now a full-on throbbing.

And then his thumbs part the lips of my pussy and I suck in a breath of air filled with anticipation as he lowers his mouth and begins licking me, flicking the tip of his tongue around my fingers, but never directly coming into contact with my clit.

"Don't tease me," I beg.

"It's not a tease. It's a promise," he whispers, his lips so close to that sweetest of spots, his words just low enough to vibrate the sensitive skin of my folds.

And then he brushes my hand away and his mouth covers my pussy, his tongue frantically flicking and licking. My hips buck and my back arches from the sudden explosion of pleasure that pulses through my body.

I want to come. Like… immediately. But then again, I never want this to stop. I want to linger in the bliss of being just a moment or two away from a full climactic release.

And just when I decide that I can't take it anymore—I can't possibly hold off the explosion that's coming—he pulls back.

"Noooooo," I moan softly.

"Don't worry," he whispers back, now kissing the inside of my thighs. "You're gonna come tonight, Belinda. At least twice. But I want to do too many things to you to let that happen yet."

He slips one arm underneath me and repositions himself between my legs so his head is resting on my inner thigh. His breath tickles along my skin and then he slides his hand up to my breasts. He pulls my bra down, exposing my nipple to the air, making it hard and erect.

"Play with that," he says, then lightly flits his fingertips down my stomach until he gets to the curve of my mound. I open my legs a little wider and bite my lip with agonizing anticipation.

He fingers my clit and I gasp when he slowly pushes his fingers deep inside me. I hold my breath as he eases them in and out. My body begins to uncontrollably squirm and then I wriggle backwards, because I'm going to lose it if he keeps going.

Vann doesn't relent. He begins pumping me harder. Faster. Slicking up the inside of my pussy until I can feel the wetness spilling out and running down towards my asshole.

I try. I really try to hold it together. Because I want to make this moment last. I want to feel this way forever and hold it in my memory. But just as I think I might have all my primal urges under control, his mouth lowers down to my clit and his tongue swirls around and around as the pleasure inside me grows. Rising with each passing moment.

And then I'm there. At the cusp of something truly and spectacularly erotic.

"Now," he whispers, his words once again vibrating against my folds.

There is no fight left in me. I am weak with my desire and I want nothing more than to obey his soft command.

I come all over his fingers as he presses his whole mouth over my pussy and flicks his tongue against my clit.

My back arches off the mattress and my lips part as a long, low moan escapes.

I lose track of everything in this moment. Sparks flit through my head. The world tips sideways and then spins. Time stops, and my mind goes blank, and everything disappears except for this one moment of pure bliss.

I lie there spent in the wake of a perfect sexual storm, breathing heavy as my heart races inside my chest.

But Vann doesn't stop. He's easing his way up my body, kissing my breasts, nipping at my fully erect nipple, then my neck, then my ear, then my mouth.

I kiss him back with lust. I grab his hair, holding his face up to mine as he knees my legs open and the tip of his cock presses into the wet opening of my pussy.

I want to touch him all over as his thick, hard cock stretches me open. And even though I'm not one of those girls who comes more than once, I feel those primal urges inside me building all over again. Like that was just the first hill on the sexy rollercoaster we're on.

One hand grips his shoulder tight. My nails dig in to the armor tattoo that covers it in ink while the other hand slides down the tight muscles of his torso and then I grab his ass through his jeans, which are pulled down just enough to give him access.

I slip my hand inside his jeans and hold him tight, feeling the muscles beneath as he plunges deep inside me and then slowly withdraws, only to do it all again.

I grip him like I never want to let go. And he fucks me hard, thrusting deep, then deeper—until he's so far inside me we become one being. Until we are no longer two separate people, but a single entity.

"Fuck," he mutters.

"Yes," I moan back.

"No…" he says. "We forgot… we're not using… I have to pull out, Belinda."

"Shit."

He goes still for a moment. And while normally this would ease the building climax, it does the complete opposite for me. The sensation of his massive cock going still inside me just makes me want him more.

I reach for his face. Hold tight in my hands as I kiss his lips. And then I come a second time. Even more of my lust spilling out all over his cock.

"Oh, fuck," he says.

I enjoy my climax for two more moments. And then I push him back.

His eyes go wide with surprise. "What—"

But I keep pushing until he falls backwards, laughing as he repositions his legs. I plant my hands on either side of his hips and smirk down at him.

"Fuck that," I say. "I'm not letting you just pull out and come. Fuck that. I promised you the ultimate sexual-fantasy experience and that's what you're going to get."

I grab his cock with both hands. It's slick with my own come. And then I grin at him as I slide my mouth down over the tip of his dick.

And then I blow him like a fucking porn star.

I'm talking a two-fisted sliding hand job.

I'm talking I take him so deep, I gag myself.

I'm talking holding myself in that position and swallowing hard so he can feel the muscles of my throat.

And then I ease back, slowly releasing the seal of my lips on his shaft until his cock pops out, a string of saliva still connecting us. "Now it's your turn," I say.

He looks at me with wild, bewildered lust.

But then he wraps my hair around his fists and pushes me back down.

I take him deeper and this time, when I make a big deal about tightening my muscles around the tip of his cock, he comes right down my throat.

He holds me there until I'm desperate for air.

But I let him.

And then he releases me and pulls my head up, come spilling past my lips and dripping down onto his bare stomach.

He grabs my arms, urging me to crawl up his body. *But I'm already there, Vann. I'm already there.*

I kiss his stomach, and his chest, and his neck. And then I whisper right up next to his ear, "We are a love story in the making, Vann Vaughn. And I expect us to get that happy ending."

He wraps his arms around my back, holding me tight against his chest. "That's a promise I will keep, Belinda Baker."

I'm a realist. I had those fears about us getting together for a reason. I know he can't keep that promise. It's not empty, but it's not his to make.

But you know what?

I decide to believe him anyway.

## CHAPTER TWENTY-ONE

*I wake up* thoroughly confused, unsure of the day, let alone the time.

I glance around and find a clock. It reads nine oh four. Assuming that's AM, since there's a hazy sunshine filtering past all her beaded curtains, I take a moment to process that.

Because... I slept. Like a real fucking sleep.

After nearly three months of tossing and turning and getting just enough sleep to get through a day, I *finally* slept through the night.

Soshee is next to me. I can feel her body pressing against mine. All soft and warm, and if I'm being honest, comforting. And when I turn my head, I see her face half-hidden by her long, messy, scarlet hair.

I smile and reach for her, pulling her into my arms as I play back the last thing I remember before I passed out.

We had sex. Really good sex. And then... nothing. Did I fall asleep after sex?

Jesus Christ. That was the middle of the afternoon and now it's morning. I must've passed out for... damn. Like eighteen hours.

I should feel great. And I do feel *better*. But I would not call it great.

It's not Soshee, who didn't wake when I pulled her close to me, just hummed a little and snuggled into my embrace. Everything regarding her is fine. At least, it feels fine to me.

So this sense of not-greatness is not related to her. It's something else.

Maybe I'm nervous because I have to leave soon? I can't stay here forever. I need to go home and get back to my regularly scheduled life.

But that's not what I'm unsettled about, either.

I don't *have* to do anything. I'm the boss of me. I own my own business and I'm pretty sure Jesse Boston is having the time of his life running that business for me. He loves the ocean. And sailboats. I'm not paying him, but he doesn't need money anyway. He wants to fit in. He told me that. He likes the Dumas family. Loves us, actually. Handling my clients for me is exactly the kind of job he needs to fill his empty days while Emma's at work.

So I'm not worried about him and that means the idea of leaving Colorado isn't what's bothering me. Jesse might, eventually, start to miss my sister and want to go home. But Emma is in Europe on business again. What the fuck else is Jesse gonna do while she's making millions of Bright Berry Beach dollars?

I could totally stay here for a while. Soshee only has… what? A month left on this apartment lease? She has to go somewhere after that. And I'm thinking about talking her into taking that crappy car of hers on a road trip to Key West. We could check out shitty tourist attractions, and eat junk food, and break down every other day. She and I could start a brand-new life together.

I smile just picturing it. Then start wondering if I'm insane. I mean, I've only known this girl for two full days and I've already got her packed up and on a cross-country road trip with me so we can shack up together in my Dumas family cottage.

Then again... Alonzo is living with a girl he virtually dated for two years before he met her. So is this *really* any stranger than that?

Besides, we've already had four dates.

OK, OK, OK. Yes. We spent the first two dates with her lusting over Vann Vaughn and me trying to hate-fuck Belinda out of my life. But they were still pretty cool dates. We had lunch, and dinner, and wine. And we talked. A lot.

They count.

Plus I slept over. And I met her mother. So these two days are like six months in new-relationship years. We jumped in with both feet and didn't even check the temperature of the water first.

Isn't that how love is done? Don't you just... *fall* into it? Isn't that the whole point?

I'm pretty sure it is.

So if it's not the business and it's not Soshee, then what the hell is bothering me?

I stare up at the ceiling for a few minutes, trying to make sense of this vague feeling of uneasiness.

It's probably the whole FBI thing. I mean, that's kind of a big deal and my family is in it up to our ears. There's the witness protection program. And the little dog from the coffee shop next to Sick Boyz has to mean something.

All that stuff is important. Maybe even very important.

But that's not it either. It *should* be it. All three of the things I listed as possibilities *should* be my major problem.

But they just *aren't*.

I push the covers off me and swing my legs out of bed. Soshee moans and turns over, flashing me her perfect breasts in the process.

"Are you awake?" I ask.

She groans and makes a face. Then cracks open one eye. "Holy shit, he's alive."

"I slept forever, huh?"

"You just flat passed out." She props herself up on one elbow and smiles at me. It takes all my self-control not to look at her tits when she does that. And when I succeed, I feel pretty proud of myself. Because damn, they are spectacular. "I was checking your breathing with a mirror," she continues. "I guess you were exhausted. Did I wear you out?"

"No." I chuckle. "I hadn't been sleeping very well over the past few months."

"Months? Jesus. You must really have something on your mind if it's lasted months. I've gone through a few bouts of insomnia." She winces. "But if I'm being honest, they were mostly all about Vann."

"Stayed up late stalking him?"

"That and... you know. It feels kinda shitty when you have a crush on someone and they don't feel the same way back."

"Yeah. I agree."

"Because you felt that way about Belinda?" She frowns. "Rosalie?"

"Rosalinda." I chuckle.

Soshee points at me. "Yeah. Her."

"No." I sigh. "I never did feel that way about her. I mean…" I don't know how to explain this. "Of course, there were lingering feelings. But they were not of the love-sick variety."

"What variety were they?"

"You know." I shrug. "Break-up hate. Or… something."

"Break-up hate."

"Yeah." I sigh again. "I can't explain it."

"No, I get it. You were stuck."

"Yeah. Stuck."

"So how did you get unstuck?"

"Do you want me to be honest?"

She sits up in bed. "Of course."

"Well, I'm not sure I am unstuck."

"Hmm," she hums.

"Are you sure you want to talk about this? It's over. Very over."

"Doesn't seem over. You just said you might not be unstuck."

"I did say that. But that's not what I meant."

"You fucked her behind Sick Boyz two days ago, Tony."

"Yes."

"And before you point out that I fucked Vann inside Sick Boyz two days ago as well, I get it. But I've sorted through my feelings for Vann. I just want to make sure you have sorted through your feelings for Belinda too."

"You sorted through them?"

"Yep. I'm totally over it. I really hope he and Belinda are soulmates. I hope they get married. Hell, I hope I get an invite to the wedding. I wish nothing but the best for them."

"And you feel that way because…"

"I have you. And having you feels nothing like not having him."

I smile and nod my head a little.

"Is that how you feel about Belinda?"

I turn my whole body to face her. Because I need her to hear me. I need to make this very clear. "I have never loved Rosalinda. I didn't love her as Rosalie and I didn't love her as Belinda. She was a cute girl I met when I was very young and we… fucked around for a few years. That's it. That's all it was. It's just… I don't know. I know you're probably getting frustrated with me, but I'm just having a very hard time figuring out what I'm doing here. Not here with you. Because I like you. I'm very sure of that. So sure, I'm picturing myself passing serious milestones with you, Soshee Ameci. But I feel like I have left something *unfinished*. When Rosalinda showed up with Alonzo's girlfriend a few months ago… I don't know what happened to me. I just… had *feelings*, but not the kind of feelings you think. It wasn't that I wanted her back. I just… didn't want her *there*. Ya know? At my fucking house. I was angry when she showed back up. She had no right to do that and I was just so fucking pissed."

"Is that when you stopped sleeping?"

I nod. "Yeah. That's when it started."

"Hmm." Soshee sits up in bed, hiking the sheet up over her breasts to cover them. "Well… I hate to break this to you, Tony, but you're right. You have unfinished business with that girl. I'm not sure if it's with Rosalie, or with Belinda, or with Rosalinda.

Choose a name and personality, I guess. But there are relationship leftovers that need to be thrown out."

"I know," I whisper. "I feel like… she and I should maybe… have a talk?"

"Couldn't hurt."

"But I don't know what to say to her. Do I say, 'Look, I'm sorry I never loved you?'"

"Did *she* love *you*?"

I shrug. "I don't know. I don't think so."

"Hmm."

"I'm telling you, it was nothing but anger and hate. Fighting and crying."

"And the sex?"

"The sex. OK, you want to hear something really fucked up?" I can't believe I'm actually gonna go here.

"Might as well," Soshee says. "We're in this together now."

I smile at that. "We are, Sosh."

"OK. Tell me the fucked-up part."

"She cried every time we had sex."

Soshee frowns. "What do you mean she cried? While you guys were doing it?"

"No. Afterward. Every time, after we were done, she cried. And I…" I sigh.

"Keep going."

"I liked it."

"You like her tears? Or you liked her unhappiness?"

I think about this for a moment. Because I hadn't realized there was a difference. "Tears, I guess. I don't want her to be unhappy. I mean, wishing unhappiness on her feels like… I don't know. An investment. Trust me. I'm not that invested."

"OK," Soshee says. "You have a weird fetish."

"No!"

"Come on, Tony. You can admit it. I'm not going to judge you."

"It's not a fetish. I never craved the tears of other girls. It was just something she did and I…"

"Got off on it?"

I sigh.

"Forget the tears. I don't think they mean anything."

"Explain."

She shrugs. "I don't think they matter. I think you're focused on them because it was weird. You liked it and you enjoyed it. But then when she was gone, you didn't pursue it. So it was a temporary thing and you left it behind you."

"Yeah, until she showed back up and that was all I thought about. I started to become obsessed with those fucking tears. I literally came here to fuck her and make her cry so I could stop thinking about her forever."

"OK. I think we're getting somewhere."

"We are?"

"Yeah, I mean, I have some experience with being in Belinda's shoes. I was totally invested in Vann and, as we all know, he didn't feel the same way."

"I don't think it's the same. Have you ever punched Vann in the mouth because you were so angry at him?"

"No," she says through a chuckle. "No. I like him. It's not hate. But it's not love either. I know that because if it were love I wouldn't be so infatuated with you right now."

I grin. I can't help it. "You're infatuated with me?"

"Totally. Ever since I sat down at your table in the restaurant and forced you to have lunch with me, Vann started to fade away."

"We stalked him that night. You fucked the next day."

"I know." She says this simply and shrugs it off. Like it's no big deal.

And, honestly, it feels very much like no big deal to me too. I don't even care that she did that. Because I get it. I know *why* she did it. It was a goodbye fuck. It doesn't even matter that she didn't understand it in the moment. We understand it now and that's all that counts.

"But back to Belinda," Soshee says. "I think you're looking for closure."

"To what? What we had was so… just… gross. It was gross. It was hate, and anger, and rage. Nothing about it was good. Trust me, I didn't think about her for years after she left Key West. I didn't spare one fucking moment of thought for her."

"Until she showed back up again."

"Yeah."

"And then what did you think?"

"What do you mean?"

"What did you feel when you saw her?"

"Anger. All over again. So much anger. Rage. I couldn't…"

"Sleep?"

"Yeah."

"And now you can."

"Well, I'm not sure one night makes a pattern, but I sure the fuck hope so."

She throws the sheet off her and crawls across the bed to sit next to me. Her arm slips around my waist and her fingertips begin rubbing small circles against my stomach. "Tony?"

"Hmm?" I say, enjoying the way her touch makes me feel.

"You were not good to her."

"I know that."

"And now you're sorry."

I think about that for a moment. "I'm sorry for what, though? Because I don't feel sorry, Soshee."

She laughs. "Damn, dude. That's harsh."

"I know! Trust me, I get it. I'm a total asshole. But I don't feel bad about the past. I just... *don't*. Like I said, that feels like an investment. And I'm just... *not* invested in her. And now you probably think I'm lying and I've got some hidden feelings. And I hate that." I turn to look at her. "I really hate that," I whisper. "Because you, Soshee Ameci? You... you... *you*."

"Me, me, me." She giggles. "I'm gonna take that as a compliment."

"Good. Because it was."

"So here's my professional ex-stalker assessment."

"Hit me. I'm ready."

"You're in a good place now."

"I am?"

"Mmm-hmm. I think you're ready to move on."

"I totally am."

"So... let her go."

"Just like that? Just... let her go? I mean, if it were that easy, wouldn't I have done that already?"

She nods. "Yep." And then she stands up and walks across the room to the bathroom. She stops just as she reaches for the door and looks at me over her shoulder. "It's a choice, Tony. Let it go and move on. Or fix it. Those are your options. But can I just say that you've already tried letting it go and moving on? And it didn't work."

"I know. I need to fix it. But *how* do I fix it?"

She shakes her head. "Well, you tried the goodbye fuck and it didn't work. So there's something else there. Some leftover feelings you need to deal with. I know you don't want to think about your past with her, but that's where the answer is. So you should probably do that."

She turns back to the bathroom, opens the door, and then looks back at me again. "I'm OK with it. I can wait. We're just getting started, Tony. So whatever it is you need to do, leave me out of it, OK? It's not about me. Now, I'm going to take a shower. And I think you should table all this angst for another time and come join me."

"Angst," I huff.

"Your choice." She smiles and disappears into the bathroom.

I sit there for a few moments, wondering how this girl went from being irrationally obsessed with a man she couldn't have to a wise woman who completely understands herself, and me, in the span of two days.

I don't know. I have no clue how she's so at ease with her place in the world, but I want some of that.

So I put Rosalinda behind me and join her.

## CHAPTER TWENTY-TWO

*The first thing I see* when I open my eyes in the morning are words.

Everywhere. Words. On the ceiling. On the walls. On the headboard when I turn to look around. Even on the windows. I don't think I ever looked up to the third-floor windows, or I might've noticed the words slashing their way across the panes. The paint or whatever Vann used to write them is faded to a dull gray. Parts of letters are missing in some places, but I can still make out the entire sentence. Part of the Pledge of Allegiance. The 'with liberty' part.

Vann is already in the shower. He left the door open to his en suite like an invitation.

I want to join him, but I can't get over this room.

I noticed the walls were covered in words after we were done having sex and Vann got up to fish an old Sick Boyz t-shirt out of a drawer so I could wear it to sleep in. I look down at the shirt now. He has worn this shirt hundreds of times since I met him and I feel lucky, maybe. That he lent it to me.

And it smells delicious. Like motorcycles and tattoo ink. Like punk music and monster trucks. It smells like Vann Vaughn.

I sigh, feeling happy and content for the first time in a very long while. Very satisfied with how this is playing out even though two days ago I was telling him we were not a thing. We would never be a thing. And now look... we're on the verge of becoming a thing.

Anyway.

There must be thousands of words scrawled across the walls, some of it in what I recognize as Vann's typical handwriting. But a good portion is done up in calligraphy. Old-fashioned letters and bold letters. Serif and sans. Every kind of lettering you can think of.

I sit up to get a better look. Because it feels so... familiar for some reason.

Then I get it.

Graffiti. I wasn't into tagging random walls back when I was a teenager in Key West. But I did my share of illegal murals. And, of course, the sanctioned one I was paid to do. Which was painted over some time during the eight years after my departure.

When Vann and Tara and I first got to Key West a few months ago we went to my mom's motel first. It was a hostel and she was gone. I didn't know it then, but the Dumas family had her relocated for her own safety. They bought the motel and used it to house the refugees they saved and they sent her up the coast to start a new life.

I was pissed off about that but they did right by my mom. I can't see her yet because it's still too dangerous. The FBI thinks she's dead or something. Out of the picture, at least. And that's how it needs to stay until we find some kind of final solution to this problem we're all wrapped up in. So I get why my mom was relocated. Hell, I even understand why I was relocated.

But that doesn't mean I'm happy about it.

"Hey!" Vann comes out of the bathroom wearing nothing but a towel. "Why didn't you join me? I was waiting for ya."

"You should've woken me up," I say, smiling as I allow my eyes the luxury of wandering up and down his body.

"I wanted you to sleep in. You look so peaceful and sweet when you're asleep."

"As opposed to when I'm awake and look... what? Crazy and angry?"

He walks over to the bed and sits down next to me, the familiar scent of his soap and shampoo a strong reminder that I know this man. I know him very well. And while this shouldn't be a revelation—eight years is no joke—it kinda is.

I never noticed that his scent was familiar until just now. And I recognized his handwriting on the walls too. Even though I've never been up here in his room before, it's all familiar. And that's comforting for some reason.

He leans in and kisses me. His mouth tastes minty and fresh. "I have never thought of you as crazy and angry." He pauses, pulling back a little. "Well, maybe a little crazy. But it's the good kind."

"I do my best." I grin.

"Yeah, so. No appointments today. Got the whole day off."

"Vinn has one. I saw it on the books." Sundays are appointment only at Sick Boyz. And the boys do their best to not make any appointments. But even if there's just one, I have to be there to run the front desk.

"I already told him he's got to work alone today."

I raise my eyebrows. "What did he say?"

"What the fuck could he say? You're mine now and if I say you get a day off, you get a day off."

"Thanks," I say. "I didn't want to go in."

"Good." He unleashes one of his most charming Vann Vaughn smiles on me.

"Why? Do we have plans today?"

He shrugs. "Coffee?"

"That goes without saying." I laugh. "Anything else?"

"Well." He looks around his room. "I was thinking I'd empty a drawer for you."

"What?"

"So you can put some cute skirts and knee socks in there."

"I literally live a hundred feet away."

"Yeah but…" He grins again. "I was thinking… I might handcuff you to the headboard and not let you go back there."

"Oh, really?"

"Makes sense to me. And I've already told my dad that you're not paying rent anymore."

"What? When? How the hell? We've been awake for like ten minutes. When did all these convos take place?"

"You've been awake for ten minutes. I've already eaten breakfast, helped my grandpa pick an outfit for his big date this afternoon with Widow Carlisle, and had the two aforementioned convos with the old man and Vinn."

"What freaking time is it?"

"Nineish."

"What time did you wake up?"

"Mm. Five?"

"Jesus Christ, Vann. What's wrong with you? Was it me? Did I hog the bed? Steal your covers?"

"No. I always get up early."

"Why?"

He laughs. "Because… because…" He looks down. And is that a blush?

"Because why?"

"I spy on you. Not look through your windows or anything. Just… you know. I want to be there when you come down."

"Hmm. That's why you were on the porch yesterday?"

"Yup."

"But you're not always on the porch waiting for me."

"No. Most of the time I work on my bike or fuck around in the garage until I hear you leave your apartment. Then I go inside and watch you from the family room window."

I almost snort. "But… *why*?"

He shrugs. "I worry about you. You've always been this girl with lots of secrets. And in the early days I always had the feeling that those secrets were trying to eat you away from the inside out. So I liked seeing you in the mornings. It made me feel better." He pauses and waits for my reaction. "Does it creep you out?"

I picture a seventeen-year-old Vann paying such close attention to me. Worrying about me. Caring about me. "No," I finally say. "No. It actually… well. It's kinda touching. To know that you were so invested. Because, honestly, after my mom and I were separated, I just accepted the fact that no one was invested in me anymore. My one true champion was gone. And I wish I had known this, Vann. I wish I had paid attention to all the ways you loved me."

He smiles. And it's a broad, full smile. "That's not why I did it." He shakes his head but the smile is still big and wide. "It didn't matter if you knew. It only mattered that I was there. Just in case, ya know? That's all. I just wanted to be there. In case you ever needed me."

Suddenly I can't breathe. It's like my lungs forgot how. And then... then... my eyes are filling up with tears.

"Oh, shit," Vann says. "Are you gonna cry?"

"No," I say, hastily wiping my eyes. "No. I do *not* cry." I sniffle. And wipe my eyes again.

"Then... what are you doing?"

"Just..." I remember how to breathe and take a deep breath and place a hand over my heart. "That's the sweetest, nicest thing anyone has ever said to me. Done for me!"

He chuckles. "Please. It was nothing. The Dumas family saved your life, got you a new identity, and sent your mom to a sweet beach town to start over with a paid-off bed-and-breakfast. I have to admit, I felt a little inadequate when I found all that out."

"What the hell are you talking about?"

"Tony and Alonzo. They set you up. That's not an example of not caring, Belinda."

I shake my head. "That's not why they did it! They did it to save their own asses and banished me to Colorado!"

"Banished you?" He makes a face. "Come on. You love it here."

"I do. But that's not the point."

"Why isn't it the point?"

"Because they didn't ask if I wanted to leave! They made me!"

"Yeah, but it worked out, right? Is that why you're so closed off?"

"What? How did this get turned around on me? I'm not closed off! I'm… perky! And peppy! I'm cute and adorable!"

"You are," he says, pointing his finger at me. "All of that. Yes. But Belinda, it took you eight years to give in to me. And I'm not saying that you should've taken less time. I was playing a long game. And I wasn't jealous when you dated all kinds of other random men. Anyone but me. Practically *everyone* but me."

"Hey!"

"I'm just saying, I didn't care. I was waiting for my moment. And it paid off. So what I'm telling you right now isn't about the wait. OK?"

"What are you telling me right now? Because I don't get it."

"I'm telling you that you were incredibly unhappy for all those eight years. And you only got happy when you went home. And Tara and I had this moment back in Key West. After Johnny Boston showed up to spell shit out for us. She said you weren't going to come back here. That Key West was your home. And I told her that was bullshit. This place, Belinda—this town— this is your home now. And I was right. Because you came back here, even though Tara stayed down in Key West. You made a deliberate, conscious choice to return."

"And you think I chose that because of you?"

He shrugs. "Maybe? I don't know about that. I think you chose to come back because you belong here now. That's all. This is home now. It's as simple as that. And I think that Tony showing up made you so angry because he was a reminder of that old life. And those old times. And that old stuff. And look, I'm not claiming to be an expert in starting over. You have definitely cornered the market on that shit. My grandpa won this house in a poker game a million years ago, back when you could look at his tattoos without wincing at the wrinkles. I've lived in this house, in this town my whole life. I will work in the Sick Boyz tattoo shop until I'm as old as my grandpa. I will die inking words on skin. So I'm no expert, Belinda. But I know it has to have been hard."

"So what?"

"So what? So… that's your hangup."

"What is my hangup?"

"Tony."

"Fuck Tony."

"I agree. Fuck that fucker. I don't care about Tony. But you do."

"Oh, my God. I do *not*!"

"Not like *that*, Belinda. I'm not worried you're into him. You just have unfinished business with the guy."

"What business?"

He shrugs. "I dunno." Then he taps my head. "That's all in there. Locked up tight so you don't have to think about it anymore. But he's gonna go home soon. I don't know why he's here, but whatever that reason was, it's over now. So he's gonna leave. And I just think… you know, before he takes off you should settle shit."

"Settle what, though? I don't know what unfinished business we have. I just want him to go away."

His eyes gaze into mine. They are bright blue today. Like a perfect summer sky. "Me too, toots. Me too." Then he slaps my leg. "Jump in the shower. Put on a pair of my shorts and grab a new t-shirt. Then meet me downstairs. We need coffee."

He gets up, drops his towel so I have a perfect view of his ass, then reaches into a drawer, finds a pair of old jeans, and pulls them up his legs. Then he slides a t-shirt over his head, grabs a pair of socks and his boots from the floor, and leaves me there without saying another word.

I sit in his bed for a few moments, thinking about what he said, trying to force it all to make sense. But all I get for my trouble is an emerging tension headache.

It's not my fault Tony is here. He should just leave. Then everything would go back to normal again.

Better than normal, actually. Because then I wouldn't have this constant reminder that I'm someone other than Belinda Baker.

What did he call me? *Rosalinda*?

Asshole. God, he is such an asshole. Rosalinda. That makes me so angry, the emerging headache becomes a throbbing one.

I turn to the bathroom and go in, then spend many minutes letting the hot water pound against the back of my neck, trying to make the headache go away.

By the time I'm dressed and heading down the stairs, it's mostly gone and I've decided to put the past behind me. Vann's probably right. I'm sure there are lingering feelings that could use some airing out. But Tony has to go home eventually. I'm certain all this angst will disappear when he does.

I'm heading around the bannister of the second floor when I notice the long line of old photographs on the hallway wall. The Vaughn family. And... wow. There are women in these pics. Women who are not the sister, Veronica.

One catches my eye immediately. A very old picture of a man, who I recognize to be Grandpa, and a woman standing in front of the mansion. This mansion. And holy crap, it was a looker back in the day. A beautiful home.

The next one has Gram and Gramps and two little boys all sitting on the front porch. I recognize the younger boy as Vern, Vann's father. But the older one, no clue.

There's more on the porch. In fact, when I look closely, I realize they've taken a family portrait on the front porch of this house every year since nineteen sixty-nine.

Fifty. Fucking. Years.

Those early ones with Gram and Gramps. Then Vern and his unnamed brother. Then Vern all grown up with a wife and a boy who has to be Vic in her arms. Then Vic and the twins. A pigtailed Veronica shows up. And finally Vann. Cherub-faced Vann. But they don't end there. No. All the kids grow up in front of my eyes. And then there's Veronica's husband, Spencer. And their baby. Then two. Then three.

Wow.

This family has lived in this house for fifty years. There are four generations of Vaughns on this wall and every single one of them has lived in this house.

I don't even know what that would feel like. To grow up in the same place. Raise a family, and watch them grow up here too.

I could've had that if I had stayed in Key West.

No. That's not right. I could've had that if I hadn't been kicked out by forces beyond my control.

"Belinda!" Vann yells up the stairs. "Come on, I need coffee."

"I'm coming," I say.

He walks up the steps when he realizes I'm right above him. "What are you doing?"

"Looking at your family photos."

He grins. "We're a good-looking bunch."

I nod. Smile.

Because they really are. A very good-looking bunch.

And I'm about to become one of them.

## CHAPTER TWENTY-THREE

*I touch her all over* in the shower. I lather up with soap that smells like the color pink looks and touch her all over. We wash each other's hair and we smile while the other takes their turn rinsing under the water. It's a calm beginning. An experience that might normally lead to sex. But we both know this shower isn't about sex.

There are big things to decide and they will need to be decided soon.

But not now. Not today. Today we wash each other, then dry each other, then get dressed. She brought my suitcase down before she went to bed last night.

I find that both bold and adorable.

I'll say this about Soshee Ameci—she is a girl who goes after what she wants.

And then, once we're dressed, we leave her apartment and walk with casual ease down the four flights of stairs to the Fort Collins Theater coffee shop.

"So what do you want to do about the little dog?" she asks.

"Shit. I forgot all about that. I don't know. Do you think I'm just overreacting and there's nothing going on?"

Sosh shoots me a sideways glance. "Do *you* think there's nothing going on?"

I draw in a deep breath. "No clue, actually."

"Really?"

"I mean I get it. I'm all wrapped up in something weird. But maybe I'm making a big deal out of nothing? Maybe they just have a coffee shop dog? Couldn't it be something simple like that?"

"A dog that they walk at four-thirty in the morning?"

"Don't coffee shops open early?"

"Conveniently past Vann's house?"

"It's only a few blocks off College Avenue."

"OK, stop." She stops on the landing between the first and second floor. "Are you really trying to talk yourself into the idea that everything's fine?"

"I'm not saying that. I'm just saying I dunno, Soshee. I don't want to jump to any conclusions."

"Conclusions? Ha! That's a good one."

"What's that mean?"

She puts her hands on her hips. "Seriously, Tony? You don't draw any conclusions. You just… drift." She puts up both hands. "Let me explain this in terms you can understand, m'kay? You're like a sailboat without sails. Just drifting in this big, wide-open sea of… of everything!"

"Sea of everything?"

"Yeah. You come here under the pretense of looking for information for your brother about…whatever the hell. Your secrets, or smuggling, whatever. Doesn't matter. You know why it doesn't matter?" She doesn't wait for me to come up with an answer. Just keeps talking. "Because that's not why you came here. You came here for Belinda."

"Soshee. I already told you. I don't—"

"Have feelings for her. I know. I heard you. But I don't believe you. It's a lie, Tony. You are so very clearly having feelings about her even I can see that."

I just blink my eyes at her for a moment. "Are we... having a fight about Rosalinda?"

She makes a face at me. "Do you really need me to tell you that?"

"Is that a yes?"

"You are having such a man moment right now, I can't even believe it." She rolls her eyes and starts walking down the stairs again.

"Wait," I call, hopping down the stairs after her. "I don't know what you want me to say. Just tell me what you're looking for and I'll answer as truthfully as I can."

She throws the door open to the bustling coffee shop and then turns to face me before she enters. "I'm not looking for anything, Tony. It's you. You're the one looking for something. I'm not sure what that is exactly. But I'm fairly certain it has something to do with forgiveness."

"Forgiveness?" I actually laugh. "From *who*?"

"From Belinda Baker, you thick idiot!"

And then the entire coffee shop—which was loud with the hum of several dozen simultaneous conversations just one second earlier—goes almost quiet. And who do I see at the cream and sugar station less ten feet away from where Soshee and I are standing?

That's right. Vann and Belinda.

"Well, that's perfect," Soshee coos at them. "Just the people we were looking for."

"Um…" Belinda says, looking at Vann for help.

"Can we help you two with something?" Vann asks.

"No," I say.

But Soshee says, "Yes, Vann. You can. You see, Tony here has traveled a long way to say something to Belinda there. Haven't you, Tony?"

"Uh… what?"

"Oh, for fuck's sake," Belinda says. "Just go away, Tony. Come on, Vann. Let's go."

She grabs his arm and starts to walk away, assuming he will follow. But Vann Vaughn does not move one inch and she kinda bounces back into place. "Hold up there, toots."

"I'm sorry," I say, cocking my head. "Did you just call her *toots?*"

"Shut up, Tony. You don't get to have an opinion about me and my life. You lost that privilege a long time ago."

"As if I even want to have an opinion—"

A shrill whistle cuts through my remaining words and once again, the entire coffee shop goes quiet and everyone looks at Soshee.

"Hey, kids," the dark-haired woman who runs the counter calls across the room. "How about you take this convo somewhere else? Hmm? We're all having a nice Sunday morning here."

"Great idea," Soshee calls back. "Let's go." She snaps her fingers at Vann, Belinda, and me in quick succession, then points to the stairs we just came down. "Upstairs. All of you. We have a messy situation here that needs to be settled. So. We're going to go up to my apartment and settle it."

Belinda plants her hands on her hips and taps the toe of her shoe on the tiled floor. "I'm not going up there."

But Vann says, "You know what, Soshee? You're right. This has gotten messy. Let's go, Belinda."

"To her apartment?" Belinda is incredulous. "No!"

But Soshee is smooth and, if I'm being honest, wearing her semi-evil Poison Ivy smile. She hooks her arm into Belinda's and beams down at her like they are the best of best friends. "You've never seen it, have you? Some people think it's over the top, but I think you'd enjoy it."

And then she's pulling her up the stairs.

"Vann!" Belinda is protesting.

I look at him. Waiting to see what he'll do. But he just waves a hand at the stairwell and says, "Let's do this."

Belinda is still protesting, but she and Sosh are already out of view somewhere above us.

"Fine," I say. "You want to do this? I'll do this. All day long, *Vann*."

"Great, *Tony*," he says, pushing past me. "Let's go."

***The girls are already inside*** Soshee's apartment by the time I follow Vann up to the fourth floor. Soshee is still talking. I catch snippets of her one-sided conversation about the décor and the view. Belinda is looking back at Vann for some kind of relief. But he must be on board with this intervention, because he doesn't rescue her. Instead he walks over to the long line of windows and leans against the window sill.

"Nice view, Sosh," he says, scanning the street below.

I hate that he calls her Sosh.

I'm not jealous. I just hate it.

"OK, I'm here," Belinda says, yanking her arm from Soshee's grip. "Talk."

She's looking at me when she says this. I look at Soshee. It was her idea, not mine. "I don't have anything to say."

"Yes, you do," Soshee says.

"Yeah. Let's get this over with, Belinda," Vann agrees.

Belinda huffs. "What the hell, Vann? Why are you pushing this?"

"Because you two have unfinished business," Vann and Soshee say at the same time. They kinda startle at the unison of their words, then glance at each other before quickly looking away.

"I don't have any unfinished business. Tony and I were never even a *thing*," Belinda snaps. "We used each other. That's it."

"I'm not going to argue with that," I say with a shrug. "It's mostly true, anyway."

"Fuck you, Tony," Belinda spits. "You're the one who showed up here trying to hate-fuck me out of your head. Do you have any idea how pathological that is?"

"Look who's talking, *Rosalinda*. You're the one who—" But before I can get the last few words out, she has crossed the room and slapped my face.

Vann quickly darts into action, crossing the room and grabbing her by the arm before she can hit me again. He barely stops her fist from crashing into my teeth. "Hold up, toots. One good slap is enough to make your point."

Belinda points her finger right up to my face and snarls, "Do not. Ever. Fucking. Call me that name again."

I laugh. She swings. Vann intercepts and pulls her back a good six feet.

"I don't know why you're so upset," I say. "That name is an accurate description of who you actually are."

"And why is that, Tony? Why do I have two names? Hmm." She pokes a fingertip into her cheek and pretends to think. "Is it because you decided to fuck up my life eight years ago? You decided that my life was over!"

"What the hell are you talking about? I saved you!"

"Oh," she guffaws. "Oh, that's a good one. You think that ripping me away from everyone and everything I know and then sending me two thousand miles away was *saving me*? Do you have any idea what it was like to get off that plane and be dropped off at the local laundromat?"

"What?"

"The laundromat, Tony! That was the job those fucked-up FBI people gave me. They made me the manager of the laundromat!"

"That's not a bad job," Soshee says. She looks at me and shrugs. "I'd be down with running a laundromat."

"I am an artist, Soshee. Or at least I was until your new boyfriend here ripped my life in two."

"Jesus Christ," I say. "You're being dramatic, Ros—"

"Do not. Fucking call me. That name."

"Calm down. I was going to say *Rosalie*."

Her whole face goes bright red. Like she might explode before my eyes. And I seriously have a little moment of worry that she's going to have a stroke.

But she doesn't have a stroke and she doesn't explode.

She begins to cry.

## CHAPTER TWENTY-FOUR

# BELINDA

*First, my face goes* burning hot. Then my whole body begins to tremble. And then the tears are there, welling up inside my eyes in great pools. The next thing I know they are falling down my cheeks.

I'm not making any sound. This is how it is with the rage tears. They are silent.

"Fuck," Tony says. "Look, I'm not here to ruin your day and make you cry. I'm here—"

"Oh, no," I say, putting up a hand. Then I point to my eyes. "Do you think"—I laugh—"do you think these are for you? These tears are not for you!"

Tony's chin juts back in surprise. "Of course they're for me. You do it every time."

"Every... what? What are you talking about?"

"When we fuck. After we fuck, I mean. You always cry. Because I'm such a disappointment, I guess."

I laugh and direct my gaze over to Vann. "Can you believe this shit?"

He looks slightly bewildered and unsure of what's happening. It's a cute look on him. But I'm in the middle of something. And not even the charming, handsome, perfectly-shaped jawline of Vann Vaughn is going to distract me right now.

Because I've been waiting for this moment. This, right here, right now, is exactly what needs to happen.

Tony Dumas needs to be set straight.

I point at him and take a step forward. Vann steps in, probably thinking I'm going to punch Tony in the teeth again, but no. I'm under control now. Because this asshole ex of mine thinks my tears were about *him*.

"You would think that," I say. "You would think those tears were about you because you're a self-centered jerk. You think the whole world revolves around you. I did cry after we had sex. Every single time. But I just want to make this very clear. I wasn't crying *over you*, Tony. I was crying for *me*. I was disgusted with myself for having sex with a man who threw me away like trash."

"I didn't throw you away!"

"Is that the only part you heard?" I laugh. "Why am I surprised? I shouldn't be. You never loved me, Tony. And you didn't come here to hate-fuck me out of your head. The fact that you tried to pull that bullshit on me—*again*—just proves what an asshole you are."

"What are you talking about?" He bellows. "I certainly didn't come here to... *woo* you!"

"Woo me?" I guffaw. I'm talking full-on throw-my-head-back guffaw straight up at the ceiling. "Shut the fuck up, Tony Dumas." Then I look at Soshee. Her eyes go wide, like she's not sure she wants my full attention. "Look, Soshee, we probably got off on the wrong foot because you were in like with Vann and he was in love with me this whole time." Vann grins pretty big at that. "And I get it. I totally understand what it feels like to be in like with someone who doesn't feel the same way back." I glance at Tony as exhibit A. "And Vann Vaughn is a fucking catch and a half, OK? He is. This man?" I point to Vann. "He's the real deal. He's everything you want in a boyfriend. He's considerate, he's honest, he's thoughtful, and yeah, he's hot as fuck. But he's more than that. Vann is patient and even though he comes from a family of tatted-up bikers who won their now falling-down mansion in a poker game fifty years ago, they stick together. They have each other's back. Do you know there's a whole wall on the second floor of their house that chronicles fifty years of family?"

I point at Tony. "This one? No. Nuh-uh. Run, Soshee. Run away from this one as fast as you can. Because he's an illusion. He's not patient. He's not considerate. He's not honest and even though he's nice to look at, there's a whole lot of ugly hiding underneath."

"You don't even know me," Tony objects. "You've been gone for eight years. I come from a good family. We definitely have each other's backs! So fuck you—"

"No. Fuck *you*, Tony. You ripped my life apart. You stole my memories. Hell, you stole my identity. And you come here, calling me Rosalinda? Fuck. You. I haven't been Rosalie for a long time now. I *am* Belinda. And you can accept that or not, it doesn't matter anymore. I'm not confused about who I am, you are. You call me Rosalinda like this is some great big joke. Some funny ha-ha shit that makes a good story that you and your brother can laugh about. And you know what the really fucked-up part is? I believed your lie. For almost a year after I got here, I believed that I was in the wrong place at the wrong time when

I saw your little smuggling job go down and lost my life as I knew it. But not anymore." I shake my head. "It wasn't bad luck. I wasn't in the wrong place at the wrong time. Because I'm right where I'm supposed to be. Here. In Fort Collins, Colorado. With Vann Vaughn. And you… you're the lost one here, Tony. You're the one out of place. You're the one who has no idea who he is, not me."

No one says anything for almost a full minute. We just stare at each other as the echo of my words becomes real and the truth of what I just said sinks in.

I let out a long, tired breath. But you know what? There are no more angry tears running down my cheeks. Because I feel just fine.

Tony Dumas will never ever steal my tears the way he stole my life.

Never again.

Vann looks at me and nods. "I think we're done here."

And then he takes me by the hand and leads me to the door.

## CHAPTER TWENTY-FIVE

*I just stand there* in the ensuing silence after her final words. I know Soshee is looking at me. I want to believe that she understands that there are two sides to every story and that she will not let Belinda's outburst cloud what we just started building together.

But one look at her… that's all it takes to see the disappointment.

"Soshee," I say. Belinda and Vann are nearly through the apartment door.

But Belinda turns back. "Are you fucking serious right now? You're going to plead your case to Soshee?" Belinda huffs. "Why am I not surprised?"

"What are you talking—" But I stop. I stop because it feels like I've been using this same, lame excuse on repeat since Belinda reappeared. And there has to be a reason for that, doesn't there?

Belinda is looking at me like I just strangled a puppy. Like I am filth on the bottom of her shoe. Like I am a *truly* horrible person.

And when I look at Soshee, I can tell she's falling for it.

It's probably not even what Belinda just said to me, either. It's probably just… *true.*

Belinda certainly thinks it to be true. She hates me. That's hate in her eyes.

I wasn't saving her, I realize. That's not why I had her sent away.

I was saving me. Not even from the FBI or anything so dramatic like what we have going on right now.

I was saving me from… her.

I wanted Rosalie gone. She was a pest. An inconvenience. A reminder of that weird tear fetish thing—that, turns out, wasn't about me to begin with.

I feel sick over that misunderstanding. Like maybe I am a truly horrible person.

I made Rosalie disappear.

Literally.

She's right. I stole her life. And then when… oh, shit. Madam Ameci's words come back to me. I hear them in my head like she's standing right in front of me. *It's not what has been said, Mr. Dumas. It's what hasn't been said.*

And suddenly the past three months of sleepless nights makes sense.

I know why I'm here and I know what I'm doing.

I turn back to Belinda and hold up a finger. "Give me one minute."

"What?" she sneers.

"I'm not done. But before I get to you, I need to say something to her."

"Oh!" She looks up at Vann. "Fuck him. Let's go."

But Vann, surprisingly, shakes his head no. "Give him his minute, toots."

I turn away from Belinda's incredulous look and gather my thoughts as I face Soshee. "Look," I say, walking towards her so I can take her hands in mine. "I just need to say one thing to you before I do anything else. Your mom was right. It's about what I *didn't* say. And I'm going to get to that in a second. But I need you to know this first, OK? I need you to hear me." I stop and point at Belinda. "What I did to her"— I shake my head—"I won't do that to you. That's all I want to say. I promise. I will never do that to anyone again."

"Ah-ha!" Belinda says. "So you admit you were a dick."

"Quiet, Belinda," Vann says. "He's about to tell you the one thing you've been waiting eight long years for. Let the man do his thing."

"I haven't been waiting for—"

But Vann cups a hand around her mouth and silences her. He smiles at me. And when he does that, I can totally see why everyone finds him so fucking charming. "Go ahead, Tony. Get it all out, man. You're gonna feel so much better when you do."

I turn back to Soshee and sigh. "I get it now."

She smiles at me and nods. "Keep going."

"What I did to her?" I nod my head at Belinda. "It was horrible. She's right. I kicked her out of her own home and had her sent to a strange place with a new name. I stole her identity. And I didn't even think twice about it. And what I need you to understand right now, before I turn and fix that, is… I will never do that to you. I will never make that mistake again. I will never throw someone I love out like trash."

I turn to Belinda and Vann removes his hand from her mouth so she can have her say too. But she stays quiet.

"I'm sorry, Belinda." And as soon as the words come out, I feel it. Relief.

This must be what religious people feel when they are baptized, I guess. Because my sin—it doesn't go away. It will never go away, but I stop carrying the weight of it.

"When you showed up on my street, Belinda, my life stopped. I'm talking I couldn't fucking eat, or sleep, or think straight. And there was so much anger inside me. At first it was because I couldn't believe you were there. I had sent you away. I had gotten rid of you. And now you were back?" I shake my head. "After all the turbulence of our relationship, when you left—and I'm so ashamed to say this out loud to you right now, but it needs to be said—all I felt was relief. I was so happy you were gone."

Belinda's face goes blank. And I almost think she will cry again. But she doesn't. She just folds her arms across her chest.

And that's not enough, I realize. Those words aren't nearly enough to keep the weight of my sin from creeping back inside me.

"I didn't understand those feelings. So I came here to figure it out, I guess."

"To hate-fuck me out of your head," Belinda says. "Just like the old days."

"You're right. That's why I came. But I didn't hate you, Belinda. I have never hated you. For fuck's sake. You're so damn cute. And mouthy. And pink. You're goddamn adorable, OK? There's no possible way I could hate you. I just…" I let out a long, resigned sigh. "I just… hate *who I am* with you."

She pouts her lips. Looks pretty sad, too.

"It's not you. It's not even me, OK? It's just…" I point to me, then her, then back at me. "*Us*, Rosalie. It's just us. We're not good together. We've never been good together. And I blamed you for that. And I'm so fucking sorry. You didn't deserve what I did to you. And I know there's no way to take that back and make it better, but I'm gonna try to do that right now anyway. So I just want you to know… I'm truly fucking sorry, Belinda."

Then I turn to Soshee. "And I know I've said it twice now, but I really need you to see that I'm being honest here, Sosh. Because you and I? You and I are like… her and him." I nod my head towards Vann and Belinda. "Does that make sense?"

Soshee sniffles a little, then laughs as she nods. "Yeah. It kinda does."

"*We*, you guys"—I look at Vann and Belinda— "*we* make sense." They just stare at me. "Am I wrong? Because if I'm wrong, just say so and I'll disappear and never bother anyone in this room again. But the four of us are connected in ways you two don't even know about yet."

"Oh, my God, that's true!" Soshee says. "Did you know I'm related to him?"

"What?" Belinda laughs.

I scowl at Soshee. "That's *not* true."

"It so is! I'm his cousin-in-law!"

"No," I say, shaking my head. "No. You're not."

"What the hell is happening?" Vann says.

"His sister married my cousin." Soshee beams. "I'm his sister's brother-in-law's cousin! And did you guys know those people at the Crappy Coffee Shop share a little dog and they're like… bad FBI or something?"

"What the hell is she talking about?" Vann says.

"I think you'd better sit for this," Soshee says, bustling towards the kitchen. "In fact, I think we need alcohol. Lots of alcohol. And frittelle. Lots of those too. Because Tony's right. We *are* good together."

## CHAPTER TWENTY-SIX

***Tony starts talking*** while Soshee starts placing bottles of Bucked Up beer on the coffee table in front of her tattered velvet couch and then serves up a whole bunch of powdery-sugary frittelle on an antique silver plate. I'm a little distracted by her apartment, because she was right when she said it might be a little over the top.

But I decide I like it. I like her version of over-the-top. I never hated Soshee. I just didn't get why she was all invested in a man who didn't feel the same way back.

However, one could say the same thing about Vann. And even though it didn't work out for Soshee, it did work out for him.

So it's about hope, I guess.

No. Not hope. Because that implies you're at the mercy of something or someone. Hope definitely conjures up feelings of desperation in my book.

So I think maybe it's more about belief. Yeah. Much better word than hope.

Tony explains what he and Soshee were up to yesterday while Vann and I were on our first date.

"A dog?" Vann asks.

"I don't understand how you didn't notice that the people who run the Crappy Coffee Shop all walk the same dog."

"Uh…" Vann looks at me, then back at Tony. "I don't really understand how you did. I mean, you've been in town for what, a week?"

"About there," Tony says. "But it wasn't just my advanced skills in observation."

I roll my eyes.

"You said it yourself. Soshee here has the best view in Fort Collins."

"We stalked you on our second date," Soshee says.

"And the first date, too." Tony laughs.

"And the third!"

"No," Tony says. "The third date was the trip to meet your mom."

"Oh, right. My bad."

"What the fuck is happening here?" Vann asks.

"Sorry," Tony says. "We were sitting up here. At that table right there, to be specific."

"And Tony noticed there was a discrepancy in the dog walkers," Soshee adds, completing his thought.

"They just seemed weird to me, ya know?" Tony says. "I see this cute college-age girl walking that dog one day, and then I see some suit dude walking him the next. And I think they were using that dog as an excuse to stalk your house."

"My house?" Vann says.

"Yup," Soshee adds. "So we think there's something fishy about the Crappy Coffee Shop."

Vann thinks about this for a moment. "They are closed a lot. And they're not friendly. I got coffee there a few times when they first opened, trying to be a good business neighbor. But they were sorta rude. So fuck it.

Life is too short to buy coffee from rude people when I can charm sexy Rook at the Fort Collins Theater coffee shop every morning. I still want to be supportive of the downtown businesses. So I go in there for sandwiches."

He winks at me so I know he's just being Vann. Which I get.

"They do serve really crappy coffee too. It's like they don't even care," Soshee says.

"They definitely don't fit in. You might be on to something. And there's that little fact that this place is a haven for witnesses."

"Tell me more about that," Tony says.

"Well." Vann stands up and walks over to the window. We all get up and follow him. He leans into it a little and points down College Avenue. "I know they hire new-in-town randos at Big City Burrito because I'm tight with the cashier, Carla. She used to give my brother-in-law Spencer line-dancing lessons back in the day. She told me they have a contract with the FBI and they hire two or three people a year in there. And then there's Renee at the Cat Call Club. Spencer was her bodyguard while she worked the club back when I was a teenager. And she told me they hire out-of-town randos seven or eight times a year too. So." He shrugs. "Who are all these random people the FBI needs to find jobs for, if not other witnesses?"

"And why do they all come here?" Tony asks. He looks at me. "When you got sent here, it wasn't my idea. The FBI made that call."

"You can't trust the FBI around here. Believe me. Spencer and his friends got caught up in some shit when I was a kid and they all got busted."

Soshee points at Vann. "I totally remember that. There was gonna be a trial? Or something?"

"Never happened," Vann says. "Important people died and Spencer's friends made sure the FBI took the heat. One of them was going to go to prison, but they killed him."

"Spencer killed him?"

"No," Vann says. Then he looks over his shoulder. Like he's afraid someone might be watching us from way up here. "That's the other top-secret part about this place. My..." He hesitates. "What to call her?"

"Who?" Soshee says.

"Sasha Aston. She's like... I don't know. Sorta like a sister because she's Spencer's best friend's adopted daughter. It's complicated. But she and these other people—who may or may not be honorarily related to me as well—they're what's called... *Company*."

"Company?" Tony says. "What Company?"

"You know that Chek dude we met down in Key West when your whole kid-smuggling thing was about to go off the rails?"

"Creepy Chek and Wendy?" Tony says. "I'll never forget those two creepy fucks. What about them?"

"Well, they're Company too. I'm pretty sure I'm not supposed to know this, and Johnny Boston would probably pay me a visit if any of you let on that I *do* know this." He pauses to eyeball Soshee. "Since, apparently, you're Zach Boston's *sister*."

"I don't even know the guy, Vann," Soshee says. "I'm not going to rat you out. I only know of him because I was snooping in my mom's stuff when we lived in the trailer park and found some old letters from my father. They mentioned I had a brother, so I snooped some more and found Zach. But we've never even met."

"Well, my sort-of sister, Sasha Aston, is one of those Company people. She's like Wendy. And her handler was a dude called James Fenici. And he rolled into town just before that trial was about to start and took care of shit. So the FBI dude who was gonna go down for the things Spencer and his friends actually did do, well, Fenici poisoned him. Bam. Whole thing went away overnight."

"Or not," Tony says. "Because they're still here."

"Not those people," Vann says. "I was only seventeen when this all happened. These people now are all new."

"Wait," I say, finally feeling like this convo has something to do with me. "Seventeen? That was the year I showed up."

Vann points at me. "Exactly. That's why I took such notice of you. One moment there is no angel called Belinda in my town. And then there was." He grins at me and I melt a little. Not just because of that grin. But... this really is real. It really does feel like destiny.

"So this means," Tony says, "that it's all connected. This Spencer dude. Chek. Wendy. Sasha. Whoever James is. Johnny. Me. Alonzo. Tara." He points at Soshee. "You and Zach. All of us."

"All of you," Vann says, "except *me*."

"How do you figure that?" Tony asks. "You're the one who knows all this shit."

"Yeah, but aside from my sister's marriage to Spencer Shrike, we're not part of it."

"You should be part of it," Soshee says.

"Yeah," I say. "You really should, Vann. How did your family stay so clean over the years?"

Vann puts his hand over his heart, mockingly offended. "Are you implying the Vaughn brothers aren't upstanding citizens?"

I roll my eyes at him.

He shrugs. "I have no clue. But if I had to take a guess, I would say... it was Gramps."

"Your grandpa?" I ask.

Vann nods. "You know he won our mansion in a poker game? Who wins a mansion in a poker game?"

We all kinda agree with this point. It's a one-in-a-billion kind of win.

"No one fucks with us," Vann continues. "The whole town might hate us, but no one fucks with us. We don't even pay property taxes."

"Shut up," Tony says.

"Seriously. I know for a fact we don't pay property taxes. It's like ten grand a year. We can barely afford the rent on the Sick Boyz storefront."

"You guys have dirt on someone," I say.

Vann looks at me and shrugs. "Probably?"

"Someone in charge, then," Tony adds.

"Someone at least in charge of property taxes," Soshee says.

"OK, hold on a second," I say, putting up a hand. "What about the bookstore?"

"What bookstore?" Tony says.

But Soshee is already pointing to it down below. "That one. Right?"

"Yeah. The blue-haired girl. She's not right."

We all crowd up against the glass to look down at the bookstore. And who comes walking out of it? Blue-haired girl herself. Her back is to us. She's locking the door, maybe?

"Not right how?" Tony asks.

But just as he says that she turns and, without hesitation, she looks straight up at our window.

"Shit!" I say. And we all duck back out of view.

"Did she just look at us?" Soshee asks.

"No," Tony says. "She was looking up at the sun."

"The sun is on the other side of the street," Vann says.

I peek back out. "Hmm. She's gone."

"I'm not convinced she matters," Tony says. "I think everyone who matters is right here in this room. And I think the people we need to concentrate on next are in the Crappy Coffee Shop."

"Agreed," I say. "It's them. I just feel it."

"Our only proof is a dog," Vann says.

"That's not the only proof," Soshee says. "It was weird from the beginning. I mean, who opens a crappy coffee shop across the street from a cool coffee shop? No one goes in there. And if the rent for an Old Town storefront is as high as you say it is, Vann, then who is paying that rent?"

"She's got a good point," I say. "And I'm convinced blue-haired girl is in on it. She's weird. I went in there to try and like... make friends with her. I was missing Tara and needed a new BFF. So I was considering all my options. But she's not real. She told me she's not into tattoos because they're too permanent. What kind of counter-culture chick says something like that?"

"Maybe she's not counter?" Soshee says.

"That's my point. Why look the part if you're not into the culture? Plus, her name is Midnight. What the fuck is that? Only people whose parents are witches have names like Midnight."

I think Soshee gets offended at that. Maybe because her mom is a fortune-teller?

"I'm not talking about you, Soshee. Your name is… practically normal." I wince at Vann and he makes a slicing motion across his throat, telling me to quit while I'm ahead.

But I feel behind. I need to justify this better. "My real point is that she was way too friendly."

Vann rolls his eyes and laughs.

"Hey, if you dress anti-establishment, you're anti-social. That's just the law. And if you break the law, then all the rest of us real law-abiding anti-social people get to question your street cred, OK? That's how it works."

"I think we should stay away from the blue-haired girl," Tony says, tuning me out.

"Agreed," Vann says. "We've got enough going on. We don't need tangents to distract us. What we need is a plan. A way to find proof that the Crappy Coffee people are really FBI."

"Or Company," I say.

"They're not Company," Vann says.

"How do you know?" Tony asks.

"Because if they were, and we got in their way, we'd already be dead."

And just as that last word comes out of his mouth, there's a knock on the door.

"Well, that's not ominous," Vann whispers.

"Who's that?" Tony whispers.

We all look at Soshee. "I don't know," Soshee whispers back, then starts to go for the door. But Tony pulls her back and puts a finger up to his lips, telling us all to be quiet.

He walks over to the door and peeks through the spyhole. But he backs off quickly and turns to us.

"Who is it?" I whisper.

"It's her," he says. "The blue-haired chick!"

She knocks again.

"What's Midnight doing here?" Soshee whispers.

"Don't say her name out loud," I protest. "That's like... calling the Devil."

Soshee huffs. "Who the fuck do you get your anti-establishment facts from?"

"Quiet!" Vann whisper-yells.

"I can hear you," Midnight calls from the other side of the door.

"Shit," Tony says. "Now what do we do?"

"Just be quiet," Soshee says. "She'll go away."

"I can *still* hear you."

"She cannot hear us," Soshee protests. "That door is made of steel."

"Hello? You crazy kids need to open the door now. We have a bug in there. We heard *everything*."

"What?" I say, looking at Vann for help.

"I'll handle this," Tony says, straightening his shirt and tipping his chin up like he's putting on his brave face.

"Good idea, Mr. Dumas," Midnight calls. "Because I'm here for *you*."

## CHAPTER TWENTY-SEVEN

**"What the...,"** *I mutter,* looking over my shoulder at Soshee. "What the hell does that mean?"

Soshee's eyes go wide. "The little dog is coming back to bite you. But don't worry. We got you. It's four against one."

I look at Belinda, feeling pretty confident that she and Vann do not 'got me'.

"Hey," Belinda says. Planting both hands on her hips. "There's no way this is not all connected. Which means Tara is probably involved too. I'm not stepping away from that fight."

"We should probably stop talking now," Vann says. "She just admitted there was a bug in here."

"I'm still waiting," Midnight calls through the door.

I glance at Soshee one more time and she nods. "We're in it together. I'm your sister's brother-in-law's cousin. We're blood, for fuck's sake."

"Soshee," I wince. "That's not even funny."

Soshee smirks at Belinda over my shoulder and shrugs. "It's a little bit funny."

"This isn't a joke. There's a blue-haired witch called Midnight on the other side of the door asking for me by name."

"I can ask for *all* of you by name if that makes you feel any better," Midnight adds.

"Bro," Vann says. Coming forward to place a hand on my shoulder. "This town might be crawling with dirty FBI and leftover Company, but my team is the one in charge. If these people want to fuck with the Vaughn family on our home turf, we're ready to roll. My sister will even get in on the action. We're one phone call away from a total Sons-of-Anarchy moment. OK? We got you. Open the door and let's get this show started."

Vann really does have a way with words. He might've watched *Easy Rider* a few too many times, but he makes me *want* to believe him. I can see why everyone thinks he's charming. "OK," I whisper. Taking one last look at the four of us. We are kind of intimidating in our own way. Vann and I are big tatted up dudes, Belinda can shit-talk her way out of almost anything, and Soshee is the supervillain in disguise.

Maybe we really are all on the same team? Maybe... I was even looking for this when I decided to make the trip up to Colorado? Belinda and I aren't meant for each other. Not that way. And I really did owe her an apology. The minute I realized that and said those words to her, everything in my life got lighter. Like all the pieces of the puzzle finally fit into their proper places. Me and Soshee. Belinda and Vann. And everything that comes with being connected to the Vaughn family.

If you find yourself thousands of miles away from the safety of home you could do a lot worse than having these three on your side.

So I nod and take a deep breath. Then walk across the room and open the door.

The girl on the other side of the door does not have blue hair. It's blonde and pinned to her head with a thousand clips. But she is twirling a blue wig on her finger. She smiles at me, then pushes past me. "Be a peach and close the door, will ya?"

I close it and turn to find her standing in front of Belinda, Vann, and Soshee with her hands clasped behind her back, sorta rocking on her heels.

"So?" Vann asks. "What do you want?"

"I'm here to give you a friendly warning."

"Is that right?" I ask, pushing past her so I can stand between Belinda and Soshee.

"Why do you think we need a warning?" Belinda asks.

"Bug. Remember?" Midnight points to the ceiling. "We bugged you weeks ago." She turns her attention to me. "I lost the bet, by the way."

"Bet?" I ask.

"That you would show up here." She juts her chin at Belinda. "But apparently there was a lot of unfinished business."

"You were listening to our private conversation?" Soshee asks. And she doesn't ask it nicely.

"Calm down, Soshee," Midnight coos. "It's just a job. I don't judge. And I don't care. At least, not about your personal lives. Though I will say they are not boring." She pauses for a moment. Makes a big deal about pretending to think. "All this personal angst might've actually saved you though."

"What?" I ask. Confused.

"Why the fuck are you here?" Vann spits.

Midnight smiles. And I can't tell if she's one of those people who just presents as mouthy—like Belinda. Or if she's hiding a deep, dark secret weapon that can annihilate the world when you're not looking—like Soshee.

"OK," Midnight says. "I see that we're all a little tense after that whole 'we had an FBI agent killed with poison by a Company assassin' conversation."

"That's not what we said," I object.

"Close enough." Midnight shrugs. She points at me. "You are going home. Tomorrow." She points at Soshee. "You're going with him. Pack your shit and show up at the Fort Collins airport tomorrow at noon."

"What?" I say. "You can't fucking—"

"I can," Midnight says. Sternly. And with a new look in her eyes that makes me pause when I see it. "And I am. You are leaving town, Tony Dumas. You've found enough evidence to assure your brother, Alonzo, that nothing is OK. That's fine. Because it's not. We'll figure out the rest when I join my people in Key West next week. Got it? Good. Now you two—"

"No, no, no," I say. Stepping forward. "You're not calling the shots here. We don't answer to you."

Vann steps forward too. "You don't run this town. *We* do."

Midnight cocks her head at him. Grins with mocking friendliness. "You sure about that, Vann?"

Vann grins back. It's his self-confident grin. The one he unleashes when things start to *not* go his way. Like he's gonna give everyone a moment to catch up to his awesomeness. "I have three brothers just like me down the street, a brother-in-law with a gang of friends who took care of you guys once already, and an ex-Company assassin called Sasha on my side. So, yeah," Vann growls. "I'm *very* fucking sure."

"Hmm," Midnight says. Her gaze lingers on Vann for a moment, then switches to me. "OK. Fine. He wants to play bad-boy biker with us? He's right. There's not much we can do about that. But you, Tony?" She shakes her head. "You don't have that luxury."

I put up my hands and shrug. "Hey, I have three brothers too. Not to mention three brothers-in-law by the name of Boston."

"And don't forget your cousin-in-law," Soshee says. Sidling up next to me and hooking her hand around my arm. "That's four Bostons. Five, if you count me."

"Right," Midnight says. Her smiles drops and her mouth forms a dead-straight line across her face. "As I said. It's *not* enough."

"Sounds like enough to me," Belinda says.

"It's not," Midnight says. But she doesn't look at Belinda. Her gaze is most definitely trained on me. "Trust me, Tony. None of that will save you or your family. Not with the shit you're involved in. That's why I'm here." She looks at Vann, Belinda, and Soshee in quick succession. "I'm trying to protect you."

"Protect us from what?" Vann asks.

"Well, not you," Midnight admits. "Your family is out now, Vann. And if you were smart, you'd keep it that way. Do you really want to drag them all back into the secrets? Spencer has settled. He has kids, Vann. Lots of them. All his friends do too. They got out and Spencer took your family with him by marrying your sister. Sasha, on the other hand." Midnight bobs her head back and forth like she's non-committal about this one. "They're not done with her just yet. Lots of missing pieces with that one."

"So what?" Vann snaps. "Tell us something we don't know."

"OK." Midnight looks back at me. "I will tell you something you don't know. I wasn't going to say anything. Didn't want you leaving town all stressed out about prison and whatnot. Didn't want you returning home and getting those brothers you have all excited. But you seem to be forcing my hand."

I don't want that sick feeling creeping through my stomach. I really wish it wasn't there.

But it *is*.

It's a deep, gut-wrenching feeling that has been living inside me ever since I agreed to help my father smuggle kids into the United States nearly a decade ago.

And I recognize it now.

It's dread.

Just thinking that word shifts my world and changes the whole idea of why I came here in the first place.

I thought it was Belinda. I really did. And for sure, we did need to sort this out. But that wasn't all of it. She was there when that shit went down eight years ago, so yeah. She was part of it.

Just not *all* of it.

The relief I felt after apologizing to her is gone now. It was never really about Belinda. Not as it relates to our past relationship, that is.

It was only about what I *did* to her.

What I brought her *in* to.

And, yeah. I understood the danger associated with what we were doing. I've heard the word prison mentioned so many times now, it has lost all meaning. And anyway, I figured the good outweighed the bad. That the righteousness of what we were doing would prevail.

So far it has.

We have prevailed. We *saved* those kids.

But we have never been the only ones smuggling kids into the United States.

We were just the only ones doing it for the *right reasons*.

So I know what Midnight is going to say before the words even leave her mouth.

"They *set you up*, Tony."

"What?" Vann asks.

"Who?" Soshee says.

Midnight doesn't say anything. She just stares at me with a very sad look on her face.

I want to object. I want to deny this revelation and make it go away. The same way I denied, for all these years, that I stole Belinda's life from her when I had her sent away.

But I can't.

Because both of those things are true.

Belinda steps forward and puts her arms out in front of her. Like she's going to protect all of us from the girl called Midnight. "You need to explain that."

"Do I?" Midnight asks. Still looking at me. "Do I really, Tony? Did you really not understand your role in all that human trafficking?"

"That's not fair," Belinda says. "They weren't trafficking. They were saving those kids. And I know for a fact that these kids were saved. I saw them! I helped them! I was *there*! They have new lives, and new names, and new families—"

"They do," Midnight snaps. Her attention on Belinda now. "You're right. The ones you saw, *do*."

"What?" Soshee asks.

Midnight looks back at me. "It's hard. I get it. It's sick. And none of us want to be involved with it. But we are."

"No," I say. Shaking my head. "Not us. We did not—"

"You're right. You didn't. You just covered for the ones who did."

"That's not true," I say. Still shaking my head. "That's *not* true."

"Hey." Midnight throws up her hands. "I'm not saying you did it knowingly. I'm just telling you that this has been happening, in your marina, for decades. And your little humanitarian missions were just cover. To make all the locals turn their heads. Blind eyes and all that good junk. If anyone got suspicious and started asking around. What do you think all those old sailors would say? Hmm? Oh, they'd be quiet about it. Make it into a big secret. Shhh." Midnight puts a finger to her lips. "Don't say nothing. Those Dumas boys are one of us. They do good works. Trust me. I've seen it. I *know* them."

I turn away and walk over to the window. Leaning against it and press my forehead against the glass.

"I didn't come here to spell it out," Midnight continues. And I just want her to shut up. "I came here hoping I could get you all back into your normal lives without having to tell you the whole truth. But..." I glance at her over my shoulder and find her shrugging. "You wanted an explanation, so here it is. If you don't do what you're told, Tony Dumas, your whole family is going to be on the news by the middle of next week."

"You're going to lie about him," Belinda growls. "About the whole family. Even though you *know* they weren't involved."

"Me?" Midnight points to herself and laughs. "Not me, Belinda Baker. I'm ex-Company, sweetie. Just like Vann's little friend, Sasha. I'm one of the good guys here. I'm trying to stop all this from happening. I didn't set the Dumas family up to take the fall for a disgusting child trafficking ring in the Caribbean. That was all them!" She points to the window.

"Who?" I ask. "Who the fuck are we dealing with?"

Midnight takes a deep breath. And is that rage she's hiding underneath all these nonchalant words? "They go by many names. Company. Silver Society. The Way. There's dozens more where those came from. But they are all the same. They are all high-ranking politicians. Celebrities. Media moguls. Just your average billionaires. Point to just about anyone at the top and they're involved. And if you don't get your shit together, Tony Dumas, the full wrath of their cover story will ruin everything your family stands for. You will all go to prison. The entire world will know your family as those nice people down on Key West who sold children into slavery. And that's the best case scenario. The headlines only get more disgusting from there."

"But they didn't," Belinda insists. "We have proof! We can show them the kids, and get the whole marina to testify—"

"Are you serious right now?" Midnight asks her. The tone of her voice rising in pitch. "I mean, I get it.

You're just an innocent girl who was in the wrong place at the wrong time. But please tell me you're not that naïve. Because if you are, we have a lot to go over before I can let you leave this room. And it's not going to be pleasant to hear."

None of us say anything. We just all stand there feeling... overwhelmed, I guess. Blindsided is maybe a better word.

Then, finally, Midnight says. "It doesn't have to go this way. We have people in place to take care of it, Tony. Johnny Boston—"

I turn on her. "He's part of this?"

"Of course," Midnight says. "He just doesn't know it yet."

We're all silent again. And we stand totally still. Like each of us is afraid to move. Afraid to hear what might come out of her mouth next.

"Listen," Midnight says. "I know this sucks."

"Sucks," Belinda snorts.

Midnight glares at her and Belinda goes quiet. "I know this sucks," she says again. "But this is how the real world operates, you guys. What better way to hide something awful? Something truly terrible that most people don't even want to admit is happening? They do it by having a *front* that seems to oppose their evil plans. If you want to smuggle children around the world for your own personal, disgusting reasons—then you start a charity for them. An orphanage. A... you know. Clean water initiative for a remote village. An adoption agency. A preschool."

"Oh, my God," Belinda says. Holding her stomach. "This can't be happening."

"You don't have to believe it," Midnight says. "But it's one-hundred percent true. I've been watching it happen my whole life."

She looks at Vann. "You think you know things because you can toss names around like Sasha Cherlin. Or James Fenici." She looks at me. "Or Johnny Boston. But listen to me. Those people?" She shakes her head. "They haven't seen anything compared to me. And I know the backstory about James. You may have heard some of it, Vann. But you don't know what really happened to him as a child. They did horrific things to him. But as horrible as they were, that was nothing compared to what they did to *me*."

Midnight shifts her gaze back to me. "Or that girl you saved a few months ago that got you into all this trouble. You did a good thing, Tony. But it's not going to help you now. They set you up. They gave you a choice to help people. The choice was an illusion. You're just another cog in the wheel. How much do you get paid? Hmm? For your good deeds?"

"What?" I say. Disgusted at the mere idea that we do this for money. "We don't get *paid*, Midnight. It's fucking charity."

"No," she says sadly. "You don't get paid. But they do. Your family does this for all the right reasons. But those people out there who really run things? They don't. This is *all* about money and leaving a legacy. All of it."

She looks back at Vann. "You seem to know a lot about what Spencer Shrike and his friends did several years back to set up, and take down, the dirty FBI in this town. But do you know the details? Do you know how they did that?"

Vann shakes his head.

"They stole money. A lot of very *dirty* money. That's how it all started. And then they used that same dirty money and simply connected it to an FBI agent. They made a money trail, Vann." She looks at me. "It's all about money. And if you want to find the people responsible for all the evil shit that happens in this world you follow the money. And if you want to set someone up to take your fall and eat your guilt—all you have to do is leave a little money trail for someone else to follow. That's how Spencer and his friends did it, Vann. They knew how the world worked. And they set someone else up to take their fall, and punish the Company at the same time."

I hear her. I understand what she's saying. But this... *can't* be true. We can't be in this fucking deep. "We don't have a money trail, Midnight. It's just not there. We never took any—"

"Didn't you?" she snaps.

"We didn't!"

"You did," she growls. "You just didn't know it. Your family is quite rich now, aren't they?"

"We *earned* that."

"Your sister—"

"My sister *earned* that! She owns a huge cosmetics company, for fuck's sake! They started it from nothing! They give away millions of dollars every freaking Christmas!"

Midnight puts up her hands. "I get it. I know how hard this is. But... I'm not saying she's not brilliant, or her partners aren't brilliant, or their products aren't superior. They are probably all those things. But come on! She's like what? Thirty years old and she's one of the richest women in the world! How do you think that happens? Hard work? *Really*?"

I... don't know what to say. But I'm not ready to accept this. "It can't *all* be based on lies."

"Your family was rich once. Right?"

I nod. I'm not into the family history the way Alonzo is. But I do know people way back in my family were very wealthy at one time.

"Families are always rising and falling in America, right?" Midnight says.

"I guess," I shrug.

"No, Tony. They aren't." She shakes her head sadly. "The *same* families are always rising and falling in America. New families striking it rich the way your sister did? That's nearly impossible. You have to know people. You have to have them on *your side*."

"So they set her up?" Belinda asks.

"They set her up," Midnight says. "They set up your entire family, Tony. And all these new connections? Boston brothers? Vaughn Brothers? Spencer Shrike, and Sasha Cherlin, and James Fenici? This—" Midnight twirls her finger around in a circle. "This is making the Company and their ilk *very* uncomfortable. We need to neutralize it and we need to do it quick."

"I guess no good deed goes unpunished. Does it?"

I turn and find Soshee looking at Midnight. Who points to her and says, "Got it in one."

Midnight waits for one of us to keep protesting, but what's left to say?

We have nothing left to say.

"All right then," Midnight says. Blowing out a long breath. "Here's how this is going to go down." She points at Belinda and Vann. "You two just need to shut your traps and go back to work. Pretend Tony left on bad terms. Pretend you don't know anything about the Crappy Coffee Shop, and—"

"Wait!" Belinda says. "Aren't you connected to the Crappy Coffee Shop?"

"Me? No." Midnight chuckles. "I am not dirty FBI. I am ex-Company. That's what I've been trying to explain for the past seven minutes and seventeen seconds. I'm on your side, OK? You just need to trust me."

Trust her? Like the way we trusted everyone else? Is she kidding?

"Let me start this again from the top. Tony and Soshee are going back to Key West. Vann and Belinda are going back to work at Sick Boyz. No one is going to pay any attention to random witnesses who show up out of nowhere. No one is going to blab to their brothers about what just happened in this room. No one is going to call Sasha Cherlin, or James Fenici, or Johnny Boston. OK? If we do that, then we all live to fight another day." She pauses to smile at us like we're children.

But we're not children. In fact, I'm fairly certain every single one of us is older than Midnight here. She can't be any older than Vann, that's for sure.

Belinda makes a noise. It's one I kinda recognize from the old days. A noise that says... *I'm gonna say something I will probably regret right now. Something cute, and sassy, but will definitely escalate the situation so maybe someone should stop me.*

I glance at Midnight and find her smiling at Belinda. And I swear to God, I know that smile. And when I look at Belinda, she recognizes it too.

"Um..." Vann says, stepping in front of Belinda. Yeah, he sees everything. And he knows that Midnight here just shot us a smile that would be totally at home on Creepy Wendy's face.

She's one of them.

She's one of those little girls.

Maybe not so little anymore, but that just makes her *more* dangerous, not less.

"I'm in a hurry here, guys," Midnight says. "Because the Crappy Coffee people are watching me too. Nine minutes and seventeen seconds ago I walked into the Fort Collins Theater, presumably to buy coffee. Which means that in four minutes and forty seconds I have to leave there with a fucking coffee in my hand. OK? Or they're going to wonder what the hell I'm up to. And while I give zero fucks if they know what I'm up to, you four should be giving all the fucks. Because they will wipe you out." She points at me. "Your family is already on the shit list after you went against orders for that last pickup job. And hey"—she puts up both hands—"I'm rooting for you guys. You saved a little girl that day. A little girl I happen to care about. So you've got that going for you. But one more suspicious move and those headlines I mentioned? They're gonna be splashed all over the world and they won't tell you they're coming. If you and Soshee don't leave town, and you two don't go back to work, all of this is out of my hands. Got it?"

We all nod. Silent.

"Good. I'm leaving now. I don't expect to ever see you again. Someone new will take over my job at the bookstore and we'll pretend this never happened. Are we clear?"

"Clear," I say, speaking for all of us.

"Then goodbye."

And with that she turns around and walks to the door.

"Wait!" Soshee calls. "What about the bug?"

Midnight doesn't even turn around. "Airport, Soshee. Tomorrow at noon. Then you'll never have to think about that bug again."

She walks through the door and leaves us standing there in silence.

None of us says anything for at least a minute.

But then Vann turns to us and says, "Follow me."

We all follow Vann out of Soshee's apartment, down the stairs, and cross the street to Anna Ameci's. Soshee lets her aunt know we're taking a table in the corner.

We all sit down and look at each other. Surrounded by the bustling chatter of dozens of conversations inside the restaurant. Safe from spying ears.

Vann's blue eyes look at each of us in turn and then finally settle on mine. He says, "Fuck this shit. You in?"

And I find myself liking Vann Vaughn.

I find myself liking Vann Vaughn a whole helluva lot.

Because I say, "Fuck yeah. I'm in."

## EPILOGUE

# TONY

***Everything about my life*** has changed since Soshee came back to Key West with me.

Wait. No. Let me try that again.

Everything about my life is *better* since Soshee came back to Key West with me.

I own a fifteen-hundred square foot cottage about mid-way down my family's street and there wasn't a single stand-out thing inside this place until Soshee Ameci moved in.

Most girls who walk away from the only life they've ever known would feel at least a little out of place, but not my Sosh. She came in, looked around with her lips pressed together, and then nodded and said, "OK. I can work with this."

I didn't understand what that meant, exactly. But I do now. Clean. Slate. As she so eloquently put it when I made a big deal about her amazing loft in Fort Collins.

She went shopping yesterday while I was at work and when I came home last night I felt like... well... I felt like I was coming home for the very first time.

I had never had that feeling before. This street has always been my home. There is nothing new to see here. Nothing exotic to discover. And I'm not complaining about that, it's just a fact.

But when I came home from the marina last night and walked into a room transformed by candles, and beaded curtains, and throw pillows made of crushed velvet. And I saw my sexy supervillain standing barefoot in the center of the living room wearing a pair of cut-off shorts and a light green bikini top that made her eyes look like flashing emeralds... well *that*?

*That* felt like coming home.

And I thought to myself... *I'm gonna fall in love with this girl.*

**Tonight when I come home** the first thing she says to me is, "I called a guy and had the whole place swept for bugs. I got your mom to let me into Luke and Alonzo's cottages too, and they're clean as well. So." She blows a stray piece of fire-red hair out of her face and nods. "I think we're good now."

And then I think to myself... *Nah. I fell for this girl the very first moment I saw her.*

I walk across the room, take her in my arms, spin her around until she laughs hysterically, and dip her backwards for one of those dramatic old-fashioned kisses.

We fall to the floor. That move is harder than it looks. But we laugh all the way down.

"Hey Sosh," I say. Once we've stopped laughing and are sprawled out in the middle of the small living room.

"Hmm?" she hums back.

"Would you like to be my partner in crime?"

She turns over on her stomach and props her hands under her chin as she grins at me. "What kind of things come with being your partner in crime? Anything cool?"

"Define cool."

"Like... do I get a costume?"

"Oh, every supervillain gets a costume. So that's a big yes."

"Does it come with a cape?"

"And a hood."

"Can we fuck in the costumes?"

I laugh. Jesus. This woman kills me. "Only if you promise to cook in it too."

Which makes her grin and wink. "I do make a good Bolognese."

"Yeah. I hear your cannolis are better than getting a blowjob in the alley."

She guffaws again. Rolls over on top of me. Kisses me on the mouth and murmurs words past my lips. "Hmm. Wow. This all sounds like a super good deal."

"We're gonna be quite the team." I whisper back.

And she replies, "We already are."

## EPILOGUE

**BELINDA**

***Winning a game is*** all about knowing when to make a move.

Go too soon, you lose momentum and the element of surprise.

Go too late and you miss your chance.

After Midnight's little visit we sat inside Anna Ameci's for a couple hours talking in low whispers as we sorted through all the information.

One thing was for sure. Soshee and Tony were leaving on that plane the next day at noon. So this was our last chance to come up with a plan.

Leave it to Midnight to save us?

Uh... no. We're not the kind of people looking to get saved by anyone, let alone some smarmy fake counter-culture wanna be. I don't care that she's some leftover assassin like Creepy Wendy. Those little Company girls might be good killers but I'm gonna go out on a limb here and say they probably have a pretty bad record when it comes to saving innocent people.

And we *are* innocent.

I reject the idea that doing good deeds will get you in the end.

It's not supposed to be that way. And fine. Creepy Midnight can call me naïve all she wants.

I don't care what she thinks. I'm not naïve, I just have high standards.

If she wants to—

"Hey, hey, hey," Vann says, wrapping his arms around me as he spoons me from behind. "Calm down there, killer. Plenty of time to plan a murder when the sun actually comes up."

"What are you talking about?" I don't snap it. But I kinda want to. Thinking about Creepy Midnight does that to me.

"I can hear the wheels turning in your head. You're making plans."

I turn to face him and match his charming grin with a devious one of my own. "You're mostly wrong. I was making plans. But it wasn't about anything dangerous. I was thinking about making your whole family breakfast this morning. I can't take another oatmeal special."

These words wipe Creepy Midnight right out of my mind. Because I live here now. In this cool, ramshackle mansion filled with tatted-up Vaughn men.

And the best part? The best part is that Vic took a picture of Vann and me sitting on the front porch and it now hangs in the second-floor hallway with all the rest. I found the frame in a box in the basement. It's not perfect. The fake gold paint is cracking and there's no glass or anything. But I wanted a frame that belonged here. Not something brand new with no history.

That's what I love most about our picture in the hallway.

I'm now part of their history and I spend a lot of time in the front of Sick Boyz Tattoos dreaming about how it could hang there for fifty years. And how one day, some girl dating one of my great grandchildren will stop there in the hallway and look at us.

And she might be a lost girl, like me. And she might say to herself... "I want that too."

And maybe she is a smart-assy go-getter with pink hair like me. A girl with nothing left until she finds my future offspring who completes her and makes her feel wanted and special.

Vann winces. Because he's still thinking about my little white lie. "Gramps really needs to hang up his apron. But you don't have to eat it, ya know. You're the only one who does."

"I can't disappoint your gramps. It's our bonding time. I'm literally like two afternoon prune-juice breaks away from making him spill the whole story about how he got this house."

He chuckles. "In your dreams. He's leading you on. Trust me, we've all tried to get that story out of him. It's not going to work. You're just gonna eat prunes and oatmeal for six weeks and see way more old-man tattoos than you bargained for."

That makes me smile and I lean in to Vann's chest. Enjoying him. Enjoying our little break from the game that's coming.

Because it *is* coming.

We know when to make a move. We're just biding our time until everything is in place. We're gonna clean up everyone's money, make that trail impossible to follow, polish their reputations, and then... bam. *We win.*

Tony and Soshee are down in Key West right this very minute pulling it all together. And pretty soon—

"What did I just say?"

"What?" I ask.

"You're thinking too loud. Stop it. You can't save the world all by yourself, Belinda Baker. And you definitely can't do it before the sun comes up. It's practically illegal to save anything before the sun comes up."

"Says who?"

"It's just the law."

I giggle. "The law, huh?"

"Yup."

"Which one?"

"The Law of Starting Over. The Law of New Things. Pretty much all the laws of second chances state it explicitly."

"Hmm. I don't remember it being in those laws. And I'm a licensed expert in both starting over and second chances."

"No."

"Yes," I laugh.

"No. That's not true. This isn't starting over. You've always belonged here."

I reach up and place both my hands on either side of his face and fall into his easy gaze. Just get lost in those blue-eyes of his.

Then I kiss him. It's a soft, slow kiss that only very familiar lovers know how to do properly. And they only happen when you're immersed in bliss.

We haven't been actual lovers for very long. Less than a week, actually.

But we are *very* familiar.

He rolls over on top of me and boxes me in with his forearms on either side of my head. So close to me, I can read the tiny circle words around the double X's on his shoulders.

I'm obsessed with him. My love for Vann Vaughn feels very all-consuming.

It's a sweet, sweet sick feeling in my stomach that makes me hungry for more.

It's a simple love too. A cliché kind of love that comes from watching too many rom com movies. Pure. And innocent, but still sexy in a fun way.

The kind of love you only find when you fall for your best friend.

The kind of love that only comes along when you're ready to accept that everything you've been craving has been right in front of you the whole time.

"And now a soft kiss," I whisper. "—Aye, by that kiss, I vow an endless bliss."

"Surrounded," he adds. "On all sides."

I am surrounded on all sides. Protected in every direction.

"You're right," I whisper. Kissing him again.

"I am?"

"Mmhm. That's the lesson I needed to learn. I was never in the wrong place at the wrong time. I was always right where I was supposed to be."

With him.

# END OF BOOK SHIT

**Welcome to the End of Book Shit, Covid-19 Edition! Also, Mother's Day Edition! It's Mother's Day, May 10, 2020 as I write this.**

If, by some weird set of circumstances, you find yourself reading this going what the fuck is an End of Book Shit, then I know you read this book out of order! Bossy Tony is book 6 in the Bossy Brothers series and it not a standalone! lol Also these EOB's are never edited, so you can focus on my typos if you'd like. But I don't give a fuck.

Anyway, this is the EOBS and you all know what it is. Just my rambling thoughts on the story. And I actually have a lot of thoughts about this one.

First of all – fuck this Coronavirus. I was originally planning on releasing this book in April. I think the original date was April 15, actually. And by the time we were all pretty certain that this virus was going to be a major disruption, and possibly even cause the end of the world, I was about 60% done with the book. I very close to finishing. But shit kinda went off the rails and I just stopped writing and started making candles! Hah.

BTW – if you want to win a cool bookish candle, and you're reading this pretty close to release day (which is supposed to be May 12, but my promo company literally just informed me a few hours ago that they have clients who have books stuck in Amazon limbo for going NINE DAYS NOW! So who knows? This book might actually release with Pretty Nightmare on May 26 by the time it goes live!) – but I'll be doing a ton of giveaways for these special bookish candles I made while I was NOT writing Bossy Tony. And they are very pretty, and smell divine, and each have their own custom label! If you stop by any of my socials or my website, there will probably be a post with info.

So that's the first thing. I wrote this book during a very strange time in the history of the world, ya know? It pretty much happened to all of us. And that's not common. That's something along the lines, as far as natural disasters go, like a fucking asteroid hitting the earth.

But I didn't really mind the break in writing. It actually gave me a lot of time to think about Vann. Because even though I knew this was a book about TONY, I was pretty sure when I wrote Bossy Alonzo that I wanted Vann and Belinda to be a thing.

This choice was kind of a risk in romance. Um… romance readers have very specific expectations about the couples in the stories. There are lots of rules and I was definitely breaking them.

But I was so convinced that Tony and Belinda were not meant for each other, and that she was meant for Vann, and Tony was meant to be with an "Ameci" girl, that I finally decided that I was just going to write my book my way, and if that bothered readers who have strict rules about what they expect in a romance story, then… oh well. I can't change the story in my head to fit other people's expectations.

That never works.

And in fact, I was listening to Veronica Roth (of Divergent fame) on a webcast a few weeks ago when her new book, The Chosen Ones, released. I felt super bad for all the authors who were releasing books during the first few weeks of Corona—especially first-time trad published authors, because this book-release timeline, for them, was like… years in the making. They can't just say—OK. Let's postpone this book for a month, like we indies can. So I was paying super close attention to the authors in the young adult sci-fi fantasy world, trying to support them by buying their books and audiobooks.

So this webcast that Veronica Roth did was replacing her book tour. And she literally had to pull the virtual tour together in like a week's time. So that's what this was. One of the webcasts she did for her virtual tour. And one of the last questions –I don't remember which webcast it was specifically; she was asked a question like—how do you deal with reader disappointment? I think we all know how Divergent ended. lol. And some people were upset. But, so her answer was "I always make sure that the loudest voice in my head is always my own." Because she knew by the end of book one, in Divergent series, that (spoiler alert) her MC was going to die at the end of the series. And that's not typically how books end in her genre. lol

And she said she debated whether or not to change that. And maybe she even came up with some alternate endings. But let me let tell you, as a very experienced writer, once you get that idea in your head—it's real. It's really hard to change things. This is why I don't "normally" write scenes in books out of order. Because my story likes to change on me. And I try not to get too attached to scenes in my head so I can change them if I feel it to be necessary.

But some scenes cannot be changed, no matter how hard you want to change them and make readers happier. No matter how much Veronica Roth knew that she was going to upset her readers, by this point this was just the fuckin' story. And it can't be changed. Or if you force the change, it ruins everything.

And maybe there are readers out there who say – "Well, she DID ruin the series for ME."

Which sucks. I get it. My favorite series of all time is Altered Carbon by Richard K Morgan. And I'm just gonna not comment on the Netflix version of it. Because I fucking hated season two. Season One was "Fine" I would not call it great, but it was "fine." But season two I just turned off. It was not the story I fell in love with.

But… lots of people did still like Season Two. They probably had not read the book, so they didn't give a fuck that the plot was all twisted up. And I did. But I'm not really the important person in this, right? As a viewer of the TV show. The writers are the ones in charge and if this was their story, fuck it. That was their story.

So even though Veronica Roth knew people were going to be upset, this was her story. And in the end, she needed to live with herself after it was over. There is nothing worse than writing a story you hate. Especially if it's a series. It feels like such a waste of energy and time. And writing books is both an energy and a time suck. Like, it sucks your life away. There is no point writing books you hate.

So when those controversial scenes or plot twists come along, and you know in your heart that this is just how it goes, you, the author, need to respect that and do your thing.

You need to be the loudest voice in your head.

I didn't have that level of angst with Bossy Tony. I definitely think having the two POV characters in a contemporary romance not hook up and get that HEA is atypical, but I didn't kill anyone. No one cheated in this book. And I will fight you to the death if you say they did cheat. They didn't.

So in the end I was still a little bit nervous about my unorthodox choices, but I'm super happy I did it this way. And I hope you enjoyed this little twist on the romance genre.

I always try and do something different. I do not write the same story over and over again. I try really hard to have something surprising or unconventional in my books. Every time. And that's pretty hard now that I've written 75 of them.

And I had never told a story like this before, so I'm really happy with how Bossy Tony turned out and I hope you enjoyed it too.

There are two books left in the Bossy Series. Luke's book and Zach's book. Luke's book will wrap up this whole mystery that started in Bossy Jesse and then Zach's book will a surprise. :)

So I'm really happy that you're still following along in this Bossy series and I hope you're ready for the big ending.

And Pretty Nightmare, which is sorta related to the Bossy series in certain ways, will be releasing on May 26. Pretty Nightmare is book two in the Creeping Beautiful series.

Creeping Beautiful series has four books – BUT THEY ARE TWO SETS OF DUETS. So that big mystery I started in Creeping Beautiful will also wrap up by the end of Book Two, Pretty Nightmare. And then books three and four will move on with, not a new set of characters, but a new set of point of views.

I'm also starting ANOTHER series next week that will be releasing in early July. I'm not going to say too much about that. But it's also a duet. And it's going to be really angsty, and dirty, and sexy.

So you have that to look forward to, as well.

OK, I think that's it for me. I'm going to go upload Bossy Tony and pray to the Amazon Corporate Gods that it doesn't take NINE DAYS to go live!

Thank you for reading, thank you for reviewing, and I'll see you in the next book!

Julie
JA Huss

P.S. – If you're into YA sci-fi/fantasy the new Veronica Roth book, THE CHOSEN ONES, was super good! I really enjoyed the story and the narration on audiobook! Five stars from me!

# ABOUT THE
# AUTHOR

**JA Huss never wanted** to be a writer and she still dreams of that elusive career as an astronaut. She originally went to school to become an equine veterinarian but soon figured out they keep horrible hours and decided to go to grad school instead. That Ph.D. wasn't all it was cracked up to be (and she really sucked at the whole scientist thing), so she dropped out and got a M.S. in forensic toxicology just to get the whole thing over with as soon as possible.

After graduation she got a job with the state of Colorado as their one and only hog farm inspector and spent her days wandering the Eastern Plains shooting the shit with farmers.

After a few years of that, she got bored. And since she was a homeschool mom and actually does love science, she decided to write science textbooks and make online classes for other homeschool moms.

She wrote more than two hundred of those workbooks and was the number one publisher at the online homeschool store many times, but eventually she covered every science topic she could think of and ran out of shit to say.

So in 2012 she decided to write fiction instead. That year she released her first three books and started a career that would make her a New York Times bestseller and land her on the USA Today Bestseller's List twenty-one times in the next five years.

In May 2018 MGM Television bought the TV and film rights for five of her books in the Rook & Ronin and Company series' and in March 2019 they offered her and her writing partner, Johnathan McClain, a script deal to write a pilot for a TV show.

Her books have sold millions of copies all over the world, the audio version of her semi-autobiographical book, Eighteen, was nominated for a Voice Arts Award and an Audie Award in 2016 and 2017 respectively, her audiobook, Mr. Perfect, was nominated for a Voice Arts Award in 2017, and her audiobook, Taking Turns, was nominated for an Audie Award in 2018. In 2019 her book, Total Exposure, was nominated for a Romance Writers of America RITA Award.

Johnathan McClain is her first (and only) writing partner and even though they are worlds apart in just about every way imaginable, it works.

She lives on a ranch in Central Colorado with her family.

www.ingramcontent.com/pod-product-compliance
Lightning Source LLC
Chambersburg PA
CBHW051950240626
47153CB00005B/1693